PENGUIN METRO READS
LOVE STORIES THAT TOUCHED MY HEART

Ravinder Singh is a bestselling author. *I Too Had a Love Story,* his debut novel, is his own story that has touched millions of hearts. *Can Love Happen Twice?* is Ravinder's second novel. After spending most of his life in Burla, a very small town in western Orissa, Ravinder has finally settled down in Chandigarh. He is an MBA from the renowned India School of Business and is presently working with a prominent multinational company. Ravinder loves playing snooker in his free time. He is crazy about Punjabi music and loves dancing to its beat. The best way to contact Ravinder is through his official fan page on Facebook. You can also write to him at itoohadalovestory@gmail.com or visit his website www.RavinderSinghOnline.com.

Also by Ravinder Singh

I Too Had a Love Story
Can Love Happen Twice?

Love Stories That Touched My Heart

EDITED BY

RAVINDER SINGH

Penguin
metro reads

PENGUIN METRO READS
Published by the Penguin Group
Penguin Books India Pvt. Ltd, 11 Community Centre, Panchsheel Park,
New Delhi 110 017, India
Penguin Group (USA) Inc., 375 Hudson Street, New York, New York 10014, USA
Penguin Group (Canada), 90 Eglinton Avenue East, Suite 700, Toronto, Ontario,
M4P 2Y3, Canada (a division of Pearson Penguin Canada Inc.)
Penguin Books Ltd, 80 Strand, London WC2R 0RL, England
Penguin Ireland, 25 St Stephen's Green, Dublin 2, Ireland (a division of Penguin
Books Ltd)
Penguin Group (Australia), 707 Collins Street, Melbourne, Victoria 3008,
Australia (a division of Pearson Australia Group Pty Ltd)
Penguin Group (NZ), 67 Apollo Drive, Rosedale, Auckland 0632, New Zealand
(a division of Pearson New Zealand Ltd)
Penguin Group (South Africa) (Pty) Ltd, Block D, Rosebank Office Park, 181 Jan
Smuts Avenue, Parktown North, Johannesburg 2193, South Africa

Penguin Books Ltd, Registered Offices: 80 Strand, London WC2R 0RL, England

First published in Penguin Metro Reads by Penguin Books India 2012

Anthology copyright © Penguin Books India 2012
Editor's note copyright © Ravinder Singh 2012

The copyright for individual pieces vests with the authors or their estates

ISBN 9780143419648

Typeset in Bembo by InoSoft Systems, Noida
Printed at Manipal Technologies Ltd, Manipal

Penguin Books India would like to thank our marketing partners—Rediff.com,
Radio City, Star Plus, Cafe Coffee Day and Flipkart.

Contents

Editor's Note

I'm not Spiderman, but I do believe in the line 'With great power, comes great responsibility', which Peter Parker recapped at the end of the film. This anthology is my way of using my power and moving a step towards accomplishing my responsibility to create a platform for many of the upcoming debutant authors. However, at the onset, it is important for me to tell you why I am a part of this project and what I think about it.

As I write this note, I want to go back in time—the time when I was a wannabe author. For me, the year 2008 was full of struggle. All I had with me was a dream—to narrate my love story. But for some reason the world around me was trying with all its might to stop me from realizing that dream. Nothing seemed to be working out. Apart from my belief in the saying 'Where there is a will, there is way', and the fact that I had a complete manuscript in hand, I wasn't equipped with anything else in my adventure to become an author. It didn't help that I had absolutely zero contacts in the publishing industry. Adding to all this was the fact that I myself had a load of questions—Where to start from? Which are the publishing houses I should send my submissions to? How best to approach them? . . . The list was longer than the word count of my first chapter! The answers I got were limited and most of them were incorrect.

Months passed by and by then only two things had changed in my status. First, my work had been rejected umpteen number of times. Second, some publishers hadn't even bothered to respond to my submission. I was still waiting for the third kind of status update—the positive one. However, I came across some people who showed me dreams but cheated me in the end. I also came across some good people who helped me beyond what they'd promised to do. In the end, I did get published and I also learnt a lot. I learnt from both kinds of people, the people who helped me as well as those who deceived me. I am still in touch with both kinds of people. My journey of becoming an author who is loved by his readers was full of frustration but also full of hope.

As I come back to my present, all this is history. And now that it is history, I have taken up a task for myself—I want to do my bit and make the road for several wannabe authors less bumpy, if not smooth. Everyone who deserves it should get a chance to narrate his/her story.

Love Stories That Touched My Heart is a great project. In my view it is a plan in which all emerge as winners—the publisher, the authors and myself. A nationwide contest gives the publisher a chance to reach out and nurture fresh talent and fresh writing, besides getting a good selection of stories. From the thousands of stories that we received, the best twenty-five have been selected for this collection. This project is also a perfect platform for debuting storytellers to compete with each other at a national level and to prove their mettle. And for me, the takeaway is to introduce these twenty-five new names to the world of storytelling. Something I set out to do in the first place.

Each and every love story that has made it to this book is unique in its own way. And as the title says, these stories have really touched my heart and I wish they touch your heart as well. The best part for me was to get a chance to experience a variety of feelings in just one book. While a few stories left a sweet smile on my lips, a few others left me emotional by the last paragraph. Some of these stories are very simple in terms of plot, but the style with which their authors have narrated them was extremely interesting. Their choice of words and their expressions won my heart. And in some cases the storyline itself was far more impressive than the style of writing. I picked them up and edited at the same time. Before I started going through the submitted list of stories I was clear about one thought, i.e., every author has his/her strengths and weaknesses. My idea was to pick up the strengths and work on the weaknesses. The idea of identifying different strengths and fixing different weaknesses is what brings diversity into this anthology, gives it that flavour and texture that can be a rollercoaster ride of emotions. And this note is incomplete unless I mention that I didn't just enjoy reading these stories, I also learnt a lot from them. Some of them showed me the art of writing an unconventional and out-of-the-box story, while some others heavily influenced me on how to beautifully write the first paragraph—something that I struggle with.

Writing a short story may be a small step in the journey

of becoming an author of 200-odd-page novels. But winning a nationwide contest is a big and crucial step. Who knows, a couple of years from now the authors of this book will be writing an editor's note, the way I am doing right now, and will recall this first step in their journey of becoming writers.

Before I end this note, I also want to thank those thousands of participants for submitting their stories—even if they did not make it to this book. And here is my strong recommendation for them—if you truly believe in yourself, don't give up. Hone your skills for, who knows, you may be the winner of the next season!

I didn't make it in my first attempt, neither did I make it in my fifth attempt. But always remember in that someone who said, 'Where there is a will, there is a way.' And no matter what, you can and will find the way!

God Bless,

Ravinder Singh

The Girl Behind the Counter

OMKAR KHANDEKAR

I leaned over the parapet of the balcony of my apartment on the fifteenth floor. The preparations for the evening bhajan ritual had begun, I deduced from the escalating hum downstairs. The building watchman was arranging gray Neelkamal chairs in a semi-circle between a sleek red Honda and a black Chevrolet SUV. I looked back up at the jumble of skyscrapers. Yardley Gardens was one of Mumbai's plushest townships that my family had recently relocated to from the humble cobwebs of Nashik. The westward sun made me squint and I withdrew to my cushy C-backed bamboo swing, resuming the novel in my hand. There are few things as relaxing as an evening breeze tickling you while you turn the delicious pages of Adiga's *The White Tiger*.

It was now nearing six and I could hear the boys playing football downstairs. In spite of wanting to join them, I stubbornly clung on to my novel. I didn't want to open my mouth and make a fool of myself. I remembered reading 'It is better to stay silent and be thought wise than open your mouth and be proven foolish'. Or was it the other way round? Immaterial, I wasn't leaving.

My tenth standard was to start in a few days' time. You could say I was a little nervous. The relocation was a little bit of, like they say, a 'culture shock' to me. My father had taken up a new job that offered thrice the pay of the previous, along with a horde of benefits like company quarters at this place, a Tata sedan and discount coupons at various dining joints. A personal pizza was no more to be shared by the family. The visit to the restaurants no more meant a strict decorum of mere daal, a paneer subzi and roti. I could unblinkingly order appetizers to overpriced Cokes without a warning eyebrow. Just the very thought of them now made me hungry. I got up from the swing.

'Ma, can I have some money? I want to go out, eat something,' I shouted as I went inside the house.

'Why do you want to go outside?' The voice came from the living room. I spotted her knitting, red and white yarn balls by her side. 'Your grandmother has packed us some . . .'

'Mom!'

'These kids of today,' she muttered without annoyance. She was quite jovial ever since we'd moved in. And in spite of being the unwilling kitchen recluse that she was, she made me take a plate of parathas to both our neighbours, without paying any heed to my 'But what do I say to them?' What happened next is something I fervently hope that twenty years later I will look back and laugh at.

She set aside the half-finished scarf for my grandmother and fished her hand into her purse that hung by the armrest of the couch. All the years we stayed with my grandparents in my native town, there was a non-stop bickering between my mother and grandma. The day we left, I sneaked a look at my mother crying in my grandma's lap and the usually stoic lady that my grandma is, even she couldn't hold back the Ganges streaming down her eyes.

'Don't spend all of it,' she said. A crisp hundred-rupee note, from which Gandhiji grinned at me.

~

The elevator doors opened to a shockingly electric environment. I mean, when you come to such a colony, you expect people to be silent and, what's the word, 'sophisticated' to the point of being considered curt. But with the noise these kids made with their Ringa Ringa and catch and hopscotch and whatnot, I almost felt like I was back in Nashik. I avoided eye contact and went to the main gate. The path to the street was blocked by a team of sweaty T-shirts and delirious outcries of boys of my age and less playing football.

Let me tell you something about me and football. First, I hate this game. Second, and by no way because of the first pointer, I am no good at it; although, that doesn't stop me from admiring a good game when I see one. And admire I did the fat guy in the midfield as he dribbled the ball between his legs. A tall stick lurched towards him. Our fatso quickly defected to his left and furiously kicked the ball at a scared teenager who turned reflexively to his side. The ball hit his elbow.

'Hand!' the fatso screamed in delight and duly encashed the free kick. I was impressed.

I looked at them from a distance, hoping they would notice and call me over. Maybe they were too engrossed in the game or maybe they didn't care about a stranger gawking at them.

I stood unheeded. Sighing, I made my way to the exit.

Spencer Mall is more of a two-floored convenience store. I was thrilled to spot an escalator and hopped right on. The first floor hosts a small cafeteria consisting of three chairs each around circular wooden tables. There is a glass counter on the left where you get 'The best Frankies in town'.

Confession—I had no idea what Frankies were. I wondered if they were so expensive that it would drive my pride of being *loaded* away.

At the first floor, one takes a U-turn to face the cafeteria. I occupied one of the empty tables and studied the menu. The contents were reassuring. A basic vegetarian Frankie cost around forty and went up to fifty five if you wanted many fancy fillings. Schezwan paneer Frankie commanded my interest. I went to place an order at the glass-top counter and there she was—the Girl behind the Counter.

'Hi! And what would you like to have today?' she smiled at me affably. It was almost a smile of recognition, as if she had been privileged to have known me since ages and that I was her favourite customer. I bit on my braces—her perfect pearly whites probably never needed dental treatment. The thick and sleek black tresses almost shone and one lock of hair hung cutely on her dusky face. Her eyes were everything the on-screen actors swoon to and poets write couplets about. You get it, don't you? She was probably a few years older than me and wore a black T-shirt that read 'Joe's Frankies'.

I tried to power up. *Speak up*, I screamed inside and mentally rehearsed what I had to say. Just order as you would normally do and say 'Thank you' when you get it. How hard is it? A question popped in my head—how is schezwan pronounced? *C and H are silent, duh*, came the answer. How can two consecutive letters be silent, I wondered. *Well, it just sounds better, doesn't it?* 'Sez-waan', I reasoned. But this is taking too long, way beyond the line that separates a customer from this pint-sized nincompoop. And was that sweat on my forehead?

'Sir?' the girl asked unflinchingly, her expressions intact. I hoped she wasn't just pretending to be calm while hunting for an alarm button under the counter.

'One plate schezwan paneer Frankie,' I said and instantly felt proud that I didn't stutter. *Smooth*, I praised myself.

'That would be fifty rupees, sir,' she looked into my eyes, smiling all the while.

I must tell you, gentle reader, that continuous eye contact is worse than browbeating. You see, girls are not intimidating. Only pretty ones are. I understand I sound shallow but I call upon the puberty-license.

Yours truly is no exception to this rule. I feigned interest in the pile of tissues in the waste bin behind her as I dug into my pocket. Finally, I produced the hundred rupee note and extended my hand to pay. At the same time, she stretched hers too and ended up accidentally touching my fingers. I cringed as my fingers tingled, feeling like a biscuit that's been dunked in the tea a bit too long. I went back to the table with eyes squeezed shut hard.

'Excuse me, sir,' I heard a voice in a couple of minutes. It was her voice. She meant me. *Me!*

'One schezwan paneer Frankie.' She gave me a roll with salad and cubes of cottage cheese lathered with sauce and gravy peeking out of the open end.

She had pronounced 'Schezwan' as 'Shej-waan'. In spite of the culinary wonder in front of me, my heart sank. I felt like stabbing myself with a spoon. *Smooth*.

'Thank you, sir,' she said. 'Hope to see you again.'

That night, I slept smiling ear to ear. In spite of having absolutely no dreams involving her, I woke up fresh as a deodorant!

~

The next day I borrowed a fifty from mother and pressed the elevator button. The same noise on the ground floor lobby, the same guys playing the football, and this time, a penalty shootout. I saw Fatso taking his position in the D and stopped walking. It was the Tall Stick taking aim this time.

'Ready!' screamed the goalkeeper from Fatso's team. The next instant, the ball was kicked. Fatso used brute force and jerked aside the guys from the opposing team standing on both sides and jumped high, his head deflecting the ball to a corner.

'Foul!' alleged a hysterical bunch. Fatso couldn't care less and bent double laughing. Tall Stick pushed him to the ground but Fatso was clearly having a time of his life. I grinned at him. I was impressed. Again.

The same traffic, the same pedestrians, the same road, the same mall, the same first floor and the same Frankie Girl. Bless her. I walked up to her and went straight to the counter. Today, I had taken special measures to make myself presentable. I was wearing my best pair of shoes and my wrist sported father's metal-strap Sonata watch. I had taken the pain of applying a small amount of face powder, just the perfect amount that separated complexion from make-up. My gait was confident and tone smooth. I went up directly at the counter and ordered without referring to the menu. She gave me her known-you-since-ages smile and asked me to take a seat. Since there were hardly any customers, the mood was relaxed. I took the seat facing her, careful not to slouch.

. She was an epitome of effortless grace. The way she fluently dealt with cash, her eased-out demeanour as she mimicked one of her colleagues, the elegance with which her features aided every word of hers and the voice that wafted, like an elixir to the ears. The more I observed, the more I was drawn towards her. *Ask what her name is*, I scolded myself. *It won't compromise the national security*. But I knew I wouldn't. I dreaded the moment I would finish my roll and walk back.

Finally, she summoned me and I went up to the counter. Taking the Frankie, I turned back. I wanted to disappear from the spot that made me feel like a coward. I hurriedly walked to the escalator. Even when I heard a minor commotion in the background, I didn't bother to check it. Like I even cared. As I was just stepping on it, I felt a pat on my shoulder.

It was her.

My heart violently jolted into a see-saw. She smiled at me. The same sunny smile. I smiled back stupidly, not knowing what else to do.

'Sir, you forgot to pay,' she said.

～

As I lay on my bed that night, I wondered how I could have been so foolish. It was embarrassing. Or was it? She gave no other indication of my lapse. What she did was exactly the opposite. She accepted the money and said, 'See you tomorrow, sir.'

I felt so *invited*!

～

Today is when this phoenix shall soar into the blue skies of hope, I decided the moment I woke up, *making up in clichés what he lacks in style*. She was not going to eat me up if I strike a conversation with her. Being well-mannered was her job description. Being myself just won't do. Besides, there is no big deal in asking a person's name. I had Shakespeare to endorse that.

'I can, I will,' was the day's mantra. I enjoyed the movie I saw, chomped up some more Adiga, laughed hard at the silliest of sitcoms and in an uber-confident mood, practised pick-up lines in front of the mirror. I enjoyed the familiar noise of the bhajans, was enthralled by one of the superb goals scored from a distance, relished the evening chirping and even helped one of the ladies from the store with her shopping bag. *This is it,* I thought as I went up the escalator.

It was yet another slow weekday. My palpitation jacked up as I noticed her. She was not at the counter though, and occupied one of the tables with a guy in his early twenties, deeply engrossed in a conversation. As I walked towards her, as if almost on cue, I saw her affectionately pulling his cheek. It was only when I reached the counter that she noticed me.

'Customer, darling,' she whispered to the guy, getting up in a rush.

'Hey, wait up,' the guy insisted, catching her by her wrist.

'Oh no,' she began to protest. 'I have to.'

'Come now,' the guy was persistent. 'I am sure he won't mind giving us a minute. Would you, kid?'

That was my call. 'Oh, n-no. Carry on.' I somehow mumbled. I wanted to look away. I didn't. I should've. I didn't.

The guy kissed her on the cheek and she responded by whispering something in his ear. 'See you soon,' she said, waving him goodbye.

She went behind the counter and adorned her position.

Giving me another of her well-practised smiles, she asked, 'A paneer-chilli Frankie?'

I didn't know what to say. Somehow, I managed a, 'Never mind,' and started walking out.

'Oh, I am so sorry,' she said apologetically behind me, her voice dipped in desperation. 'It's schezwan paneer, isn't it?'

I didn't respond and followed a chirpy middle-aged couple out on their grocery shopping down the escalator. I rehashed the events in my mind and tried to articulate what I felt being the unwilling witness. Was I sad? Nope, that was not what it felt like. It was a *funny* feeling. I cursed myself—funny won't do, such words are what stupid people resort to.

I did like her, yes sir, most definitely I did. Or did I? What was it that I felt for her? I stopped on my tracks as the word hit me between the eyes—fascination. I turned and looked at one of the stained glass windows of Spencer Mall. I was captivated by her, by the novelty she was, like a Da Vinci painting, like an amazing novel. I turned to look at the stained glass facade of the mall. She was my white tiger. So why did I turn back? Wasn't today one of the most confident days? Why should it be a 'was'? What if she has a boyfriend? What was I hoping for anyway?

Nothing! a happy voice rang inside me. I like the Frankie, I like the Frankie Girl; so what's stopping me from having both of them just now?

Nothing! came the reply again, even happier.

I retraced my footsteps. There was no audible heartbeat this time, only pangs of joy, of inexplicable ecstasy. I went to the counter and smiled.

'Hello,' I said.

'Hi, sir,' she replied, for once, more surprised than rehearsed happiness.

'Name's Arora. Nikhil Arora.' I am the king of clichés, I smiled wider.

She followed suit. 'Right, Nikhil,' she said. 'And you will have one schezwan . . .'

'. . . paneer Frankie,' I shared the moment with her. 'That's right.'

'Right away, Nikhil,' she said. 'Please have a seat.'

'Sure,' I said and waited till she called me.

And eventually, call she did. 'Nikhil, your Frankie's ready.'

'Oh yes, thank you,' I took the roll from her. 'By the way, there's something I've been meaning to tell you.'

'Yes?' She looked into my eyes inquisitively.

I took in a deep breath. *Yes, I can.* 'I love your smile,' I said.

'Thank you, sir,' she beamed, gracefully bowing her head a little. 'Oh, and there's something I've been meaning to tell you too.'

I stared at her. This was unexpected. 'Yes?'

'My name's Roshni,' she grinned, extending her hand forward.

I shook it. This time there was no long lasting tingling sensation, no desperate urge to smell the palm for a residual fragrance. It was just a warm handshake, the way it is meant to be.

~

I went back to my building. All the football players had evaporated but for one guy. Fatso was shooting against the wall and chasing the ball as it bounced back. I felt inclined to talk to him but zeroed on procrastinating it—I had socialized too much for a day already. As I walked towards the lobby,

I heard a 'Dude!'

I turned around to see the fatso calling me.

'That,' he said, pointing at the Frankie in my hand. 'That has paneer in it?'

'Yes,' I said, slowly, wondering what the guy was up to.

'Then share it, no? Don't be so selfish,' he said and grabbed at it. I didn't mind it. Nothing about his tone was forceful. On the contrary, it was friendly.

'By the way,' he said; his mouth full, 'I am Aditya. And you?'

'Nikhil,' I said and extended a hand forward.

'Good, man,' Aditya said, almost moaning at the taste. 'This shit's good.'

I was amused. The guy was ravenously friendly. Somewhere, not far off, I saw a figure running towards us. That thing was skipping, almost bounding toward us in excitement. Aditya recognized the figure and his eyes lit up as the figure too gave a squeal of joy.

'*Dude!*' he said and, dropping the Frankie, hugged her. The girl was about my age, a few inches shorter than me but extremely attractive. She hugged him back. 'Oh my God, where've you been for so many days?'

Awkwardness started flooding inside me again. Aditya noted my presence and quickly released her. 'Dude,' he said. 'This is my cousin.' Then he noticed the mess he created by dropping the Frankie. 'Oh shit, I dropped it, did I? Wait, I am going to run and get one for each of you. Hang in there. Won't be long . . .'

'Well,' the girl turned from a scampering Aditya to look at me. 'What's your name, did you say?'

'I didn't,' I said almost reflexively. 'Did I?'

'Let's try again,' she chuckled. 'What's your name?'

'Nikhil,' I said.

'I am Roshni,' she said, extending her hand.

My face brightened. 'Roshni, did you say?'

'Yeah, why?'

'*Pleased* to meet you,' I beamed and offered my hand. She shook it.

Was it a tingling sensation I felt?

A Train to My Marriage

VANDANA SHARMA

I am afraid of heights of all kinds—valleys, mountains, rivers, railway station bridges and even relationships make me sick. And today I am going to experience all of them.

'Krishna, come fast, we will miss the train!' Mom shouts, breaking my train of thought.

'I would be glad if I could,' I mutter, putting on my dark brown blazer.

One more addition to my Hate List is this goddamned winter season. I am very sensitive to getting a bad cough in this season and I cannot bear the chill. So I have put as many woollens in my bag as on my body.

Here comes the auto rickshaw.

'Come, come, everyone get inside,' Dad says.

'What the hell, Krishna! How many clothes have you stuffed in your bag? It is way too heavy!' screams Anoop, my brother.

13

'Don't worry, I will take my luggage myself. You don't have to bother about it.'

I immediately regret the sentence after saying it. It is heavy! Uff!

Soon we are in front of a big—no, actually a monstrously huge—railway bridge.

'Okay, I can do this.'

I try to be a brave girl. I am not going to look down. But the combination of loudly hooting trains and my immense fear of heights makes the situation more horrific. When it comes to heights, I can be a total freak.

'Here are our seat numbers,' says Mom when we board the train.

I take my laptop and climb on to the upper berth. As it is an all-night journey, everybody will be asleep soon and I am going to watch the Korean movie *My Little Bride*. I love romantic Korean movies.

By the time it's 3 a.m. I feel sleepy. But first I have go to the loo, so I just wait for the train to stop at any station. That's one more addition to my list of phobias—I cannot go to the loo when the train is moving. Now you must be getting a clearer idea of my freakishness.

I doze off later. Then suddenly it's raining and I'm all drenched; a wave of water comes to drown me and I'm awake!

'Holy shit, Anoop! Are you fucking out of your mind!' It turns out to be part of a dream, and Anoop was trying to wake me up by pouring water on my face.

He laughed stupidly and said, 'We are almost about to reach Ambala.'

Yes, we are going to our village which is located in Ambala. It's always been very exciting for me to go there

but this time it's a little different. I am going to face my
fear of relationships.

We are going to meet D.S. Sharma Uncle and his family.
And I am sure of the real reason we are meeting the
family—they want me to marry Sharma Uncle's one and
only son who lives with them in their farmhouse. Their
family is very affluent but I never wanted a man who lives
in a remote area and is a farmer. I think he must be barely
a graduate—a narrow-minded control freak. Men in villages
want housewives, not working girls.

The train arrives at the station. Coolies are competing to
get into the train. Everybody rushes out of the train except
me. I am struggling with my bag and suddenly I tumble on
to the platform, head over heels. Shit! I just fell from the
train. God! Can I do this any better? Fuck, fuck, fuck . . .

Before I can manage to get up myself, a hand comes through
the crush of bodies to my rescue. Without looking at who
it was who offered to help me get up, I grab that hand and
pull myself up. Having stood up, I immediately start brushing
my clothes. Then I look up to thank the man who helped
me . . . I'm struck dumb. He is dangerously handsome.

'Thank you.' This is all I manage to say.

He is wearing a white kurta–pyjama. The top buttons of
his kurta are unbuttoned. His perfectly trimmed muscles can
be seen; his biceps give the perfect shape to his arms. Is he
not feeling cold? May be he is already too hot.

Suddenly his voice breaks the spell, 'Are you okay?'

'Yes, thank you again,' I say, hesitant and embarrassed.

'How many times I have to tell you to be careful!' chides
Mom.

My brother is laughing as usual. Now he has got my 'new
train scandal' to talk about for at least this month.

I then realize that Sharma Uncle's family has been there all this time. And the handsome man is none other than his one and only son. I still don't know his name. Now this is more embarrassing.

'Please give me your bag,' he says softly.

'No, I can manage,' I muttered.

'Yes, I have seen that already,' he grins as he almost snatches my bag from me.

Soon we are in their car—an Endeavor. It is cozy inside. He is driving the car and I can feel butterflies in my stomach. I still don't know his name.

Finally we have arrived at the farmhouse. It is beautiful, completely surrounded by nature. The entrance gate is covered with some kind of flowering creeper. There is a nameplate: SHARMA'S RESIDENCE. The building itself is breathtakingly gorgeous. Could there be anything else that one can want in life?

We are in our separate rooms now. I am feeling very sleepy so I just snuggle under my quilt and sleep.

When I wake up, it's dark outside. Looking out the window, I'm trying to recollect my thoughts and then I realize that this is not my room. I get up and go downstairs to the main hall.

Everybody is there having dinner. Crap . . . I realize I slept all day.

'Come, dear, have dinner,' said Aunty.

Mrs Sharma is a beautiful lady and anybody can see where her son gets his good looks from.

Mr Perfect is also there, sitting beside my mom and talking about his work. Huh, what attitude . . . He didn't even notice me? As if I care . . .

After dinner, we return to our rooms. Now everybody is going to sleep when I'm wide awake . . .

Thank God I have my laptop with me.

Somebody knocks at the door. 'May I come in?'

'Yes,' I answer,

And here he is—Mr Perfect.

'Mom has asked if you need anything.'

'No, thank you,' I say, smiling.

He is about to leave when he suddenly turns and asks, 'What are you doing on your laptop?'

'Nothing, just watching a movie.'

'Can I join you?'

'Oh! Okay,' I say. I'm surprised, especially after how he totally ignored me at the dinner table.

'Korean movie, haan . . . That too romantic?' he says, grinning.

'I like romantic Korean movies,' I say abruptly.

'Don't you have horror movies?'

Okay, I got you. You are trying to flirt with me. Although, I think, he has succeeded to some extent. I am impressed.

'Yes, I have them, but it would be better if you don't watch it with me. I scream while watching horror movies although I don't even watch most part of the movie. I cover my eyes all the time so that if any thing shitty happens I can close my eyes immediately.'

'Okay, then let's watch your romantic Korean movie,' he says, grinning again.

'By the way, what is your name?' I ask.

'You don't know my name?' Now he does not seem very pleased.

'We didn't have a moment to get properly introduced before,' I explain.

'Hmm . . . Okay . . . My name is Daksh,' he says, stretching out his hand towards me.

'And I am Krishna,' I say, reaching out to shake his hand. As I touch his hand, a quiver runs through my body. His hand is warm, in sharp contrast to my cold hand.

It is always risky to watch romantic movies with parents or with a hot guy like him. Suddenly, the hero and heroine are getting closer on the screen, and I begin to feel very conscious, even embarrassed. I try to move so that I can fast forward the movie, but I just cannot. Now they are kissing each other ferociously. The hero unzips the heroine's skirt and moves his hands all over her thighs. The heroine then helps the hero to unbutton his jeans, after which the hero mounts her, and is then inside her. And after both of them are fully exhausted, they fall into bed and hug each other tightly. The hero kisses the heroine gently on her forehead. Oh . . . this forehead-kissing scene is my favourite. And thus the movie goes on.

Slyly, I try to peek at Mr Perfect's face. He is calm but I can see his facial muscles clenching as he tries to hide his smile.

The movie finishes at 1 a.m. He gets up to leave.

'Goodnight, Krishna.'

'Goodnight, Mr Perr . . . err . . . Daksh.'

Narrowing his eyes, he leaves the room.

The next morning I get out of my room, brush my teeth, pick up my sneakers and head out to the fields. It is a very cold, foggy December morning, so I'm wrapped up in thick woollens.

What was I doing last night? Talking to myself. Even now, my thoughts are focused on him. I know he is handsome but still I'm sure he is a narrow-minded control freak.

As I remain lost in my own thoughts, my foot suddenly slams against a heavy stone. I stumble into a slushy part of the path. Apart from landing like a fool into the slush, I realize I have hurt my foot.

'Need any help, Miss?'

Oh, it is him! What is he doing here? Why is he always there to rescue me from my own disasters? Oh!

I clear my throat. 'I can manage . . .' I say, trying not to look at his face.

'You are very stubborn, Krishna. Just give me your hand.'

I offer my hand hesitantly. He clutches it tightly to help me get up; again I can feel the cold even more . . .

I stand up, stumbling, holding on to his shoulder for support.

As we enter the house, everybody is surprised to see both of us.

'Hey, what happened?' asked Mom.

'Nothing, Mom. Your dear princess fell again,' he says, grinning. Everybody laughs at this.

Huh! How dare he? And why is he calling my mother 'Mom'?

Oh, my suspicion was right!

Or maybe not?

I must know for certain. So the next time I find him alone, I confront him. He is sitting at a desk, doing some accounting work.

'I want to talk to you,' I say.

'Krishna, I am busy right now. Can we talk later?'

My big negative point is my egoistic attitude.

'Why did you call my mother "Mom"?' I ask.

He looks up. 'Is that a problem?' he asks, keeping his

accounting book aside. Standing up, he then comes close to me.

'Yes,' I said, stuttering. 'She is my mom, so you cannot call her that.'

'Oh, really?'

He walks a little closer. Crap! I cannot move. . . I want to step back but I find myself simply unable to move. I need water; it is getting too hot here.

Suddenly he pulls me into his arms. My mouth is so close to his. He is looking into my eyes. I am trying to look down, afraid that he can read my eyes and can see into my soul. He lifts up my chin and gently runs his thumb over my lips. For that moment I forget everything around us. All I can focus on, apart from the sensation of being held by him, are his dark brown eyes. Oh boy, he is the only man around whom I can feel mushy without even watching a romantic movie.

'Krishna . . .' a voice comes suddenly from another room.

I push him away and manage to calm myself.

It was Anoop asking me to come to the hall. 'Mom is calling you.'

In that moment, my heartbeat thuds very rapidly. I rush to attend to my mother.

Later in the evening, we all make a plan to go to a famous restaurant in the city. As we get ready for the outing, I consciously try to ignore what happened with Mr Perfect that afternoon. But still I ensure to put on my best dress—and I realize how very pleased I am to have taken the pains of bringing so many dresses with me on this trip.

Am I trying to impress him? No way! Everybody is trying to look their best, so why shouldn't I?

But I find that I'm more nervous than usual.

Soon, everyone is ready and it's time to leave.

'You two, go in the other car,' says Mom.

'What?' I am surprised. Mom is asking me to go alone with a boy! I insist, 'No, I will also go with you.'

'Yes, Mom, there is no need of another car,' says Mr Perfect.

Thank God! I cannot bear landing in one more scandalous moment after that afternoon.

'No,' says my mother. 'You will go in separate car. That's it.' No more discussions.

I know what mom is trying to do. Seriously, Indian mothers can be such a headache sometimes!

We take another car—this one's an Audi!

The streetlamps look beautiful this foggy evening, between the mist and dark night.

Mr Perfect doesn't say a word. So to end this awkwardness I start a conversation.

'How about your higher studies? You don't want to study further?'

'Krishna, I have already done my MBA and I have also been a research scientist at the Indian Institute of Agricultural Sciences. So now I am working on increasing crop yield methods while simultaneously learning the ropes of my father's business and also doing some actual farming. What else you want me to do?'

My jaw almost falls to the ground.

'Oh!' I said. 'So you would want a wife who can stay with you? I mean, a housewife.'

'Yes, I would definitely want a wife who can stay with me, Krishna.'

I knew it! A narrow-minded control freak. Huh!

'But, he continues, 'if my wife wants to work, she can work with me in our business.'

He never ceases to surprise me. I am feeling good about it. But still I am confused about why he wants *me* to marry him? He can get any girl he wants.

Suddenly, the car stops and I notice that we are near a hill.

'Where are we? Don't tell me that the car has stopped working.'

'No, Krishna. Please stop watching those romantic movies in which the hero–heroine get stuck in a car and then their romance starts,' he says, grinning.

'Whatever! Just a thought; it has nothing to do with romantic movies.' I say, annoyed.

'Let's go.'

'Where?'

'Up there. To the top of the hill.'

'Are you kidding me? I'm not going there.'

'Huh! Stubborn girl.'

He takes my hand and we move towards the hill. As we reach the top, I can see the river on the other side. This scene is breathtaking. Although it is far below us, the sheer height does not seem to scare me. Instead, I feel great—so amused and thrilled.

A cold breeze blows my hair over my face.

'It is so beautiful, nothing can be more beautiful,' I say.

'I knew you will like it.'

Suddenly, Mr Perfect gets down on one knee, pulls out a ring and says the world's most magical words: I LOVE YOU, KRISHNA. WILL YOU MARRY ME?

I am dumbstruck at that moment. Here is Mr Perfect—and that too on his knees, asking me to marry him!

This cannot actually be happening. All this only happens in the movies. I wish I could hold on to that moment forever.

'Krishna, please reply, my knees are hurting and it's very cold out here.'

I smile, my eyes wet with tears, and say, 'YES!'

Thrilled, he gets up and slips the ring on to my finger. He then hugs me tightly. I can hear his breath in my ears as he says, 'I liked you when Mom showed me your picture . . . And I liked you even more when you fell from the train.'

'Then I should fall every time,' I laughed.

'I wanted you right there while watching that movie,' he whispered in my ears. 'I love you! Be mine. Be my wife.'

I look up at him. He lips come close to mine and then he softly kisses me on my lips.

'I love you too,' I responded gleefully.

And, like every other love story with a happy ending, 'we lived happily ever after'.

A Love Story in Reverse!

SUJIR PAVITHRA NAYAK

Sunday, 12 August 2012

And They Lived Happily Ever After!

'If the only prayer you said was thank you that would be enough.'—Meister Eckhart

And I mean it from the bottom of my heart. The benevolence and support that you all have showered upon this tiny blog has brought colossal contentment to our beloved Ramanima.

Mumbled in between sobs and sniffles, she said, 'That stupid new tenology (technology) and that fish net (Internet) . . . Say thank you to them, Putti . . . (*Sob! Sniff!*) . . . I don't know how they knew! Truly God's blessings; I thought I will die from a heart attack rather than old age. My Krishna has come back to his Radha. Hare Krishna!'

And that is how Ramanima expressed her gratitude to all of us.

I realized that love is not just about being romantic and mushy, but it is about strength and respect at the age of fifty-three.

The meeting finally took place at Cubbon Park, beside the big rock. The first reactions of the lovers took the whole crowd by surprise! Instead of a warm, yearning embrace, they looked at each other peculiarly. It was like watching two chimps in a zoo being moved into the same cell for the first time. Singhji curiously took Ramanima's hand and started to peel off the band-aid that covered the tattoo off her wrinkled forearm whereas Ramanima kept brushing the long-pepper salt hair off Singhji's forehead to check for the mark. Age had worn and withered both their physical appearances but some marks were forever. After they were satisfied with their findings, they suddenly locked themselves in an embrace, just like the audience had first expected. Cheers and claps followed, and the couple broke away from their embrace, suddenly conscious and overwhelmed by their surroundings. After a light-hearted speech everyone left for their respective homes, knowing that what they had witnessed that day was nothing short of a modern Cinderella fairytale.

Thirty years of hope, three lives, two hopeful lovers, and a modern fairy godmother and her ever so obliging helpers—these are the perfect ingredients for a contempo-antiquated love affair!

Sunday, 15 July 2012

It's the Final Countdown

'There are certain moments in life that are moments of impact. These are the moments that will affect your entire life.'—*The Vow*

My evenings are only filled with blogging, probing and watching romantic movies on a minimized window on my laptop. My friends tell me that I am insane, my parents have given up on me and my bosses at the office would sack me without hesitation if I weren't employee of the year! Only you, my readers and supporters, understand what I am going through. It is because of you that two lives will be changed forever!

I know this journey has been lengthy and tedious, and I won't deny that more than fifty times I have decided to give up. But you, my readers, have been my motivation, and today I want to share with you the greatest surprise of all!

We may have finally found Singhji, and this time I did check out his story. I am 99 per cent sure it his him. After all, only Ramanima can be the judge of that. So I am going to share the story of how we finally were contacted by the 'real' Singhji.

Nearly two weeks ago I received a postcard from a chap in Dublin, Ireland. It read: 'If you want to know the truth about Singh, then you must first hear a story. I will be available from 11.30 a.m. to 7 p.m. IST on this number +353 894 ### ###.'

Strange! At first I thought this was a prank by yet another one of the many pranksters who have sent us fake letters, mails, emails, postcards, etc. But there was something intriguing about this card. So I called the number. What I heard next I would not have anticipated in a million years.

The voice at the other end was hesitant and had an unrecognizable accent. But there was also willingness and a sense of relief; like a heavy burden was being lifted off this man's chest!

'Errr . . . Hello, am I speaking to Miss Alicia? . . . ..Great!

Hello again . . . Before you ask me anything, let me tell you my tale.

'About thirty years ago, when I was a hot-blooded young chap, I roamed the free streets of Punjab with not a care in the world. I had no job, not much education, and like most young, hot-blooded Sikh boys, I would eat, spend time with my friends, run in the fields and tease girls. I had a way with the ladies and secretly dated many girls during my day, which was not accepted by society then. My father had heard a lot of rumours about my activities and wasn't pleased at all. He decided to send me to the south of India—to Mysore University—to get a good education and a job so that I wouldn't squander my life away. I was very unhappy about this decision but I respected him enough to obey his orders.

'The university life was completely different from how I had lived in Punjab. I learnt about new things like discipline and respect for fellow students. There were very few girls who studied with us. But there was this one girl, Ramani. Even to this day my heart skips a beat whenever I think about her. She was the only one who could turn a hooligan like me into a little puppy with just her words. I had instantly fallen in love with her charms. It was hard to court a girl like her. She was the most beautiful of all the girls at the university. I courted her for ten months before she finally reciprocated my love.

'Within a week of this development, I received a call from my brother. He said that our father had been killed and that riots had begun all over the north of India against the Sikhs. Devastated, I had to leave Mysore immediately. I left a friend's address with Ramani and told her to keep sending me letters to that address. She was heartbroken when I last saw her. Little did I know that it would be the last time I saw my beloved.

'When I went back to Punjab, the state was in absolute disorder. People who considered each other brothers had turned into bitter foes. As soon as I reached home, I was met with a rude shock. My eldest brother was forced to join the Sikh extremist group. Currently, the members of this group were forcing my middle brother to join as well, saying that our family's lives were at stake. Within a month my eldest brother was killed and my middle brother was once again asked to join the group. When he refused, his wife was burnt alive. They also threatened to kill me, so he was forced to join the group.

'A few days later, I was approached by a friend of my brother's. He told me that my brother had been captured by the police and they were coming after me since they did not want to leave anything to chance. He told me that the only way to get out of this mess was to leave the country in a shipping container and flee to the USA. All this while I was in touch with Ramani and we exchanged letters often. But I knew that I would never be able to see her again, so I wrote her my last letter. That same night I left in the container with forty other men heading to the USA. We travelled for twenty-seven days with limited food and water. But when we finally saw the light of day we were not in the USA!

'We had landed in a strange country. Later, we were told that we were currently in Portugal, and the container would be shipped off to Mexico immediately, without food!

'After another journey of twenty days we finally arrived at a port close to the USA–Mexico border. To cross over into the USA, you had to cross a river and a forest illegally. On the river, a bridge was being constructed, and the workers took a break for fifty minutes every day. This would have to be our time to move. All in all in a span of fifty minutes, we had to swim across the vast river. After that we had to cross the forest at night. Little did we know that the forest was not only home to wild animals but also Mexico's most feared mafia gang!

'We lost about seven men in the waters, and another five to wild animals. The survivors ran for their lives through the forests. As expected, we were captured by the gang and held for ransom. Everyone was asked to get approximately a lakh of Indian rupees in exchange for their lives. Those who did not have anyone back in India were shot on the spot. The rest of us were held captive. Then one night, when the leader and his troops had gone out and the men guarding us had relaxed a bit, we managed to kill them all and escape.

'We fled to the border only to be greeted by a fresh round of firing bullets. The border guards!

'We screamed and begged and lifted our arms to signal surrender. We lost two of our friends to the bullets. The police then captured the remainder of us and held us at the police station for questioning. It was then that I saw a clock and a calendar for the first time since I'd left India.

'It had been almost five months since I last ate a decent meal. Looking around, I saw that only twelve of my friends had survived! After that we asked for political refuge in the land of dreams. We were granted it, but we didn't realize that we were bound in the USA forever. It was only after another ten years that we finally were helped by a non-government organization. They fought for our rights and we were granted citizenship. After that, I joined a few other Indians and set up a small spare-parts business. And from there, there was no turning back. Today I head the Europe zone of the company. I have never travelled to India, nor tried to contact Ramani.

Call it spinelessness or cowardice, but the truth is that I never wanted to see Ramani with any other man. Somewhere deep down, I was still that same hot-blooded Sikh.

'Then about three months ago, my friend from Punjab called me up to say that some girl had come to our old home and had been asking about me. He sent me the details from the business card you had left. I used the Internet to find you, and what I came across was simply unbelievable! How much you had dedicated your life to finding me! I was ashamed. It took me three months to decide if I should contact you and I am glad I did. Alicia, I know this must be too much to take in; and if you still don't believe me, just ask Ramani to show you the tattoo on her hand. It will read 'SHYAM', which is another name for Lord Krishna. And tell her you have found her Krishna for her. Also, don't forget to add that her Krishna has a scar on his forehead from the day he cut himself while fighting thirteen boys in college to prove his love for her. You believe me, Alicia?'

I was flooded with emotion; I actually had a lump in my throat. It was different—it was victory mixed with a sense of witnessing true love unfold. And I justly have to thank and give most of the credit to my friends who supported us through our blockbuster journey which we made together.

The wait has finally ended for all of us. The location is booked and the message has been spread. We all gather at the rock in Cubbon Park, near the Victoria statue, at 4 p.m. sharp on the 12 August 2012. Let us all be dressed in something red, symbolizing love, when we bear witness to this stunning moment in front of our eyes.

Oh God! I am so wound up! I'm finding it difficult to get myself to wait for a month. Imagine having to wait for thirty years!

Sunday, 1 April 2012

I Am a Love Fool!

What a coincidence? Today is the first of April and here, at our tiny NGO office, we have already received twenty-nine prank postcards (I must applaud the timing!), sixteen emails (all pranks, of course!) and even seven prank calls. And in good humour I thank all our readers for cheering us a bit with all these pranks.

But I am nowhere close to finding Singhji, I just returned from my fourth trip to Jalandhar and unfortunately it has still yielded no results. The only good news is that I finally tracked down Singhji's original house, which is now occupied by some other family. This piece of crucial information was shared by a Miss Harpreet, our dedicated reader from Punjab. She even helped us track down the house. I am really overwhelmed at how much support we have been receiving from all our beloved readers. Thanks again, guys. I can never really thank you guys enough!

Let me tell you why this story is so important: I have been in and out of relationships and no one has really stuck on. And I am sure that most people today think that commitment is something that weighs us down. I see marriages breaking up around me and people already on the 're-bound' after such great commitments—even before they have time to call their friends and family. Society has advanced so much now that we have no time for anything!

When I first heard Ramanima's story, I felt like I was being told the plot of a movie. We study the examples of Romeo and Juliet, or Salim and Anarkali, as part of history and literature. Epic love has always been referred to in the past tense since we have no such examples to provide in the present!

Personally, I feel that all of us are slowly losing faith in the great love story, and the Prince Charming theory now only seems applicable to the real-life royal families!

My cause is a little selfish, I must state. I have never found true love. Even so, a part of me has always wanted to be a part of one great love story. So when I heard Ramanima's tale, I decided that I was going to become the modern-day Fairy Godmother to this ever-so-hopeful Cinderella, and help her find her true Prince Charming.

This Fairy Godmother is on a mission!

Sunday, 4 December 2011

The Very Beginning!

I have a mission to embark upon. A chance encounter on my trip to Mysore has left me with no option but to use this medium of mass reach to start a hunt. No, it's not duck season, but it is the season of love. I had met a woman who told me her story of lost love—and it was so heartwarming that I got swept away by it.

For the past five months I have turned hundreds of pages of directories, and used various people finders and search engines. I've travelled three times to Jalandhar, Punjab, and even carefully tracked the Mysore University records from 1982 to 1985 *just* to be thorough in finding a Mr Gurmeet Singh—the hero of our love story.

I was driving from Bangalore to Mysore with a couple of friends, when one of my friends suddenly had to pee. And since we were passing a village we randomly knocked on the door of a pretty house. A sweet middle-aged woman opened the door and welcomed us into her home! We had an instant connection with her and told her that we were on our way to the Mysore University, and one thing led to another and suddenly we were listening to a story which changed our lives.

Ramani—lovingly known to us as Ramanima—was a student at the university thirty years ago. While studying there, she fell in love with a Sikh boy. She had her best memories there and she narrated her story with such passion that we got lost in the details. In fact, right from the first moment she laid eyes on him, she knew he was the one! (How can anyone know that?) But while India may have got her freedom, society was still bound by tradition and love was misunderstood. The stolen glances, the meetings in the park, the large group of friends accompanying them on their outings—it was all like a 1960s' movie!

Incidentally there is even a part where she put Singhji through a test to prove his love. One thing led to another and he was made to beat up thirteen guys, cutting his forehead in the process, and was nursed back to health by Ramanima. (So cute!)

Their love story was cut short when he suddenly left for Jalandhar when the riots broke out there. The two of them were in touch for a while, writing letters for a few weeks. But then he disappeared completely from the face of the earth!

She told us that in her heart she knew he was out there somewhere. She had been waiting for him for about thirty years.

When she showed us the letters, we were stunned! On our way back, as a joke, we took up the mission to find Ramanima her true love. But today I have realized that the mission has become an obsession for me. So I have a request, my dear readers. I need your help! Anyone interested in helping me out can post their comments on this blog or write to me at mission_r_s@gmail.com! I am also starting a Facebook page. Please 'like' it and spread the word!

Together we can make a miracle happen, and we will!

Flirting

VINAYAK NADKARNI

'Has the bus E104 already left?' I breathlessly reached the bus stop and asked the man standing there.

He was taken by surprise, as if I asked him for his wallet. After a pause he replied, 'No.'

I heaved a sigh of relief. As I returned to my normal breathing speed, I asked again, 'I see your tag, do you also work for Reuters Software Solutions?'

He replied 'Yes, I do.'

His voice was strong yet polite. Dressed in neat formal clothes, he was clean-shaven and looked like a well-cultured man. I quickly glanced at his fingers. No rings. All this is fine but what's with these short answers. I wondered if he was simply shy by nature or just plain arrogant. I was also not one of those who would give up easily. There's something strange with women like me—when someone ignores us, we tend to get more attracted to them. It's a classic flaw introduced by the naughty Almighty, but still I could not resist talking to him further.

'Hi, my name is Naina, I joined RSS recently.' I extended my right hand hoping to involve him in a conversation.

'Oh, that's good to know, I am Abhishek.' He rendered a rather weak handshake and did not bother to extend the conversation.

'So which department you work for, Abhi? I guess I can call you that, right?' I continued, moving closer to him. Wow! He smelled great as well. I was hoping we at least end up having a couple of dates, if not more.

'I am in the training department; actually, I am one of the coordinators.' After a small pause, he continued, 'And ya, Abhi is fine.'

With those words, he looked into my eyes for the first time. For me, that's all it takes. Once someone looks into my eyes, they get lost as if they are hypnotized by a magician. The eye contact lasted exactly five seconds before our brief, interesting little moment was abruptly ended by the arrival of the bus. Needless to say, I sat next to him.

After the brief quixotic moment at the bus stop, I was sure that he would be the one to restart the conversation.

'How about you, Naina? Which department do you work for and how do you find our RSS?'

There you go! It was the magic of my earthen-pot eyes and my charm that was putting those words in his mouth. I gave him more details than he asked for, talking about my department, work, colleagues—and I did not stop there. I also hinted that I am the girl to party with. He listened with great interest but I could also sense that he was a shy and quiet person.

Time is heartless. When you want it to move slower, it

flies and when you are waiting for something important, it crawls. Though we travelled almost twelve kilometres for about thirty-five minutes, it felt like less than five minutes. We reached the office and went to our desks. For both of us, the day had started on a bright note.

~

After I reached the office, I went to my desk, checked my emails, had coffee with my colleagues and then returned to my desk. Being a new member, I had very few responsibilities to handle. I was almost through with my day's work within first couple of hours. My crazy mind was recollecting the time spent with Abhi and my logical mind was telling me it could take more effort from my side to make things work. My thought flow was disturbed by the loud voices I heard from the corner of the room. I put my head up to see what was happening. A muscular man, with his shirt torn, was walking out. Curiosity took over and I went to investigate. I learnt that he was involved in an argument with one of the staff members and had left the scene furious. I saw him going towards the men's room. I casually walked in that direction and he came out. He looked very confused as if he didn't know where he wanted to go. Being a responsible employee, I stepped in.

'Excuse me sir, may I help you?' I asked him.

'Er . . . I don't know. I am not sure why I am here. Is there any artists' association or something like that?' he asked.

I was right, he was confused—but even more than I thought. There was no mention of the events that had transpired minutes earlier I chose to carry on with the momentum.

'Yes, but not in this office. It's just a couple of blocks away. I can help you with that.'

'Oh! That's so sweet of you. I am Rohan, a columnist for one of the monthly magazines, called *The Impression*.' He introduced himself by extending his left hand.

'Hi, I am Naina. I . . .' But before I could complete my sentence, I was struck dumb by our handshake. What a firm handshake, strong and confident. I could see the veins distinctly visible on his strong forearm. Either he was very angry or he hits the gym regularly. I continued after returning to my senses. 'I am glad to help you. I was going out for lunch anyway. So you are a columnist for *The Impression*? What do you write about, Rohan?' Unwillingly, I ended the handshake and walked with him towards the exit door. I had gently mentioned about having lunch as well. I was curious to see if he was sharp enough to catch it. I had heard that physically strong people are usually dumb.

'It's mostly philosophy, Naina. We can talk about it more over the lunch,' he replied with his head slightly tilted towards left. His left hand stretched out to open the door for me and there was a smile on his face which read: *You are so gorgeous!*

It was hard to believe he was the same angry young man from a few minutes ago. He took me to a Bavarian restaurant. It was expensive but worth it. He asked me whether I was in a hurry to get back to office. I assured him that I was not. So we walked all the way back instead of hiring a taxi. I left him at the Vintage Artists' Association and returned to office.

~

After a rather eventful day, I was sitting at my desk playing solitaire. The clock showed 6.10 p.m. I was waiting for my cellphone to buzz. Usually it beeps between 6 p.m. and 6.07

p.m. Just then, my phone beeped and the message appeared on the screen:

Cm out baby, I wil b there in 5 mins.

Involuntarily, a smile appeared on my face and I gave a *blow-kiss* in reply. Within five minutes, the white Volkswagon arrived. I stepped in and kissed Gautam on his forehead.

'So how was your day, sweetheart?' he asked with the same enthusiasm, same undying love and same everlasting care as always.

'Wonderful, honey. Let's grab some dinner on the way,' I replied.

'Yes, dear, we don't have time to cook tonight, I am all excited about our big trip starting tomorrow. Finally you can meet my childhood friend!'

We stopped at McDonalds. He ordered two Happy Meals for takeaway. The person at the counter asked, 'What would you like to have as a drink, sir?'

He replied, 'I will take organic milk.' He turned to me and asked, 'How about you, sweety?'

I said, 'Diet Coke.'

He ordered, 'So one organic milk for me and a Diet Coke for my *wife*.'

～

We reached home and ate our dinner watching some sport I am barely interested in. My husband, Gautam, tried to explain to me how different rules apply in different formats. I acted as if I cared. I saw his face brighten with excitement when he thought one of the rules was particularly tricky. I nodded but hardly listened.

I love him. He doesn't know how much. After dinner, we finished packing and Gautam was as excited as a little kid whose summer holidays were about to start after long-and-hard exams. Once he slept, I poured myself a glass of red Bordeaux wine. It takes a lot out of you when you meet different people and try to connect with each of them emotionally. I opened the balcony door of our apartment and stood there staring at the dark sky. Even some of the stars which were usually visible were missing. It was completely dark. I took a couple of large sips and revisited my day in my mind. So it was a day of three persons. Usually it would be two, but today was three. I took one more sip and sat on the chair with my legs up on the table. A cold breeze had picked up. Unknowingly my eyes got moist. I gulped my sorrow along with my wine. Abhi, Rohan, Gautam—I am living a fake life but I chose it. Dr Reddy's words crossed my mind as I closed my eyes and took a deep breath.

'You have to make a choice, Naina. You can leave Gautam here and we will take care of him like any other patient, or you can take him with you.' It sounded insensitive but doctors can't be diplomatic.

'He is the only one for me, I love him. I want to take him, doctor.'

The doctor explained, 'I understand the emotions behind those words, Naina, but it's very complicated. We have observed him over a month now and clearly he has shown us two distinct personalities. Some days even three. The accident has made him develop an MPD. Though it was an accident, Gautam thinks he is responsible for the death of his childhood friend Abhishek. Every morning he wakes up thinking he is Abhishek. In some of the situations where he is put under stress, there is another angry personality, Rohan. As we discussed earlier, I have no idea where this personality has come from. The most important thing is that Gautam's memory is limited only to the day before the accident.'

'Yes, doctor, but multiple personality disorders have been successfully handled by treating every personality with equal respect and attention. Proper love and care make things work,' I argued with hope.

The doctor replied agitatedly, 'Yeah, but you don't know what you are signing up for, Naina. There can be more personalities than we have seen so far. Rohan can be more dangerous and destructive. It demands round-the-clock attention and, more than that, you are putting people around him in trouble as well. Naina, you are flirting dangerously with life!'

'I understand, doctor, but what's life without an impossible challenge? I can do it. I will get the chance to meet two different persons every day. I will make sure he will get the attention that he needs,' I said.

'Naina,' the doctor warned, 'you have to keep him engaged in every personality, you have to care for him, make life interesting for him in each of them.'

'Doctor, I love Gautam—I love him in every form. I love the challenge of making him fall in love every day or rather twice a day.'

I knew it was not for a day or a month. It could take years, or worse—it might never end. Before taking Gautam with me from the hospital, I had to do a lot of preparation. I spoke to those in RSS to carry out this drama daily; I checked with the Vintage Artists' Association about occasional visits whenever Rohan comes up. More than that, I had prepared my mind to act, to involve, to love.

The cold breeze had now become even colder and they broke my chain of thoughts and brought me back to the present. The tears had soaked my cheeks and the wine glass was empty. I went inside, washed my face and went to bed. I had to get ready again to meet Abhishek the following morning.

~

'Has the bus E104 already left?' I breathlessly reached the bus stop and asked the man, Abhishek, standing there.

The Divine Union

K. BALAKUMARAN

Have you ever been alone—truly alone?

Have you ever been in a place that was massive, cold, kind of whitish, calm and serene with a tranquillizing ambience? Lacking human presence, completely enclosed and thereby administering a strong dosage of claustrophobia in you right away?

Have you ever been subjected to the cold embrace of loneliness?

Do you know what it means to be secluded?

Have you ever smelled isolation?

Is this going to be one hundred years of solitude for me?As such thoughts slowly start to take over me, I see her standing there, probably waiting for me, her lips parted slowly to flash that magnetic smile!

~

'As your friend, I'll have to tell you that you're never going to get married, my dear Arun! The kind of girl you are looking for probably doesn't exist, never existed and will never exist. Even if someone like that exists, why in hell would she choose you? You are greedy and your superiority complex is going to keep you single for eternity! Listen to our advice. Stop looking for something ideal and accept a girl that will work out for your family and get settled!' Thus shouted my friend before alighting the train when it arrived at the station. Most of his advice had anyway been swallowed up by the screech of the arriving train.

The girl he'd suggested sometime back—I'd conversed with her the previous day for ten minutes. She was faltering throughout because of her inability to answer any of my questions coherently. General conversation between me and the so-called prospective brides would go something like this:

'Hello.'

'Hello.'

'Your name?'

Prompt response.

'What does it mean?'

'Father kept it/Mother kept it/It's my grandmother's name/ It's fashionable/It's the name of a goddess.'

'Whatever, it should mean something?'

No response.

'Do you read books?'

'Yes,' I would hear a feeble voice.

'Good! What kind of books do you read?'

After few moments of hesitation, 'Cookery, self-help books and some Tamil magazines.'

Some of them would mention some commercial English authors and some of them Paulo Coelho. But when questions are asked about the novels themselves, mainly theme and plot, there would be an incoherent, unintelligible response.

'What do you think about Indo-US nuclear deal?'

'Well, er . . .'

'Do you think we should go for it, given the fact that we will be bound by the 123 agreement?'

'US is a bad country. We shouldn't go for it.'

'Bad means?'

No response.

'Do you think we should sign the NPT?'

'NPT?'

'Non-proliferation treaty.'

No Response.

'Like literature?'

'Yes!'

'Favourite book or author?'

'Thirukkural.' Some of them will say this, as it seems like a safe and smart answer.

'Your favourite *paal*, rather, section?'

No response, most of the times. Some people would gather courage to mention the sections *Aram* (Virtue) or *Porul* (Realities of Life).

'Your favourite *kural* (couplet) and its meaning?'

No response.

'Thank you,' I would say and hang up the receiver.

Almost the same happened yesterday with the girl my friend suggested. Neither did she answer any of my questions coherently nor did she say anything that intrigued me. It seemed that all she had done until then was to get herself ready for marriage by learning to cook, do house chores and other such stuff. When I asked her if she had read John Skelton, she got scared and hung up. She'd informed her parents later that I was asking her about skeletons and black magic. Her parents had admonished my friend and, obviously, he was getting back at me with his advice.

When I was naive, I insisted upon having a girl who was beautiful, with at least the ninety-fifth percentile or higher on a standardized, supervised intelligence test. Later, I slowly relaxed and agreed to compromise on the looks of the girl who should still be intelligent enough to converse with me on a wide range of subjects. This relaxation probably tricked people into believing that I would slowly become as regular in my preferences as any other guy; but I stuck firmly to my ideals, like dried-up glue on one's fingers. This infuriated them.

I never went to people voluntarily and requested them to find a suitable partner for me. It's they who came to me and asked me about my expectations; and whenever I expressed what I wanted, it angered them. They felt that I was being a snob, a prig, a haughty egomaniac who never understood the importance of a girl capable of running a family. I've never felt superior to girls who are trained for marriage. It's just that I felt I wouldn't be compatible with those kind of girls. But nobody seemed to understand this.

I was fed up with these beaten-to-death, clichéd bits of advice. Not that the offensive statements hidden (or sometimes explicit) in the advice hurt me any more. I was clearly far beyond getting hurt by silly statements. But, increasingly, their sheer frequency and repetitiveness bothered me. I requested them—my friends, colleagues, family and 'why-don't-you-marry?' interrogators—not to repeat the same thing again and again. I asked them not to worry about my marriage or my life. But such requests only made them rephrase the same age-old advice—and that's all they did. The content almost remained the same. I sincerely hoped they would understand that I couldn't let myself fall in love with or marry 'just another girl'. However, over time, I found that I was growing weak in the face of this repetitive advice. I was afraid that I would give in at some point, owing to the pressure.

I decided not to discuss my marriage with anybody any more. As they had started chanting in news channels, 'Enough is enough!' But thanks to all the brainwashing of my friends and well-wishers, I had started to get that deep, hidden, uncomfortable feeling in me. Pain? No, pain is too big a word. Fear? Yes, I was starting to get afraid that what these people said—that I may never get married—was destined to happen. Were they words from God thrown indirectly through some random strangers selected as messengers? I started contemplating the idea of spending the rest of my life without a girl. Would it be really bad? It couldn't be worse than what it would be if I were to marry someone who didn't match my tastes, I concluded. I cursed myself for having wasted time by forcing myself into a vicious cycle of depressive thoughts—this always ended up giving me only a heavy measure of negative energy.

I pulled out a medicine strip, pushed the tablet gently as it slowly tore the plastic sheet and came out. I swallowed the tablet at once. I was used to popping pills without water.

~

I opened *The Castle*, the novel that seemed to be getting increasingly difficult with each page, probably due to the fact that I was getting exponentially depressed as my thoughts took over. But before focusing on the novel, I looked around the compartment and understood that I was alone. It was not something new, considering my office timings. Starting at 7 a.m., my office operated until 2 p.m., enabling me to catch that empty train at 2.30 p.m.

As I prepared myself to spend the next one-hour journey alone, a girl entered the compartment and sat down beside the window on the extreme right side. My only other companion in the compartment. Clad in a white dress, she was reading a book by Eco, one hand covering the book's title (although it didn't take much time for me to guess it was *The Name of the Rose*, Umberto Eco's magnum opus) while the other adjusted the strands of her hair that were longing to kiss her face. Something attracted me to her. I mustered some courage, shifted myself and comfortably settled opposite her.

She didn't bother to look at me. She was lost in the book. I gathered myself, cleared my throat and said, 'Hello!'

She slowly lowered her book, smiled warmly and said, 'Hello.'

She was very pretty. There was this air of nobility about; I would sound like a crazy man if I told you that I could even see a thin halo behind her. Her supernatural aura cast a spell on me.

'It's boring being alone, especially when you know the next one hour is going to be like this!' I said, trying to strike up a conversation—and attempting to make it sound as sensible as possible.

'Is it? One hour?' Her voice was just more than a whisper. Any hypnotist would die to become the owner of that voice.

'This is an odd timing. Nobody will board the train at this time. I am used to travelling alone at this hour. By the way, my name is Arun—Arun Selvam. It's a pleasure meeting you!' I said and offered my hand.

'You seem to have no respect whatsoever for Edward

Lorenz, Mr Arun Selvam,' she said casually and reciprocated the gesture.

'Excuse me, what . . .?' At first I didn't get it, then it suddenly struck me what she'd meant. My prediction that nobody would board the train at that time was obviously disrespecting Lorenz's 'Chaos Theory'. I didn't bother to continue my question. I just smiled.

She continued, 'Arun means brilliant, Selvam means wealth. Are you the repository of all the intelligence and brilliance in the world?' She smiled. It was a perfect smile. It was like she couldn't overdo it even if she wanted to.

'Your name?'

'My name is Nila.'

'You mean "moon"?'

She threw me an odd look, probably for having asked something that was so very obvious.

'Yeah, "moon" in Tamil, "Nile river" in Latin and "champion"—'

'In Irish,' I completed. This probably earned me some respect.

I continued, 'Where are you getting down, Nila?'

'A good traveller has no fixed plans and is not intent on arriving.'

'Lao Tzu,' I said at once.

'Good!'

'Yeah, even I firmly believe that "No one realizes how beautiful it is to travel until he comes home and rests his head on his old, familiar pillow"'

'Lin Yutang,' she said immediately.

I held her book in my hand and said, 'You know there's a theory that William of Ockham got inspired by this book and came up with Ockham's razor.'

'Interesting! Are you an atheist?' She asked me without delay.

'Yes! How did you know?'

'People who talk about lex parsimoniae and Ockham's razor are generally atheists!'

'Are you an atheist?'

'No! No! I am a theist. I was convinced by Kurt Godel by his ontological proof,' she said and flashed that killer smile again.

There I was sitting and ogling a girl shamelessly like never before. What was with her that attracted me instantaneously? I realized, with each passing second, I was slowly but surely becoming her slave.

'You are native?' I asked.

'*Yadhum oore yaavarum kaelir* (All the world is my world, all humanity is my fraternity),' she quoted the Sangam poet Kaniyan Poongundranar as she stretched her hands above her head and continued. 'Have you read Sangam works?'

'Yes, you?'

'Yes, thanks to Dr Kamil Zvelebil. If not for him I wouldn't have even touched Sangam works.'

'Your favourite Sangam work?' I inquired.

'*Kurunthokai.*'

It seemed a rather odd choice.

'Oh,' I didn't know what to say.

'Have you read this song by Korikorran in *Kurunthokai*—*Panai thot kurumnagal paavai thaiyum*?' Her diction astonished me.

'Yes, I have. It's the one about the hero's blackmail, isn't it?' I asked and started to watch her again, deciding to maintain silence for some time.

'Good! By the way, why do you go to some dream world

every now and then? Don't expect me to do an interpretation. I am not Freud!' She winked.

How would I let her know that I can exchange anything I possess for that wink?

'Do you believe that Freud's *Interpretation of Dreams* still holds good?' I queried her.

'Don't ask me anything about Freud. You will only get a biased opinion. I firmly believe that whatever he said holds good till date. These modern psychoanalysts—they did nothing but just reinterpret whatever he said in their own way. Concealing the source smartly, then called it their own theory, and as if that was not enough, they rubbished some of Freud's interesting theories.'

'But his Oedipus complex was indeed nonsense!' I was quick to retort.

'Maybe. That's the reason why a group of people started opposing whatever he said.' The sadness in her voice was not well concealed. She was silent for the next two minutes.

'Who is your favourite philosopher?' I asked, trying to break the uncomfortable silence.

'Søren Kierkegaard and Friedrich Nietzsche,' she intoned, without finding the pronunciation difficult.

'Why them?'

'They laid the groundwork for existentialism long back. Didn't they?'

'But, what is so special about existentialism? Again, it says like all other theories that "Life is meaningless". Isn't it?'

'Yes. But it at least gives some importance to the human subject. It's good that somebody at last said, "Stop looking at the thinking subject. Concentrate on the human subject."'

It was already evident that I'd fallen for her. Now, when do I let her know that?

We were then silent for some time—a long time, in fact.

'If life is meaningless, why do you think we all should live?' I asked in an honest attempt to conquer the silence.

She took an eternity to answer.

'Enlightenment,' she finally said and stopped for a moment as if examining something.

The medicine strip in my pocket had caught her attention.

'What's that? You are not feeling well?' There was genuine concern in her voice.

'No, nothing! Just some mild anti-depressants.' There was an awkward pause. 'By the way, you were saying something about enlightenment?'

'Yes, of course. What do you know about enlightenment?'

I spat out the definition without further ado: 'Enlightenment is man's release from his self-conferred tutelage. Tutelage is the incapacity to use one's own understanding without the guidance of another. Such tutelage is self-imposed if its cause is not lack of intelligence, but rather a lack of determination and courage to use one's intelligence without being guided by another.'

'Don't tell me what Immanuel Kant said.' she reprimanded. 'Tell me what you feel about Enlightenment!'

'It's the ultimate goal of every man.'

'Have you tried it?'

'No! I must say I didn't give it much thought.'

'Have you ever tried jumping off a running train?'

I wasn't sure if I heard her right.

'Excuse me?'

'Do you want to taste enlightenment?'

'I don't get you!'

'Have you read the Katha Upanishad?'

'Yes!'

'Do you want to attain enlightenment the same way Nachiketa did? Have you heard of the Nachiketan fire?'

'Yes. The fire-sacrifice for three-fold knowledge, the fire that is burning inside each one of us, named after the boy who confronted Lord Yama himself!'

'Don't you think you have to meet somebody like how Nachiketa met the lord of death?'

She held my hand and led me to the door. Then, smiling, she let my hand go and slowly whispered in my ears, 'Only when you get to meet him, will you be able attain the ultimate goal. After all, what's life without trying to achieve the ultimate goal?'

I just stood there, frozen, trying to comprehend. She blinked for couple of seconds and continued, 'You don't believe me, do you?'

Then she suddenly jumped off the train.

All my senses went numb. When I regained my composure somewhat, I slowly peeped out of the train to see where she'd fallen. She was nowhere to be found.

I understood that she had gone to the same place where Nachiketa went in the Katha Upanishad—to seek enlightenment, to achieve the ultimate goal, to meet her almighty.

As the realization dawned upon me, I stood at the edge and prepared to take a leap.

~

Cameras and reporters were seen everywhere. There were probably a thousand flashes, all at once, with reporters grilling the RPF Deputy Superintendent of Police. Constables were finding it difficult to control the huge crowd gathered there.

'Is it true that the TTE threw this young man Arun Selvam out from a running train for ticketless travel?' It was the millionth time the question was asked.

'See, please understand it's only a rumour. Someone has spread this lie with malicious intent. Mr Selvam certainly had a ticket. We got this from his shirt pocket and the TTE never examined tickets during that time.'

'How did he die then?'

'We have with us here a senior physician, Dr Shankar. He will give you an explanation.'

Dr Shankar adjusted his spectacles as he addressed the media, 'The Police have recovered strips of Clozapine from the victim. Strong dosage—i.e., close to 500 mg—suggests positively that he could have had severe visual, auditory and olfactory hallucinations. The victim could have also suffered from paranoid and bizarre delusions. So, undoubtedly, this is a case of "Sui caedere".'

Reporters left the place, content with the explanation from Dr Shankar.

'Thanks, doctor. We could never have convinced them.' The DSP shook hands with the doctor, and thanked him with all his heart.

~

Is this going to be one hundred years of solitude for me?

As such thoughts slowly start to take over me, I see her standing there, probably waiting for me, her lips parted slowly to flash that magnetic smile!

That was a smile that can belong only to her.

I go near her, labouring hard in the process. Holding her hands, I say, 'You didn't think I would come. Did you?'

She doesn't answer. She just smiles, holding me in her gaze.

Holding me for eternity.

'Did I tell you something?' I ask her, not expecting an answer.

'Hmm . . .' she whispers softly.

I feel the magnificence of the anticipation that filled the air.

'I love you!'

I can hear wild explosions. I hug her gently, push some of the hair that covers her face aside and plant a soft kiss on her cheeks!

Just Because I Made Love to You Doesn't Mean I Love You

ANJALI KHURANA

People half her age knew the difference between sleeping with someone and actually marrying them. Mitali didn't, she never did, and maybe she never would. She'd try hard not to mix sex with emotions but, in the end, would mess up both.

I met Mitali via Aditya who was my colleague when we worked together with UTV. Aditya headed an animation project with the company and Mitali was into film marketing. Mitali hailed from Kolkata. Not many knew she was divorced and had moved to Mumbai in search of a new life after separating from her husband. She didn't socialize much with her team, once out of office. She made fewer new friends and spent more time with her existing ones. Her dusky complexion and brown eyes attracted a lot of male attention at work; but otherwise she looked very average. She was like an obedient child who arrived on time, left on time, did as directed and never opposed her bosses. A simple and straightforward girl, she didn't want any complications in her life, which is why she never took up any competitive role in her team. She ate and slept on time with no demands and no regrets. She earned enough to feed herself in the harsh city, never asked for increments and never desired a lavish lifestyle. She seemed content in her one-woman kingdom.

Aditya and Mitali often worked on projects together but Mitali's reclusive behaviour never gave Aditya a chance to speak about anything other than work. He wondered why she was so unfriendly with him. Aditya Krishnan was doing exceptionally well in his career. He earned a fat salary, lived in a plush house in Bandra, worked only a few hours a week and went on holiday every three months. There was nothing average in his life. He did things in extremes—worked hard, partied harder, took on the most competitive tasks at work and accomplished them before deadlines. He was never alone; his evenings were full of women and wine. He felt drawn towards Mitali perhaps because she was the only woman who repelled him.

It was quite late that night when Aditya packed his stuff and was about to leave. He passed Mitali's desk and saw she was fiddling with an Excel sheet on her computer. He thought of stopping by to ask if she needed help but then recalled how rude she had been each time he offered help in the past, so he carried on. Just when he exited the gate, he realized she was the only one sitting in office at that hour. He somehow gathered the courage to go back and stand behind her. Astonished, she raised her eyebrows suspiciously.

'Isn't it quite late?' he said. 'How will you go home?'

Continuing to add formulae to her Excel sheet, Mitali said, 'I have work to do. Will manage, thanks!'

Aditya wasn't surprised at her answer. He was wondering what to ask her next. At the moment, she seemed very puzzled while calculating the payment to be released to an artist who had raised an invoice of Rs 21,90,000, with an added service charge of 10.3 per cent. Ideally, the total amount raised would be Rs 24,15,570, against which she was supposed to deduct TDS at 10 per cent. But for some unexplained reason, the results on the computer screen were different from her own calculations on paper.

Aditya prompted, 'Rs 21,74,013.'

Mitali looked back and he repeated the digits. She was neither angry nor surprised. She knew he was sharp with numbers, but *why* he was helping her was her concern. Unwillingly, she went with his calculation and corrected the figures on the sheet. For the next ten minutes, Aditya helped her with all the calculations without actually having a conversation with her. He continued to stand behind with his heavy laptop bag hung on his right shoulder, leaning towards the computer screen and prompting the digits. He used the computer's calculator only when Mitali's hand freed the cursor. Finally, they were done. Mitali heaved a sigh of relief and Aditya had a chance to stand straight. He wondered at her discourteous behaviour—she didn't even ask him to sit all this while.

Then, looking into Aditya's eyes for the first time, she thanked him. Aditya felt honoured. Swelling with some confidence, he asked if he could drop her home. For the first time ever in her stint with this company, she agreed to be dropped home. She held a record of not letting anyone do her a favour at work or in general. That's how she was, disciplined and firm. While in the car, Aditya made constant efforts to probe more into her personal life—for instance, whether she lived with a boyfriend, roommates, family, etc.—but Mitali chose selective listening and selective answering. The only time she spoke was when she had to guide him to her house. When they finally reached her old, worn-out, about-to-collapse building, she simply looked away, muttered, 'Thanks' and went inside the building. Aditya said to himself, 'The building compliments her personality so much and vice-versa'. He drove back to his house.

Next morning at work, he again stopped by to see if Mitali remembered that he had dropped her home the night before. Maybe she did, but that was it—she didn't think it was important to smile at him just because he dropped her home. She was indifferent, so Aditya went straight to his cabin and followed his routine. Aditya's colourful life had suddenly become ensnared by Mitali's sadness. The more she avoided him, the further his interest grew in her. He stayed back till late to see how puzzled she remained with numbers. He also visited her Facebook profile to see who she was committed to, who her friends were, or whether she socialized at all, but he found nothing to his avail. She was just as introverted online as offline. One fine evening, Aditya was struggling with a presentation on his laptop when Mitali noticed that his cabin lights were on. She thought to herself, 'This guy never stays back so late, especially on a Friday.' It was 7 p.m. Aditya's usual timings were 11.30 a.m. to 5 p.m.

Unlike Aditya, she didn't mull over whether she should offer him help or not, she simply knocked at the glass door and entered without even giving him a chance to say 'Come in.' He thought he might have committed a crime, judging by the way she walked inside. He went blank.

She asked, 'Isn't it quite late? Why aren't you going home?'

Aditya was pleasantly surprised and had wanted to say, 'I shall stay back every day if you walk into my cabin the same way' but he ended up looking at the presentation and said, 'I'm supposed to mail this across today but my team has made it just as bland as pasta without cheese. So, I'm adding the seasoning to it—my way, of course.'

'Okay,' she said and tried to exit the cabin when he exclaimed, 'Won't you help me? I'm stuck with these creatives just like you were stuck with numbers that evening.'

Mitali turned back to help the poor guy. She knew he was lying—he headed the animation business, so he couldn't *not* know his creatives. While she scrolled down the PPT, he checked her out from top to bottom. Her stats seemed all right to him but this girl wasn't about her body, she was about something else, something Aditya hadn't known himself. He knew for a fact that he had dated one of the best chicks in town and Mitali was so ordinary by contrast. However, he was drawn towards her, especially by her indifferent attitude. Her hair was tied up with just a thin banana clip in several circular knots right above her neck. Aditya was tempted to untie it. He wanted to see how she looked when her burgundy streaks tumbled down. Mitali caught him looking at her hair.

'What do you want me to help you with?' she asked.

'A lot of things,' was his quick reply. But Mitali's hard stare made him change his answer. He said, 'I am yet to decide which of these slides go with text description . . . See, ah . . . here . . . umm . . .'

And that evening, both spent time in that cabin shuffling slides around in that PPT, resizing images, Googling new ones—basically not doing anything fruitful but making the most of each other's company. Aditya evidently liked having her around in his cabin. Mitali seemed to feel at ease too, but she was careful with her expressions and tried being indifferent, this time deliberately. Aditya dropped her home once again but this time she did look into his eyes when she thanked him.

Things were clearly shaping up between them. Aditya really had to struggle a lot to look inside Mitali's hard shell. Only one out of ten times would his efforts make the dusky girl smile, talk and flirt. Like a Hindi film hero, Aditya pleased her with something new every day. For Mitali, tangible things didn't matter, so Aditya couldn't gratify her with expensive wine-and-dine options, luxury watches and imported perfumes. He learnt that she really enjoyed was spending 'real' time with each other—for instance, sitting on the shore together and looking at the sea, whether or not they talked to each other. She liked keeping quiet most of the time; her listening skills were great. It took Aditya almost three months to come close to Mitali whereby she confided in him about her past and present.

Once it so happened that Mitali's empty house and lonely evening were graced by Aditya's surprise visit. Mitali made a quick coffee and they began talking. When she was reciting the incident of her broken marriage to him, he felt so shaken inside that he wanted to hold her tight and say, 'I'm here for you.' Mitali wasn't sobbing or crying; she had let go of her past, she was out of it, but Aditya felt the need to comfort her. He was more heartbroken than her on learning about her past. He saluted the spirit of womanhood, realizing how tough women could be when they needed to be. He had till date only been with sexy, suave and urban women who liked dancing, drinking and making out with him. Mitali was distinctively different. He was now sure of his feelings for her. Just as Mitali finished reciting her story, she said, 'So . . . this is me, ordinary and average at my best.'

In response to this, Aditya came so close to her that she couldn't repel him any more. He kissed her before she could know what was happening. He held her tight, wrapped both his arms around her, and she reciprocated by surrendering completely. That night, Mitali's gloomy house lit up with joy. Mitali hadn't been loved like this in a long time. Things had started to change thereafter. Mitali's life was changing for the good—just as she always deserved.

Aditya's happiness knew no bounds when he saw Mitali transform from a reserved and uptight girl to a chirpy sparrow. She laughed and giggled more often these days. She met people with glee and the radiance on her face said a lot about her new relationship. Even her colleagues had started interacting with her freely, unlike before. With a new wardrobe, a new smile every day and a new relationship, Mitali became a rockstar. Aditya took the credit delightfully. Though no one talked about their affair in front of them, people discussed it behind their backs.

Aditya was happy with Mitali. In the evenings, either he was at her house or she was at his. They cooked and ate together. They made love like nobody's business. Aditya had disconnected himself from other women. He drank very little these days. He partied even lesser and listened to soothing music with Mitali. He was quite okay with his changed lifestyle. Mitali thanked God for her separation from her husband because she realized she was destined to meet Aditya.

Nearly a year had passed. Mitali's parents made a visit to Mumbai. Aditya and Mitali both went to receive them at the airport. Aditya made her parents feel just as comfortable as he would have made his own. They were happy with their daughter's choice. They spoke to her candidly in Aditya's absence and asked her to take the relationship to the next level. She was a little reluctant, considering what had happened in the past, but her parents explained to her the difference between her earlier choice and Aditya. They said, 'Your earlier choice was someone whom *you* loved, cared for and wanted to marry. He had no career, no dreams, no concern towards household responsibilities; but you still convinced him to marry you. It didn't work and hence you both fell apart. Aditya loves you, takes care of you and does everything to make you happy. He is doing well in his career and can ensure a healthy life for both of you in the future. If we were to find a match, it would've been him.'

Aditya undoubtedly made their stay a memorable one—he took them around the city in his car, spent time with them speaking about his family and career and assured them that he would take care of Mitali once they went back. After her parents left for Kolkata, Mitali and Aditya were having a casual conversation about what kind of marriages lasted forever and which ones fell apart soon. Mitali expressed a desire to remarry, to which Aditya gave a blunt answer, 'Marry? Once again? Are you mad, what's wrong with you?'

Mitali was taken aback by his sudden reaction. She responded, 'What's so wrong about remarrying? Just because it didn't work in the past doesn't mean it won't work in the future.'

Aditya: 'Come on, Mitali, I thought you were out of this ceremonial nonsense—that you had moved on . . . Why do you want to marry again?'

Mitali: 'Ceremonial nonsense? Are you saying your parents and mine are putting up together because of some ceremonial nonsense?'

Aditya: 'Let's not drag parents into this! Who do you plan to marry, or rather, who wants to marry you this time?'

Mitali was stunned at his question. For the next one minute, she wasn't sure if he had actually said what she had just heard. She mumbled, 'Don't you?'

Aditya looked at her and asked, 'Do you mind repeating your question?'

Mitali's trembling lips managed to ask him, 'Don't you want to marry me?'

Aditya's eyes were full of anger. He somehow modulated the tone of his voice and answered, 'When did I say that I wish to marry you?'

Mitali's world went blank. She had no answer. She was looking at him and praying to God that he was kidding.

He repeated his question, 'When did I say I wish to marry you?'

After awaiting an answer for a minute or so, he continued, 'Listen to me very carefully, Mitali. I don't recall an incident when I have expressed a desire to marry you. If you have misunderstood my care and affection for love, then I'm very sorry for you. Just because I'm not sleeping with other women doesn't mean I'm committed to you. Even if I were committed to you, where does marriage come into the picture?'

Mitali wasn't shedding tears but her expressionless face clearly depicted that her heart was crying aloud in distress. She chose to stay quiet and listen.

Aditya continued, 'And please don't tell me that you are so old-fashioned that just because I met your parents and greeted them nicely, you assumed that I am pleasing them so that they agree upon our match and some crap like that. Mitali, if it is so, then I regret treating them so well; I would have done that for any friend's parents.'

Mitali uttered her first word after a long pause, 'Friend?'

Aditya: 'Why, do you not know that we are friends? Do you not know how wonderful a host I am for all my friends and their folks?'

Mitali: 'Now I know . . . We were friends!'

Aditya was full of animosity by now. He got up and screamed at the top of his voice, 'Mitali, don't talk like a sixteen-year-old! If you were under the impression that you are my girlfriend, that's your fault, not mine.'

Mitali was very subtle and well behaved when she replied to his last comment, 'Why did you make love to me if you didn't love me at all?'

Aditya was terribly perplexed at her useless questions. He said, 'Have you lost it or what? Just because having sex is called "making love" in your language, it doesn't mean I actually love you. Please Google some expert comments on sex so that you don't talk like a dumbo the next time.'

Mitali got up from the couch into which she had sunk all this while and proceeded towards the door. Aditya asked, 'Where are you going?'

Mitali opened the door and replied, 'I'm showing you the way out. It's my house, please leave.'

Aditya carried his shoes in his hands, picked up his wallet from the table and left in the next thirty seconds.

Just as he approached the main gate, he received a call on his cellphone. It was Mitali.

He picked up and said 'Hello' in the most impolite manner, possibly thinking that she had called to apologize. But instead she had called to say, 'You forgot your car keys, come back and collect them from the foot mat. The door will be shut.'

One Night Stand in Hariharapuram

MOHAN RAGHAVAN

'Achamma, shall I turn on the AC?' asked my grandson Raman.

'It's fine as it is, Raman.'

Raman was very attached to me and couldn't bear to see his eighty-three-year-old grandma distressed. I rarely showed my emotions but today was different.

'Want some water, Achamma?' he pressed on, worried that the tension might affect me.

As the car picked speed on the flyover, the wind blew on to my face. I saw the horses galloping on the race course far away. I could distinctly hear the clatter of horses in my mind's ears. My mind galloped too—backwards in time . . . more than six and a half decades back . . . to the royal palace of Hariharapuram . . .

~

I was fifteen. The year was 1944. I belonged to Moolapuram, but frequently visited my aunt who was married into the royal family of Hariharapuram—a scenic principality high on the grassy slopes of the Sahyadri Mountains in northern Kerala. The palace was a large two-storeyed wooden structure amidst the woods and faced the green rolling hills. The rooms surrounded a central quadrangle with a small lily pond. The durbar was a large hall on the first storey. The women stayed in rooms on the second floor. Just next door was the ancient Hariharan temple which gave the kingdom its name. The Hariharapuram kings were the custodians of this rich temple with valuable treasures hidden deep in its vaults. The kings on their part used the riches only for the temple upkeep and to provide relief to people during natural calamities. They considered themselves the servants of Lord Hariharan and the people of Hariharapuram. It was this humility that endeared the royal household to the people.

That day I was loitering alone in the garden when voices from the durbar above caught my ears.

'Has the Resident been informed?' It was the frail voice of the ageing king Periya Thamburan. Thamburan was an honorific for 'prince' or 'king'.

'Yes, Thamburan . . .'

'What was the reply . . .?'

'The Resident refused to interfere in our internal matters . . .'

'Hah . . . Like they never interfere,' came the sarcastic reply. The Resident, Lord Iemmington, was the representative of the British crown. The kings looked after routine administration but didn't maintain armies for which they depended on the British.

'Thamburan, they are doing it on purpose . . . They are aware of Ramachhan's revolt. But they would rather have him finish us off, so they can take over Hariharapuram.'

'Yes, Thamburan,' said another voice, 'I have heard too . . . that they want to raise resources for the war against Germany . . . .and . . .'

'And what?' Periya Thamburan's voice betrayed alarm.

' . . . the treasure of Hariharapuram temple is on their minds . . .'

'Never! As long as the last man of Hariharapuram is alive, it will remain here . . . and will be used for the people of Hariharapuram!' Periya Thamburan thundered.

'But what can we do, Thamburan? If Ramachhan raids the palace and the Resident remains silent, we are no match for them . . .'

There was a deathly silence.

'Listen . . . ' Periya Thamburan broke the silence. 'As per the treaty they can take over the temple only if there are no male heirs . . . Even if a single one of us is alive, they cannot take over without inviting the ire of the people . . . which they won't risk at this time.'

'If Ramachhan were to attack, half of us will stay back to defend. The rest will go different ways . . . May Lord Hariharan be with us!'

I was too scared to hear any more and ran away to my aunt.

～

As night fell, mist covered the green hills. The croaks of the beetles and other insects in the woods made grim music. Little oil lamps flickered in the room. I was sitting with my aunt by the window. There was pitch darkness outside. The sky was cloudy and the moon peered out occasionally, throwing a dim light on the valley. The temple bells rang incessantly as the day's last service came to a crescendo. Hundreds of flickering lamps in the temple courtyard were the only source of light on the dark night. The villages around were fast asleep. I don't know how long I sat glued to the window before I had dozed.

Suddenly I woke up. There was a commotion and loud voices. The sound in the foliage outside was unmistakable. Was it an army of elephants? Or . . . Was it Ramach—! I froze in fear. There was no one around. I rushed downstairs. There was mayhem.

'Ramachhan is here! The traitor!' a loud voice screamed. 'All women rush to the temple!'

I ran out of the door behind the womenfolk. Before I could reach the temple gate there was a loud clatter and suddenly a bunch of horsemen with faces covered rushed towards us. Scared out of my wits, I ran back into the palace. The men rushed out with swords in hand to meet the invaders. I could only hear the screams and roars of men fighting outside.

'We've been surrounded . . . For the sake of Hariharan! Go! Go!' screamed a voice. It was Periya Thamburan . . . Immediately five men rush back into the palace and made for the side door that opened out into the dense forest. That's when I was spotted.

'What are you doing here? You should have been in the temple!' screamed their leader.

And without waiting for my answer, he dragged me out with him. We had barely taken a step when I heard a gunshot and my rescuer collapsed in a pool of blood. I ran behind a boulder. There were dozens of men dressed in local costumes, but their faces were European. As the gunshots raged, I ran into the woods. Behind me, I could see all except one collapse in a heap, hit by bullets. I didn't go far before I tripped and fell.

'Get up and run . . . or else we will both be killed!' ordered a voice behind me.

I ran behind him, taking a mud path into the woods. I didn't know where it would lead, but my companion seemed to know. After running for almost an hour, we came to a small clearing. I turned back to see that we had descended into the valley in front of the palace. High above me I saw the raging fire in the palace.

'Traitors! They are burning the palace!' said my companion. Then, with some urgency, he hissed, 'Let's go!'

We walked an hour more before we came to a small house in the dense forest.

'Get in,' he ordered.

We opened the creaky door and entered to see a small dark room with no windows. I could see nothing inside. My companion entered and, running his hands around the wall, produced an oil lamp and lit it. We immediately closed the door so that nobody could see the light from afar. I collapsed in exhaustion while my companion sat grimly by the oil lamp. For the first time I got a glimpse of his face. He was not yet a man, probably just a little older than me. I recollected seeing him at the palace occasionally. He was one of the grandsons of Periya Thamburan.

'Scoundrels . . . they planned this all . . . to exterminate the line of Hariharapuram!' he intoned, furious.

'Anyone else escaped?' I asked.

'I doubt it . . . They surrounded the palace. They knew all the exit points. That traitor Ramachhan!'

I thought of my aunt and uncle. Tears flowed down my cheek. For the first time that night I had time to weep.

My companion had a stony expression on his face. 'We won't be safe here for long. Soon they will realize that I have escaped and come looking.'

'But where can we go?' I asked.

'Nowhere . . . We are probably safe till early morning, and then they will search the woods. We have to get out of here in a few hours time.'

He sat there with eyes closed, facing me, motionless. His handsome features were silhouetted by the light of the oil lamp. The long straight nose, hard cheeks, a large forehead, a broad chest, slightly muscular frame.

Suddenly he broke down. 'Periya Thamburan, we have failed you . . . We have failed you . . .' he repeated as he shook his head and hid his face in his palms.

Looking at him cry, I could cry no more.

'They won't spare the males—those dogs! I could see them shoot all those who came out of the side door.'

'Was your father among them?' I asked.

'I don't know . . . and it doesn't matter,' he said, resuming his grim posture. 'It just doesn't matter who died, but someone must survive. We promised Periya Thamburan . . . for the sake of Hariharan . . . and the people . . . or else all the treasures will be gone! The people will starve!'

Amidst my fear and grief I couldn't help but marvel at this man. He had seen his entire family wiped out in front of his eyes, but yet grieved only for the people.

'Don't worry, you will escape,' I said weakly.

He remained silent.

'I don't think it very likely . . . Anyway, you are the one from Moolapuram, right?'

'Yes . . .'

'All right, listen. I'll take you to a family of hunters who live some distance away. They'll escort you safely to Moolapuram. No guest to Hariharapuram should be harmed. Let's go.'

'No, I am not going away anywhere,' I answered stoutly. 'Moolapuram is not a home for cowards.'

'But what can you do? . . . Fight? With a sword against their bullets?' He was enraged at my audacity.

'No . . . But I can make sure that at least a male survives to serve Lord Hariharan and his people.'

'You can't save me.'

'I didn't say so . . .'

'Then get going . . .'

'You are not the only one who can serve the people. Your forefathers did and so will your descendants . . .'

'You!' he shouted, shaking in anger.

'I didn't mean to belittle you!' I said sheepishly.

He fell silent, probably ashamed at having raised his voice.

'Listen . . .' I continued.

'You may not survive, but your son may live to do what you want to.'

'My son? I don't have one.'

'I know . . . but you may have one tomorrow . . .'

'Are you mad? I am only eighteen and not yet married . . . Which son are you talking about?'

I moved closer to him and looked him straight in the eye and whispered, 'We have time till morning . . . If Lord Hariharan wills, you may have a son. *We* may have a son . . .'

The last part of the sentence jolted him. He remained dumb with an expression of horror on his face.

'See, as you said, they are after males, so I may escape alive even if caught, and so will my son—our son.'

A long silence ensued.

'Do you know what you are saying?' he exclaimed, finally breaking his silence.

'Yes.'

He stared at my face long and hard. Our eyes met, and stayed locked in an inexplicable bond. My heart was almost still. I hardly breathed. Neither did he. I don't know how much time passed. Neither of us blinked. Time seemed to have come to a standstill . . . until he lunged forward and clasped me in a tight embrace. His broad shoulders seemed to me like the trunk of a huge banyan in which I happily nestled.

With tears in his eyes he looked at me. 'If you succeed, Hariharapuram will worship you forever,' he said. These were his first words in a long time.

'If Lord Hariharan wills, it will happen . . . my Thamburan,' I said.

Gently he ran his fingers over my moist eyes and wiped them.

Swiftly he ran his fingertip over the streak of kumkumam on his forehead and brought it close to my forehead. As I looked into his eyes, he pressed his finger hard on my forehead a little above where the brows meet. I could feel the neat circular mark of his finger on my forehead that had been washed by torrents of sweat. He placed the oil lamp between us. Clasping my hands tightly in his, he whispered into my ears.

'We are one . . . May Lord Hariharan be the witness . . .'

I continued to look into his eyes in half amazement and half stupor.

He gently placed his hands on my head and then slowly

and firmly on my breasts—as if to say that our hearts were one from this moment. The small shack was glowing in the golden hue of the lamp. Everything seemed golden—the lamplight, his face glistening in the light beams, my gold-bordered sari . . . . just everything. It was the golden moment of my life.

I just realized that my sari was completely dishevelled after the run, and had become miserably loose. He noticed it too.

~

We were woken by the sound of waterfowl in the distance. I couldn't move an inch. His strong arms had firmly woven a net around me. Soon he woke up too.

Quickly he jumped up and peered out of the crevice in the door.

'It's about to be dawn. Quick! Let's move.'

In a trice we were out and moving. We walked for about half an hour when we came to a small stream by the mountainside.

'You need to go down that slope and through the estates. The hunters—they are our people; they will escort you safely to Moolapuram.'

'You?' I asked.

'I can't come in there . . . The place will surely be watched. I will move into the denser forests on that side.' he said, staring into the distance.

I felt my heart sinking. But before it did, I sank into his arms again.

'Do not waste any more time,' he said as tears streamed down from my eyes.

I walked silently down the path, but I kept turning back.

He stood there looking straight at me. Then I looked back one last time, and ran away sobbing heavily. I could take it no more.

~

Screech! The tyres screamed as our car came to an abrupt halt.

'Sorry, Achamma! The dog came right in between.'

'It's okay,' I mumbled. I was jolted back to the present.

As the car picked speed, I leaned back into the seat again.

The years following that eventful night had gone by in a blur. People said the entire household was put to the sword. My Thamburan was caught and exiled to Andaman. The temple was ransacked. But the treasures weren't found; except for the idol of Hariharan which was promptly shipped to England. Our son Udayan was born soon afterwards.

After 1947 I came back to Hariharapuram and lived there like a commoner under a new identity. With the help of the local people we formed a trust and revived the temple. Udayan grew up to be a businessman of repute and then we had much more funds to manage. Ten years ago, with the help of archeologists, the treasures were located and put under the custody of the temple trust headed by Lakshmi, Raman's sister.

Once things stabilized, I moved over to Bangalore where my son lived. Last year we found the idol of Lord Hariharan going for auction at a British museum and brought it back. But for all these years there was no trace of my Thamburan and I was fast losing hope. Then, just two days before the idol was to be reinstalled in its original place, Raman saw a report in the papers about some person who had been brought into a Mysore hospital with third-degree burns. The person supposedly had identified himself as belonging to the erstwhile royal family of Hariharapuram.

Immediately Raman and I headed for Mysore in his car.

~

'Achamma . . .'

'Yes?' I knew he was itching to start a conversation.

'You spent just seven hours with a man, but have lived seven decades living his dreams . . .'

'Our dreams,' I corrected.

'Okay, but . . . it was just a . . . a one night—'

'One night stand?' I smiled. 'That is the difference between love and infatuation, Raman,' I said gently.

'But don't you think you have just been a doormat . . .?'

'Yes I was . . . but so was he . . . We both were doormats at the temple of Hariharan and his people.'

'You think he will remember you—if at all we find him?'

I smiled.

'It may be a question for you, but for me it is a fact.'

He fell silent.

Soon we were at the hospital. I walked as fast as my old legs would carry me. An old man with a long beard met us at the door. Apparently he was the one who had brought in the patient to the ICU. He had a few words with Raman, who then came back to me with a somber face.

'Achamma, you have to be brave . . .'

'Don't teach me bravery. What's the matter?'

'He is no more . . .'

'Where is he?'

All three of us walked through a few doors. At one corner was a stretcher. I gingerly moved the bedspread away. The body was charred beyond recognition. I gently put my hands on his forehead. With tears streaming down my cheeks copiously, I stroked his head again and again. Oh! If only he could have been alive one more day, to see his dream fulfilled . . .

I could take it no more. I put my face close to him and whispered, 'Thamburan, we kept our promise to Periya Thamburan . . . Lord Hariharan will be back in his place tomorrow.'

A few minutes of silence ensued.

'Thamburatti . . .' I heard a voice behind me. I was startled at being addressed as 'princess'.

The old man who had brought us in was standing just a few inches from me.

His eyes were moist. I looked into those eyes—those very same eyes! Unmistakable!

I fell into his arms.

'Forgive me for this. I didn't know how else to find you!' he said.

'Thamburan, we kept our promise . . . we kept our promise,' I said again and again as I wept uncontrollably.

'*You* kept our promise . . . my princess! O princess of Hariharapuram!'

May God Bless You, Dear

YAMINI VIJENDRAN

The small, hard grains of rice were now soft, white and flaky. Cooked. The steam—that had till then swirled inside the stifling confines of the pressure cooker—now prepared to make a grand exit, announcing to the world that its goal was accomplished and it was free to become one with the universe. It gathered momentum and gave one final victory whistle—the intensity of which would have given the Hogwarts Express a run for its money—and escaped into eternity.

The neighbour sat up in consternation, cursing the jobless, thoughtless and sleepless old lady who had no better work than to cook at three in the morning! 'But the old lady is not so thoughtless every day,' a part of his brain reminded him, and he remembered the delicious rasgollahs she had prepared for him a couple of days ago. Indignation simmering down to a grumble, the neighbour reached for his earplugs and dived into his half-completed dream again.

'That's four. Should be enough,' thought Brinda, counting the whistles while adjusting the red coin-sized orb of kumkum on her forehead before walking over to the kitchen to switch the stove off.

She worked on a raita and ten minutes later, sure that the steam would have completely exited the cooker by then, she opened the vessel. The mouthwatering aroma of kashmiri pulao wafted through the early morning breeze, making the neighbour smack his lips even in sleep. Perfect, just as Rajan would love it.

She had worked very hard yesterday on today's menu, finalizing and changing it three times, before she finally decided on it. It had to be kashmiri pulao, rajma, aloo paratha and raita, Rajan's most favourite dishes. Nothing else would fit the occasion. She had carefully remembered to get all the ingredients required for cooking the lunch yesterday itself, and was now breezing through her cooking, already past the halfway mark.

A while later, the hot parathas, spicy rajma and other dishes sat on the dining table, all neatly packed—first in aluminum foils and then in Tupperware boxes—waiting for their creator to dress up.

Brinda chose a peacock-blue Kanjeevaram, the MS blue, named after the Queen of Carnatic music, M.S. Subbulakshmi. Rajan had gifted it to her on her retirement and it had looked perfect on her. All of sixty years, she had looked resplendent in that sari, commanding respect and exuding warmth as she sat through her retirement party.

That was the thing with Rajan. Everything he did and said was perfect, or at least nearly so. Be it in business or personal life, his decisions were always bang on. He was a master of people management and he exhibited his skills both at work and at home, adeptly guiding his son without being authoritative or imposing. It was this amazing trait of his which made him a hero in the eyes of his son and wife. Unlike other young men who thought it was unfashionable to pay heed to their father's advice, Arvind still hung on to his father's every word. So did Brinda. Rajan was like the magical mirror in Brinda's life, one she looked up to whenever she wanted an opinion.

Brinda appraised herself as she wore a string of jasmines over the bun she had tied her hair into. Rajan had come to love this look of hers in recent years. Before that, she remembered, gently pushing a hairpin into the bun to hold the jasmines in place, he had liked her plaiting the hair and letting a foot-long double string of jasmines hang from the top of the plait. His love for seeing flowers in her hair grew mostly in the later years. When they were young, during courtship and right after marriage, he liked her to let her hair loose. The scent of her hair gave him a high that no joint in the world could match, he had told her on many occasions.

Placing the lunch basket carefully beside her on the back seat, Brinda nodded to the driver. He had already revved up and kept the car ready for Madam. He had been with the household for many years now and knew the importance of this day. Therefore he certainly didn't want the car to cause any kind of hitch by failing to start in the early morning chill.

The car was just turning the end of the lane when Brinda's phone rang. Even before she looked at the screen she knew it was Arvind.

'All set?' he asked, emotions constricting his voice. 'Did you make any sweets?'

'No, son. Your father does not like sweets, remember?'

'Of course. Just asked. Hope everything goes well. Take care, Ma.'

It took just twenty minutes to reach the place, thanks to the empty morning roads. As the car entered the compound, Brinda could hear sounds of Suprabhatam in MS's voice floating through the morning breeze. Rajan loved these verses.

She got down from the car, which the driver then drove away towards the parking lot, and walked towards Rajan's room. As she neared it, she could hear the nurse's voice, 'Good morning, Mr Rajan. Hope you slept well.'

She did not hear any response.

Rajan was sitting on his bed, in the posture the nurse had made him sit. His eyes were lost in some far-off, unknown realm, searching answers for questions that did not exist. Brinda fussed over him for some time, changing his sheets, making him wear a new shirt and dhoti, combing his hair. Then she sat by his side and read the Gita the whole morning. Every now and then she looked up to her husband's face to see if there was any sign of cognition. None whatsoever was forthcoming. She collected herself and went back to reading. She maintained a stoic appearance and never showed signs of the pain she felt seeing her dear Rajan in this state—right from the day she came to know of his ailment.

Dementia. That's what had hit the Rajan family. When the dynamic and flamboyant Rajan began to get lost in mid-sentence, everyone was amused at first. The amusement soon turned to horror when the condition was diagnosed. As he degenerated and increasingly became a vegetable, Brinda and Arvind had no other choice but to leave him in a palliative care centre, since Arvind's job required him to travel extensively and Brinda was no longer strong enough to single-handedly take care of everything. That's how Rajan landed in this place.

Though Brinda knew that this disease was degenerative with no proper cure, she had hoped for some sort of recovery. The doctors had told her it would be possible only through a miracle. But God was not in any mood for miracles just then. Rajan's condition went from bad to worse.

It wrenched Brinda's heart to see her husband like this. He seemed a shadow of his former image. Or perhaps a previous birth. She hated to see him undergo the agony and pain the treatment was causing. The self-made man Rajan now dependent on another person to even pee. Unable to bear Rajan's plight, Brinda had made the decision after consulting Arvind.

It was mid-day. Time for lunch. Brinda took out the lunch basket and laid the items on the table beside Rajan's bed. She put a little of each item in a plate and repacked the rest. Giving the rest of the food to the nurse, Brinda said, 'It is my husband's birthday today and I made some special food. I would like all you good people who take care of my husband to have some. Please take this and distribute it among your team of nurses, would you?' The nurse happily obliged and went to share the treat with her colleagues.

Brinda closed the door behind the nurse and returned to Rajan. She sat for a moment near him, wishing for his lost eyes to turn their focus on her, just once. Closing her eyes, she planted a soft kiss on Rajan's forehead, concentrating the full intensity of her love into those two little arcs and stamping them on to his skin. A minute later, Brinda took a small vial from her handbag and added some of its contents to the food on Rajan's plate. She started feeding her loving husband spoonfuls, singing softly:

'Happy birthday to you, happy birthday to you,
Happy birthday dear Rajan, happy birthday to you.
May God bless you, dear, may God bless you, dear,
May God bless dear Rajan, may God bless you, dear.'

Tears streamed down Brinda's eyes. The red orb on her forehead somehow resembled the setting sun, as if it knew this would be the last day it would shine on Brinda's forehead. From tomorrow, white would be the only colour in her world. Praying, 'May God bless my husband with an easy and painless death,' Brinda went on feeding the poisoned food to the person she loved the most.

Cheers to Love

RENU BHUTORIA SETHI

I, Trisha Mehta—twenty-seven, blogger and screenplay writer—-have achieved all that I had hoped to achieve. And yet there is something missing. Friends said that it was love that I was missing. I didn't really think so; I was never a romantic person by heart. I frankly think the whole concept of love is completely rubbish and overrated. Love is just a tool where you use your partner and your partner uses you, each to their own benefit. In short, love is selfish.

I am travelling to Delhi to meet my mom. My parents are divorced. My dad lives in Chandigarh with his partner and my mom lives in Delhi, married to a businessman. Every year, my mom sends me a ticket to visit her on her birthday. Usually I avoid, because I can't really stand that man and my mom together. This time I agreed, as I have an important bloggers' meet in Delhi. What's better than getting your trip paid for? I am surprised that finally she has understood my aerophobia. This time I get a first-class train ticket to Delhi. I switch on my laptop, thinking of updating my blog. The door of my cabin is open and a guy—somewhere in his thirties—enters. We exchange smiles. He sits on the seat opposite mine. He too takes out his laptop and gets busy with it. After few minutes the guy asks 'Hey, what time do we reach Delhi?'

'10.30 a.m.,' I tell him.

I can feel the guy looking at me. Finally he says, 'So what do you do?'

'I am a writer.'

The guy smiles—whatever be the thing, the man does have an amazing smile.

'So what do you write about?' the man asks.

'I write short stories on human relationships,' I say.

'You mean love stories?' he asks, looking interested.

'There are no love stories and I don't really believe in love stories,' I spoke my mind .

The man said thoughtfully, 'You have to see one to believe in one, let me tell you a story . . .

~

June 1973. Uday Singh was just twenty-one years old when he became a chartered accountant, the first boy to study beyond metric. The villagers had no idea about the enormity associated with becoming a CA. His family, instead of celebrating, was busy mourning that he was of no more use to them. According to them, he was ruined because he would never become farmer and help his father. Uday wanted to shift to Calcutta and join a nationalized bank. His parents were a little sceptical about his decision, but finally relented on the condition that he'd get married before that. He agreed.

Within a couple of days his parents even found him a girl. Her name was Asha. She lived in a small village near Bhiwani, Haryana. It was Uday's aunt—who also lived in the same village—who had suggested that girl. Uday went with his family to see the girl. When he reached his aunt's place, he saw a girl in a shabby salwar–kameez—but with spotless fair skin and beautiful green eyes—washing utensils outside her home. She looked at him briefly and again went back to work

In the evening, he got ready to meet Asha, the girl he was there for. When he came out, he again saw that green-eyed girl playing with other kids and laughing. Her laughter was as beautiful as her face. The girl too looked at him and again went back to playing. He thought about her eyes, her skin and the way she looked. With that thought he entered Asha's house.

'They are rich people, they have twenty-four cows and buffaloes and a big piece of land, and she is their only daughter,' his aunt said. 'They would even give a good dowry,' she insisted. But Uday was not even listening to her; all he thought about was that girl, that beautiful green-eyed girl. He didn't even know when Asha came and left. His thoughts were somewhere else. The girl's father confirmed that they were ready to give Rs 25,000 and one kilo of gold as dowry. But Uday was not even interested in the money. He just sat there, expressionless. When everybody started leaving, he too got up and left.

The moment he reached his aunt's place, everybody surrounded him. They wanted to know what he thought about the girl. Uday finally said, 'I didn't even see the girl . . . I want to marry *that* girl.' And he just pointed out of the door towards the green-eyed girl in the shabby salwar–kameez, playing and laughing. His aunt was shocked. She said, 'She's

Sarita. Her father passed away three years back and her mother stitches clothes to make enough money to feed her children. They won't even be able to give Rs 2000, leave aside Rs 25,000 and one kilo gold.'

But Uday wanted to marry her only and nobody else. He knew he was in love. He put forward an ultimatum to his parents, 'It's either Sarita or nobody!' Finally, with a heavy heart, his parents agreed. Sarita's mother was called and was given the proposal. She said she did not have much money to fund the marriage. Uday reassured her and said that they were going to have a temple wedding with only his immediate family and Sarita's immediate family in attendance. Uday's parents got up to revolt but, seeing Uday's stern expression, they sat down.

The next day he married Sarita. She looked stunning in a red zari sari with jewellery. Uday couldn't take his eyes off her. As they were about to exchange garlands, she looked up and smiled her captivating smile; Uday smiled back. He loved her more and more with every passing minute. He promised himself that he would do his level best to see this beautiful face smiling always.

After they returned to his hometown, the young couple left for Calcutta the very next week. As they came out of the Howrah station, Sarita was amazed to see how big the city was. Cars zoomed past her. She had never seen anything like that before. It was nothing like her village. She was astounded by the vastness of this city and beauty of it too. In Calcutta, initially they stayed in a hotel, until they found a house to live in. And till then they did not sleep together. Sarita insisted on sleeping separately on the floor. At first, Uday thought she was perhaps nervous, so he did not question her. But finally, he asked her why she wasn't sleeping with him on the same bed. Sarita's eyes grew big and she spoke very innocently, 'Ma had said if I slept with you on the same bed, I would get pregnant . . .' Uday was speechless. He didn't say anything. He knew she was young and that he had to wait. He had no problems with that. But he couldn't see her sleeping on the floor every night.

The very next day, he got a sofa for his place. Sarita was very excited as she had never seen anything like it. By the time the delivery men left, she had climbed on to the sofa and started jumping on it. Bouncing on the sofa's springs, her laughter and playfulness was infectious. Uday too climbed on to the sofa and jumped with her. Finally exhausted, they sat on it and laughed uncontrollably. Sarita got up to prepare dinner, but Uday wanted to take her out for dinner and a movie. *Anand* was playing at the Metro then. He made her wear a green-and-red sari and no make-up. Like always she looked ethereal. They boarded a tram from Bhowanipore to Lindsay Street. It was Sarita's first film. She watched the entire film and it seemed she didn't even blink her eyes. Sarita cried inconsolably, seeing Rajesh Khanna die at the end. She thought everything that was happening was for real and Rajesh Khanna had really died. Uday had a tough time making her understand that it was just a movie and not for real. Uday was taken aback by her sheer innocence. Crying made her eyes become very big and very angelic. For the first time he hugged her in public and she hugged him back. He took her to a very famous restaurant called Moulin Rouge in Park Street. There were live cabaret dancers. Sarita stared at the semi–nude ladies. Uday had no idea what she was thinking. Her face went through series of expressions—surprise, shock, embarrassment, shyness, wide-eyed amazement. From time to time she looked at him. Uday couldn't even remember if he looked at the dancers; like always he couldn't take his eyes off his wife.

After they were done with their food, they came out of the restaurant. It was a lovely night and a cool breeze blew from the nearby Hooghly river. Uday suggested they walk back home instead of taking a tram. They walked silently and then Sarita started talking, and went on about the restaurant, the food, the city . . . She just looked like an excited child. As they reached home, Sarita started putting a mattress on the floor. Uday stopped her and made her sleep on the bed, while he slept on the couch.

Days passed, months passed, and finally the week arrived when Sarita had to visit her mother. Uday had been dreading this for months. He knew he couldn't live without her. He spoke to his boss and took leave for a week. He visited his parents and then took Sarita to her mother's place. He ensured that they met everybody within a week, after which he brought her back home. This time she was very angry as she wanted to stay longer with her mother, but Uday wouldn't let her. Uday reasoned, 'Who will cook for me? Outside food doesn't agree with my stomach.'

Once Uday and his wife were invited by his boss for dinner. Sarita saw they had dinner in glass plates. As she returned home all she talked about was the glass crockery. The following weekend she got a dinner set which cost them half of Uday's monthly salary. Like his boss's wife Sarita too hanged them on the utensil rack. But within minutes the whole rack came crashing down, breaking all the pieces of the set. Sarita, out of nervousness and fear, went and hugged Uday and cried bitterly. Uday didn't scream at her; instead, he consoled her and helped her clean up the mess. Then he took her to Prinsep Ghat for some pau bhajji.

Sarita too cared for Uday. She would make sure Uday had no problems throughout the week. She would wash his clothes, starch his shirts, iron his clothes; she would try to learn new recipes because of her husband's love for good food. They had made a routine every morning that they would go to Victoria for a walk, and then would have tea together. After tea, Sarita would prepare breakfast and tiffin for Uday, while Uday would clean up the house. Uday made sure Sarita had a maid who would do the rest of the cleaning. He hated to see Sarita work, but Sarita insited on washing clothes herself. In the evening, sharp at five, she would get ready before he came back from office. Every Sunday, they had to go out—either they would go for a movie together or he would take her out to shop for clothes. Nearly every month Sarita would get a new sari.

Their fourth wedding anniversary was approaching. Sarita was about to turn eighteen. Uday knew it was time to take the next step—consummating their marriage and starting a family. They hadn't gone out on a holiday since the time they had got married. So he decided to take her to Kashmir, the Heaven on Earth. He booked the best hotel possible. When they reached the hotel he refused to take the electric heater. He knew that when she'd start feeling cold, she would automatically come to him for some warmth. It happened exactly as he planned, and that night they were finally husband and wife. Exactly ten months after their holiday, Sarita gave birth to a healthy boy. They decided to name him Agastya. Now Uday's small, happy family was complete.

Uday was made the regional manager of his bank. Uday was now on top of the world. He had everything that he desired. Years passed and he was promoted to the post of assistant general manager, and after that, general manager.

His love for Sarita was still the same. It was not that they never fought. They fought nearly every day, but for things that could only make Uday smile. Uday had a pretty-looking secretary and Sarita hated that she wore short skirts. Sarita would display her possessiveness every now and then. Uday never had any friends. He would always laugh that his wife was his friend and that he didn't need any more—she was a handful already!

Years later, when Agastya was twenty-three, they decided to send their son to the US for further studies. After Agastya left for the US, Sarita started keeping unwell. She would get dizzy spells, she would sleep a lot, she became forgetful. Initially, both Uday and the family doctor thought it might be because she missed her son.

Then one day, she fainted while working. Thankfully, Uday was around. He immediately took her to the hospital. Lots of tests were conducted and the reports showed only one thing: she had a tumour on the right side of her brain. He took her to all the best hospitals in Calcutta, Mumbai and even Delhi. All the doctors said the same thing—the tumour was getting worse. Uday had never felt this lonely and helpless in his entire life. He had well-wishers all around but nobody he could speak to and share his fear of losing Sarita. Sarita knew there was something very wrong with her. She could see it in Uday's eyes. She wouldn't complain and would joke around Uday to make him smile. Uday would smile too. But both knew that their mirth wasn't genuine. He couldn't concentrate on his work. Sarita was getting weaker day by day. She would sleep most of the day. Uday couldn't see her like that. All of a sudden his picture-perfect life was breaking into pieces. Doctors tried explaining to him that it was too late to do anything—she was already in the fourth stage and that was literally the final stage. Uday knew he was losing her with every single passing minute. She had lost a lot of weight. Uday thought it was time he called his son. He called Agastya and he told him everything about Sarita. Agastya did not say anything; he returned to India the very next day. By that time Sarita was sleeping nearly twenty hours a day. Agastya was home, but Uday couldn't open up to him. He had so much to say to Sarita but couldn't.

That night, Sarita woke up for a while. She asked Uday how he was and why he wasn't sleeping. He had to go to office and Agastya to school. Uday looked at her and smiled. Sarita moved beside him and hugged him with her frail hands. Uday hugged her too. He so wanted to protect her, save her, not let her go. When she looked up at him, her eyes shone brightly and she smiled. Although her cheeks were hollowed and eyes sunken, her smile was as mischievous as it had been on their wedding day. She shut her eyes and went to sleep again.

She didn't wake up the next morning.

Uday had lost his wife—his companion and best friend. After the cremation was over, Uday went to his room to lie down. His son came to his room to talk to him. On seeing Agastya enter, he sat up. Agastya had no idea what to say—he too had lost his friend and mother; he too missed her. Uday broke the silence. He said, 'I never told your mom that I loved her, and even she forgot to tell me that. Since our marriage we've never slept without each other; we've never been apart. This is the first time I am going to sleep without her. I never even let her stay at her mother's place without me. She can't even go to heaven without me. I hope she'll wait.'

Agastya was too dazed to listen to what his dad had to say. Finally Uday said 'I want to sleep now'.

Agastya left and went to his room. By the next morning his father had passed away in his sleep . . .

~

'Love stories exist,' says the guy sitting opposite me, concluding his tale. 'You just have to meet the right person.'

He then shows me a black-and-white picture of a very beautiful lady with a very handsome man. They look happy, more like buddies. 'Sometimes you meet someone and before you even know their name, before you even know what they do or where they're from, you get that hunch that sometime in the future this person would mean something important to you.' Flashing his gorgeous smile again, he extends his hand. 'Agastya Singh here.'

Well frankly, I feel the same way about this guy. Okay, now I can safely say, I do have something romantic in me.

'Trisha Mehta,' I reply, smiling, and truly hoping for a new love story to start.

Synchronicity

JYOTI SINGH VISVANATH

Tasha fought the urge to straighten the painting on the wall. It was what made her notice the man sitting below it. He was tall. She could tell by the way his frame folded on the low seating. Good-looking too, despite the creased brow. She surprised herself by her observations and returned her attention to the painting. Drew rubbed her back to let her know he was there. She turned to look at him, her son, her beautiful sixteen-year-old. Then the nurse walked in . . .

The man unfolded himself. Tasha stood up. The nurse waited. Then a doctor came up to Tasha and said, 'I am sorry, Mrs Miller . . . we did all we could.' Tasha sank to her knees. The nurse took over, while the doctor walked over to the man. He didn't have to say anything. The man's deep voice resonated across the hospital's waiting room, 'Not even her?'

The doctor shook his head. The man just stood there, arms loose by his side.

It took a moment for it to make sense to her, then Tasha just launched into the man, hammering his chest. It was ineffectual. He just stood there, taking it like it was deserved.

Drew dragged her away, apologizing to the man. 'She killed him . . . she killed him!' Tasha screamed. She looked into the man's face and saw the tears, her own eyes were dry. She wanted to cry, too.

That's all she remembered of the fateful night she lost her husband. The man, Brad King, she later found out, had lost his wife and daughter that night. One accident ended all three lives. Greg was heading home from work and Brad's wife and daughter were heading out for some ice-cream.

~

The week after the funeral Tasha went to the GP for a review of her prescription for sleep medication. She saw Brad sitting in the waiting room of the surgery. Her heart skipped a beat. She didn't want to face him but her GP's room was just past where he was sitting. He looked up and as their eyes met, Tasha knew she had no choice. She took the seat next to him. Brad shifted uncomfortably.

'I just wanted to apologize for my behaviour that night,' she began.

Brad didn't say anything, just nodded his head.

'Is everything okay?' Tasha continued.

'I can't sleep . . .' Brad finally spoke.

'Me neither.' His eyes met hers in understanding. A strange arc of awareness shimmied down her spine.

The doctor popped out and signalled to Brad. He rose and walked into the office. The door closed.

Brad's eyes were red when he came out. The doctor patted his shoulder and asked Tasha to come in. As she brushed past Brad, he put his hand out. She looked up at him. 'Will you have time for a coffee after?' he asked. She nodded and walked towards the doctor.

The waiting area was empty when she came out. Tasha was angry at her disappointment. What had she expected? She searched the pocket of her cashmere coat for her car keys and marched out of the surgery.

Brad was in the parking lot, leaning against his Bentley Ghost. He straightened up as he saw her. Tasha walked towards him.

'I have to pick up my prescription from the pharmacy,' she said, as she fiddled with her car keys.

'Me too. I'll follow you there. Then we can go to the Fox and the Hound,' his deep voice was smooth.

'For coffee?' she arched her brow.

'Just need something stronger right now,' he said.

Brad was already following the waiter to the table when Tasha walked in. She weaved her way to him. Brad helped her out of her coat, and then held her chair as she sat down. He was a gentleman, like Greg.

The waiter took their order and left.

'How've you been?' Brad asked.

'I don't really know . . . Right now, it's all about getting through the day, one moment at a time,' Tasha felt the tears begin to gather and blinked furiously to fight them, 'What about you?'

'Am back at work. . . it's busy right now,' he looked into her eyes. A tear rolled down her face. He wiped it with his thumb and cupped her cheek.

'It will get better. It *has* to get better . . .' he murmured.

The waiter came with their drinks. Brad dropped his hand and Tasha touched her hair self-consciously. They were both still married—to dead people.

Even though they did not actively seek each other out, the weekly visit to the surgery and the stop at Fox and Hound became a ritual. They didn't talk much. It was an odd connection, where the shared pain didn't need to be explained. Once they drove away from the pub, they went back to their separate lives.

Two months later, Tasha stirred her Pimms absently as she looked out of the window.

'Something on your mind?' Brad asked.

She turned toward him and said, 'I've made a decision.'

Brad leaned forward.

'I'm going home,' Tasha looked into his eyes.

'Home?'

'Yes, I'm going back to India,' she said.

'Why?' he reached over and placed his hand over hers. She turned hers around and laced her fingers through his.

'Family . . . Drew . . . It's so difficult without Greg . . .'

Brad's fingers tightened, as a muscle twitched in his jaw. 'You seem to be doing okay,' he said.

'Look at me, Brad. I've lost more than twenty kilos. I struggle to get through the day. The bank wants the house back . . . I just can't do this anymore!' Her eyes filled up.

'Is there anything I can do?' he asked.

'No,' she said with conviction.

'Tasha. . . '

'It's done, Brad. I'm leaving next week.'

The waiter came to the table and Brad withdrew his hand.

Brad rested his hand on the small of her back as they walked to their respective cars. As she made to walk away, he tightened his hand. 'Tasha. . . '

She turned toward him and looked straight into his grey

eyes. She couldn't read them in the dark but something told her they were stormy.

He touched her face gently, pushing back a tendril of hair from her forehead. 'Don't leave.'

'Brad. . . I have a home in Delhi, people who'll help me get back on my feet and right now, what choice do I really have? I have to think of Drew.'

He said nothing, just leaned in and placed his warm lips on hers. They tasted of his favoured single malt. Tasha felt a pleasant tingling before stepping back. She had been kissed by only one man in the past eighteen years—Greg. Her guilt got the better of her and she ran to her Jag, fumbling her way in. As she reversed, she saw Brad still standing where she left him. Her heart wrenched.

She could not take the leap. She understood that neither could he. They had been brought together by circumstances, not desire. Kindred souls. The yin and yang of personal loss. The healing was yet to begin.

She didn't see Brad again before she left London. The memory of him standing in the parking lot of Fox and Hound was etched in her mind.

It had taken two years for her to gain some semblance of sanity after Greg. Setting up roots, getting Drew through school and reintegrating with family after many years away. Every day was a challenge. It did not help that she loathed Delhi with unbridled passion. She thought of Brad and wondered how he was doing apart from the girls, parties and wild abandon she saw in his Facebook posts. Sometimes she thought he was doing it to thumb his nose at her . . . but at others, she understood that his pain must be harder to contain than hers. She at least had Drew.

One night as she worked late on her laptop, Skype

messaged Brad was online. It was quite alarming how much they were connected even though they did not talk to each other. She tried to concentrate on her work but Skype's familiar ringtone filled the silence. Tasha hesitated, before clicking on the call.

'Tasha . . .' the deep echo of his voice saying her name sent a frisson up her spine.

'Hi, Brad . . . All well?' she replied as if they talked every day.

'Sort of. Have been thinking of you,' his disembodied words made her shift in her seat.

'Activate your video, I want to see you,' Brad had never been this forward in all the time she had known him.

'Can't, sorry, the call quality drops . . . Are you drunk?'

'Not yet, but that is the aim,' he replied.

'Maybe we should talk some other time, Brad.'

'You are always leaving . . . Don't go. I have something important to tell you.'

'I'm here, not going anywhere. What is it?'

'I'm moving to Delhi for the next three years . . .'

Silence.

'Tasha. . . you there?'

'Why, Brad?'

'Work . . . The recession's a bitch. We bankers are having a pretty rough time,' he sounded frustrated.

'Good,' she didn't really know what else to say.

'Bad . . . I don't know a soul in Delhi. You'll be there to hold my hand, won't you, Tasha?'

'Of course, tell me what you need . . .'

They talked for a long time after. Made plans, something she hadn't done in a long time . . . In fact, there had been no plans after Greg. It was just one day at a time.

That changed when Brad arrived. It was like a whirlwind had swept her off her feet. Every day, something or the other turned up. He found a house close to hers. She helped him settle in—furniture, curtains, domestic help. It was a welcome distraction from her usually staid life. Drew did not take well to the change. She sensed his aggravation over how Brad had invaded their lives.

'You're going out again?' he'd say petulantly.

She discussed his anger with Brad. 'I want him to understand that there is nothing between us.'

'Isn't there?'

'Stop it, Brad. Just understand. I am his mother.'

'I know, Tasha. Just want you to know that you're also a very beautiful woman and most importantly, not dead. At least, not yet.'

'Brad . . .'

'Want me to talk to him?'

Brad had reached out to Drew several times since he had come to Delhi, but the boy had shut him out.

'Do that. He just doesn't listen to me.' Tasha left it that.

The following week, Brad and Drew returned from playing rugby with a group that got together on Saturdays. Drew blustered in and threw things around. He turned on Tasha, 'What's wrong with you?'

Tasha was surprised into silence.

'It's my time—my time to have girlfriends and fun. Not yours!' he screamed and marched off.

Tasha was distraught. Brad gathered her into a hug and let her cry.

When she could think again, she moved away from him and asked, 'What did you say to Drew?'

'I told him I was in love with his mother and as the man

of the house, I needed his permission to ask for your hand in marriage.'

'Get serious, Brad. What *did* you say?'

'Just that, honest. He should know I am going to be here a long time and needs to get used to the idea of having me around.'

'Get out, Brad! Now!' Tasha walked to the door of her flat and held the door.

Brad walked slowly up to her, reaching out with his hand, 'Tasha!'

'Are you kidding me? Just go, Brad.'

It took all of the next week to get Drew to even talk to her. She had no time to process what Brad had said, all she wanted was her boy back. The flowers came every day, holding little notes of apology. He called but she did not want to talk to Brad.

Two months passed by. One day, Drew came home with Brad. 'Mom, marry this man. He's not Dad but he's a good man and he loves you,' he said. Then, smiling mysteriously at Brad, he left the room.

'Brad, explain . . .'

'For the rest of my life, my dear.'

Love Is Also a Compromise

MANJULA PAL

I was screening the medical records when I stumbled upon a file that caught my attention. It read:

Patient's name: Aditya Raj
Age: 62
Diagnosis: Tuberculosis.

He had been registered in the hospital only a month back and was being given anti-tubercular treatment. I was confused. Who could this person be? Could it be him? The person I knew by this name had migrated to the US a long time back and we'd not been in touch for the past thirty years or so. This was during my new job in a private hospital—I'd recently taken it up post my retirement from a multinational. I was supposed to develop a software that would facilitate displaying patients' complete data online.

Out of sheer curiosity, I took the address from his file and, on the following weekend, found myself standing in front of a DDA HIG flat with his nameplate on the gate. A maid responded to the doorbell. She let me in. I saw a man sitting in an easy chair in the front room. He looked weak, unshaven, unkempt.

'Yes? Who is this?' he asked.

A thirty-year gap. Obviously, he had not recognized me. But it was indeed him. Disease had aged him beyond his years. but his trademark boyish grin was just the same. I decided not to disclose my identity. Using a fake name, I introduced myself as a social worker from the hospital, and said that I was filling a pro forma required for the follow-up of TB patients. Like any other lonely, elderly person he appeared eager to talk—particularly to a woman—and he furnished me with all those personal details that were not really asked for.

He told me that he and his wife had returned to India about a decade back to take up a job in Delhi. He described in detail what happens when a loving life partner of many years dies. His wife had died a year ago, leaving him both physically and mentally drained. Thereafter he'd neglected his health totally. It was during that time that he had contracted TB. His only son, a worthy one, was settled in the US, and had wanted Aditya to migrate there to live with him; but this had been delayed by one year owing to Aditya's medical treatment. He hoped to get completely cured of his disease while still in India.

I felt sad and returned with a heavy heart. The last time I'd seen him was when we went to the airport to see him off.

My memory went into a flashback of the time when

Aditya and I were classmates in MBA. Our friendship had slowly blossomed into a love affair. Fortunately, our parents also did not disapprove of our relationship.

After passing out, we got employed in two different companies in Delhi. While I liked my job, Aditya was dissatisfied in his. He changed his job at the first opportunity and went to Bombay.

Three years passed and my parents started insisting on marriage. However, Aditya was not prepared, because neither was he liking Bombay nor was he feeling settled in his second job. He also wanted to try his luck abroad. In fact he had already fixed up with some company in the US and had decided to migrate. I did not seem to fit into his plans—at least for the time being. In any case, being the only child of my parents, I was not eager to migrate in a hurry.

Months before he was to leave for the US, he came back to Delhi, so that we could spend some quality time together. Our parents performed a small engagement ceremony. The process of getting my passport made was also initiated. After completing his formalities at the passport office, we went on a short pleasure trip to Simla.

Merely a few days after he'd left, I learnt that he had given me the most unacceptable parting gift! I panicked and wanted to get rid of the unwanted burden as soon as possible. Thanks to liberal abortion laws, I got it done on the sly, without having to explain anything to the doctor. Half an hour's job at the hospital and two days of rest was good enough to get me back to my routine.

I decided not to tell anyone about my pregnancy, not even Aditya—firstly, because I did not want to bother him at that stage, and secondly, because I was the one who had actually messed up with the baby pills and therefore felt solely responsible. No one, not even my mother, suspected anything. And I also forgot all about it afterwards.

In those days, international calls were very costly. Therefore we stayed in touch with each other mainly through letters. But with the passage of time, I found that our demanding jobs and long working hours were slowly taking out much steam from our long-distance courtship. I had no choice but to wait for him till he got somewhat settled.

On the other hand, my professional life was good. With no responsibility, and with all the pampering from my parents, I was doing much better than many of my colleagues who had to look after their families along with their jobs. I was giving my hundred percent to my work and was suitably rewarded too. I realized that once I married and went to the US, I would definitely be missing my job here. After all, the husband's job had to be given a priority.

It was at that time that we learnt through someone that Aditya had married. I clearly remember how, in complete disbelief, my parents and I went to his parent's house to inquire about the truth. It was not a rumour. He had indeed married an Indian-American girl. My father fumed at his apologetic parents and called their son's behavior totally opportunistic and deceitful.

It was a big blow to all of us. For me the humiliation of rejection was much more than the loss of love. The unscrupulous fellow had dumped me without even giving me an explanation. I hated him! Even then, it took me some time to move on.

However, things gradually began to return to normal. My parents started looking for matches for me, but somehow, nothing worked out.

After facing disappointment in love, and with the kind of

responses we received from proposals that my parents were negotiating, I felt extremely frustrated. I was also experiencing a change in my attitude towards life, particularly towards the institution of marriage. Widespread marital discord was apparent among my contemporaries, not only in arranged marriages but equally in love marriages too. I was alarmed by the increasing rate of divorces in my peer group—particularly amongst the so-called metrosexual couples. So, by that time, I became so disillusioned that I decided not to marry.

Frankly speaking, I was so busy with my job that I did not have any time to think about my single status. Moreover, I had no opportunity to mingle with men with whom I could have thought about marriage—some of the men I liked were already married while others were not the marrying type. My social life was limited to my parents and a selected few colleagues.

Years passed by. My parents' health was deteriorating. Frequent hospital trips—and the growing realization of living all alone when they were gone—depressed me.

While I still had five years of service left, both my parents passed away. Life was not the same after their demise. The loneliness was excruciating. Luckily, my habits of regular exercising and yoga kept me physically fit and mentally sane. During those days, I often thought of my unborn child and sometimes imagined caressing my baby in my arms. How I wish I had told Aditya about my pregnancy and forced him to marry me—not for anything else but for the sake of our child.

I retired in due course of time and, thankfully, soon after my retirement I got this hospital job, which I not only liked but which also kept me gainfully employed.

Then this Aditya episode happened.

I made it a point not to meet him when he visited his doctor next. But, as the luck would have it, during his next monthly visit, he came looking for me in my room. Entering, he pulled a chair, sat down in front of me, looked into my eyes and called me by my name, 'Venu.'

I was shocked.

He laughed, 'I've done my homework well and know that there is no social worker in this hospital. I had a doubt, after you left my house, but it was not difficult to find out the truth. Why did you have to hide from me?'

Then he almost forced an invitation out of me. He announced that he would visit my house on the coming weekend, and then left without even waiting for me to react.

He came as expected, but brought with him a big bouquet of flowers and a basket of fruits and other eatables. It was evident that he had taken special care to dress well. I was full of anger and pain, and got very irritated with his remorseless, aggressive attitude. He was like an intruder, not welcome in my house. I needed an explanation. Why did he ditch me in the first place? And now, why had he stormed into my life again? Stunned at his behaviour, I kept sitting rigidly, avoiding his glance.

All of a sudden he squatted on the floor in front of me, cupped my knees with his hands and put his head on my lap and started sobbing. 'I have wronged you. I am an offender. Still, I want to share the circumstances which forced me to behave like that. My job contract had expired and I was not getting an extension or another job. I was facing deportation. I hated to come back as a loser. I already had a marriage proposal from Ria, who was an American citizen of Indian origin. It was tough for me to decide. Besides, I could not see you marrying a person with such low self-esteem. I was not worthy of your hand, I thought. I became selfish and opted for the easier route. I married Ria to escape deportation. I could not muster the courage to talk to you directly, so I sent the news of my marriage through someone else . . . However, I could never imagine, even in my wildest dreams, that you would remain unmarried. As for me, I was lucky to get a wife like Ria, who had a traditional Indian upbringing and was intelligent, loving and caring. I was blessed with a son and a happy married life.'

After he finished his explanation, he gently took my hands in his and said that he was ready to do anything and everything that would make me happy. He repeatedly begged to be forgiven. I did not respond. With tears in his eyes, he left.

He phoned me the next day and again expressed his wish to see me. I could not refuse. An opportunist he surely was, but he did not pretend. He was genuine, honest and transparent. I reasoned it out and forgave him. My long lost love for him also started blooming. The big gap of thirty years was bridged before we could realize what was happening.

We started meeting often and even began going out together. Having a protective male escort by my side was flattering. I liked his exuberance and optimism. He used to look for excuses to pamper me. My heart pined for him in his absence. Our intimacy, however, was limited to holding hands and uttering sweet nothings to each other. He probably knew the limitations of his disease.

Our love affair was like that of two teenage virgins—restrained and yet eager to explore. We hardly quarrelled and never even argued the way we had in our youth. We believed in giving rather than demanding. In a way, our love was an untold compromise between the two of us. The feeling of belonging was beautiful and divine. Life was all honey and roses.

He was recovering well from his disease and had started gaining the weight he had lost. With his salt-and-pepper hair and boyish grin, he still looked handsome to me. I noticed that I too was getting compliments on my dressing sense and my good looks.

One day, after about a year of our memorable togetherness, he declared that he would not be seeing me for some time because his son was coming to wind up everything. Most likely, since he was fully cured of his disease, he would now go away with his son. I felt depressed. I took some time off from my job and stayed home to get over this low phase.

It struck me that he had used me again. I felt cheated.

After a couple of days, the unexpected happened. He was standing at my door.

'Sorry, I did not come before, because I was busy winding up,' he said.

'So you have come to say goodbye. When are you going?'

'I am not going anywhere, but I am going to shift into your house, as your house is better than my DDA flat, which I have already sold off.'

'Means your son did not take you back with him, and instead took away all your money?'

'No, that's not true. He wanted to take me along, but it was my decision not to go. And he did not take any money, because it has to be deposited in your account. I do not want to be living off you.'

'But why did you not tell me all this before?'

'Tell you what? Did you not see how madly in love I am with you? You silly girl, I need you more than you need me.'

He embraced me, with a hug that was tighter than ever before, and started passionately kissing me.

'Venu, I have the doctor's permission. I do not want to stop here.'

I did not mind it anyway.

A Village Love Story

HASEEB PEER

Sogam was beautiful, just like a fairy-tale land, located more than 150 kilometres from the main city of Srinagar on the rim of Indo–Pak border. Apart from the Yaarbal, a local rivulet, Sogam housed gorgeous paddy fields that looked like a sheet of green during summers and were stripped bare during the winters, when we often played cricket on those frozen acres. Icicles drooping down from the naked branches of apple trees were often chomped greedily, making a crunching sound whenever we took a bite.

During the summers we often sat down on the muddy pavements flanking the fields and watched the men work tirelessly for the whole day. In the middle of the day, women accompanied by their little girls brought boxes full of rice and mutton. The hungry workers ate heartily and often pounced on the food like famished dragons. Quite customarily, we too joined them in the feast. The view of the paddy fields that stretched on for acres—until it was stopped by the sweep of the mountains—often flavoured the food. At four in the afternoon, it was time for nun-chai (salty Kashmiri tea). Homemade ghee chapattis were consumed along with the traditional Kashmiri *satt.*

My friends and I often sat down on the banks of the local rivulet that snaked its way through our village. We would often watch the waters, arguing as to whether snakes inhabited the Yaarbal or not. 'I have seen a black snake in this water,' one of my friends would often say. We would in turn laugh at him and often wonder what made our village so beautiful. We would sit down with Showket, one of my friends who would smoking his Panama cigarettes bought at the local grocery store. Occasionally, we would take a puff too, but Showket would warn us against taking more than one.

The summer was also the season when we would spend most of our time waiting for the girls who would accompany their mothers to the fields. The girls would habitually catch hold of their mothers' arms and walk adjacent to them. I would wait for a girl, Sumera, who had this flair and flamboyance that was hers alone. As she entered her adolescence, she often covered her head with a round scarf, wrapping it so tightly as to stop even a small strand of hair from peeping out. She would sit between her father and mother under the shade of the green-apple tree; and as her father tore into the mutton pieces, she would sit their quietly looking at him. I would often climb the tree overhead before they sat underneath it so that I could catch a closer glimpse of Sumera. They never seemed to notice my presence overhead even though I would keep munching the toffees I had in my pocket. I would wait there until lunch was over; and after both the mother and her daughter disappeared, I would slowly crawl down and run towards my friends who would then laugh at my daredevilry. When nun-chai time came, I followed the same routine once again. It was during these days when Sumera first noticed me. One day, she saw me climbing the tree and my secret adventure of looking at her no longer remained a secret.

Sumera often played with her girlfriends in the big kitchen garden of Habib Kaka. I often saw them playing hopscotch or house-house while I peeped from a small hole in the wooden door of the kitchen garden. She often came to the Yaarbal to play in the water and I would often reach there before her. Finally, after so much hard work on my part, she too began to look at me with her almond-shaped green eyes and I felt love in the air. I followed the same routine during the day and she too reciprocated by looking back at me most elegantly. It often made me go wild.

After the day was over, I would often sing alone in my own room in a low voice. Ours was a typical Muslim village that outlawed any sort of Western culture. We never had a television, but we did have an old radio that my grandfather had bought when he had gone for his Hajj pilgrimage. I would often strike a conversation with my grandfather about Islam and then concur with his views to keep him in good humour, so that he would lend me his radio for the night.

Sumera would often search for me with her eyes while playing hopscotch on the days when I didn't come to the Yaarbal or the fields. I observed this as I lay hidden behind some obstacle to watch her movements. After my eighteenth birthday, Sumera suddenly vanished. I had never talked to her, but not seeing her for days began to make me as restless as a child. Now she wouldn't come to the fields, the Yaarbal or the kitchen garden. I searched for her everywhere and spent many sleepless nights on my bed thinking about her and wondering at her sudden desertion. Her green eyes began to fill my imagination and the thought of her being confined to some place made me sad.

A month passed and then another. I spent the days roaming around in search of her—I had already explored the places she visited regularly but I did not give up. Finally, after three months of being deprived of her presence, I caught a glimpse of her. I was sitting on the concrete stairs that formed a path up to the Yaarbal when I noticed a girl dressed in a complete burqa on the other side. Her eyes were visible through the narrow slit on the burqa. I recognized her—those almond-shaped green eyes were speaking to me, asking me a question. She wasn't alone at the Yaarbal. The other girls formed a circular barricade around her. We couldn't look at each other directly, but I had found a way to look at her—I was continuously staring at her reflection on the shiny waters of the Yaarbal.

For the next few days, I followed the same routine of not looking directly at her face, but at her reflection instead. I was so mesmerized by her reflection that I often forgot that there were other people who were passing by and looking at my eccentric behaviour. Sometime later, Sumera understood my idea and she too started staring continuously at the slow waters, focusing on my reflection. Often I smiled while we both stared at each others' reflections. Every day I went home, thinking about the next day and her splendid beauty. I would reach the Yaarbal bank fifteen minutes prior to her arrival and take the best possible position to have a look. She came in every day at her usual time with a group of friends; and while the others filled their pots, we continued with our routine.

Every day I greeted her by closing my eyes for a brief moment and she reciprocated by doing the same. Her friends had begun to understand her feelings and they would fill her pot of water while she sat with me. We couldn't do the routine directly because of the continuous presence of the village elders and the women who often flocked to the Yaarbal.

Our village wasn't a modernized hamlet but I had seen on the TV in Rahim Kaka's house how people approached each other if they developed feelings for one another. But our village was different. You weren't allowed to talk to the opposite sex; you couldn't even stare at them directly. Call it extremism or the extent of darkness. This was how it was. No one had the fortitude and the backbone to transform the current system and change it with something that appealed to the present generation.

A few days later, I stood on the banks of the Yaarbal and Sumera stood on the other side. I was staring at her eyes, reflected on the rivulet's surface, when she slowly lifted her burqa and washed her face with the water of the Yaarbal. This brought her adolescent face into view. A round face shone in the sunlight and its image sparkled on the water; a trick of the light caused the reflection to playfully change colours like a chameleon. Her lips resembled the petals of a freshly plucked tulip, but unlike a tulip's fragrance and beauty that last for just over two weeks, I knew the beauty of her lips was there to stay. Her nose resembled the newly blossomed flowers of the Kashmiri spring season. With every splash of water that hit her face, I felt like I was living in my own dream. A few moments later, the burqa was back in place, covering the magnificent face that had brightened my day. I smiled. I knew that she wanted to break out of this barricaded existence and come away with me. I in turn knew that something had to be done. The glow of her face had stoked the passion in my heart, and I felt as though I must speak to her. At least greet her directly, my heart said. I was sceptical about this, and it took me some time before I finally decided what to do.

Time passed and one day, I decided to hop on to the other side to have a direct talk with her. I started to cross the rivulet directly, the slow waters helped me sail across to the other side. All her friends stood up and she stood in the middle of that huge contingent of girls. I wanted to talk, but my lips froze and my tongue didn't support me.

'*Rishta bhej do* (Send the marriage proposal),' her friends said in unison.

I stood there like a frozen lamb. She didn't speak and kept her head down looking at her chappal. I too kept staring at the ground, hoping that she would speak up. But she didn't. I wondered whether I should initiate the first round of talks, but I kept on beating around the bush, until it was time for them to leave. The attempt to talk had failed and I cursed myself. A few days later, I again crossed over to the other side to talk to her. She was alone this time and the setting was awesome. But this time she ran away as soon as she saw me and disappeared from the scene. I looked around and saw Gul Khan, a chowkidar from the local apple orchard, coming towards the Yaarbal. I left.

A few days later, I again saw Sumera, sitting and filling her empty pot with the clear water of Yaarbal. I vowed to myself that I would speak this time to her. I crossed over to where she was and stood in front of her, gazing at my feet, until she broke the awkward silence.

'*Rishta bhej do*,' she said without looking at me.

The words hit my ears like a swirl of cool breeze ruffling the leaves of a tree. I left so as to avoid anyone's eyes from catching me in front of Sumera. It felt like I'd crossed a barrier and had finally heard what was in her heart. But I had acted like a coward since I hadn't talked.

Days later, as I was standing on the Yaarbal bank, I noticed Sumera writing something on a wooden slate or *mashiq*. She left without even looking at my reflection but kept the *mashiq* on the ground. Curious, I crossed the Yaarbal and saw that the news written on the *mashiq* was devastating. Her parents were planning to get her married and she had asked me to do something about it. I spent the next few days in torment. Finally I talked to Ammi. I told her I wanted to get married to Sumera, daughter of Majid Dar. Ammi told me that they were of a lower caste and we couldn't have a relation with them. I protested, saying that no castes existed in our religion, but she wouldn't listen.

A day later, I wrote on the *mashiq* about what had happened and passed it on to Sumera. She looked at it and didn't reply. A teardrop was clearly visible at the corner of her eye. Devastated, I ran back home to once again raise the question of marriage with the household. Ammi refused my pleas once again and didn't succumb to any of my protests. The next day, Sumera wrote on the *mashiq* that her father had fixed the marriage date. I wept as soon as I read those lines. I couldn't write anything. I started to cry loudly. I wrote back to her in a miserable condition stating that I was helpless. She cried as she read the words and threw the slate back. But the worst was yet to come. Gul Khan, the chowkidar, saw us crying and quickly informed her father about it. The whole village gathered in a matter of a few minutes; a few elders came forward and slapped me. I was also beaten and abused by her father. She was asked to leave and she did so, grudgingly. Her father caught hold of my hair and took me to my house. He shouted at my parents. I stood there, dazed and shocked, worried about Sumera. The memory of her reflection suddenly came to mind, but everything was now shattered to pieces. I had never expected the locals to react so ferociously. I stood there, gazing at my feet and thinking about my next step. My mother and father started to cry due to her father's rude behaviour. They had blamed my parents for everything. I was thrown inside the house and caged.

A few days later, I came to know that Sumera had also been beaten brutally. The narrow-mindedness of our village had taken its toll on our lives. Sumera's marriage had been set to the nearest possible date. I spent my days alone in my room, thinking about her. Her friend informed me through the window of my room that she did the same. I had the *mashiq* as her memento; she had nothing but a basketful of memories. I heard that she kept crying day in and day out for me. I did the same. I kept on craving for her presence. Her thoughts filled my mind.

The day of the marriage finally arrived. I couldn't bear the fact that she was getting married. I wanted to kill myself but the thought of her getting married virtually killed me. I turned insane. After that day, I spent my days staring at the *mashiq*. I held it tightly to my body; if anyone tried taking it away, even for just a second, it made me go wild. I shouted at people without any reason and didn't even touch food for several days. I paced up and down my room for several hours, circling around without any purpose. Her almond-shaped green eyes made me cry every time I thought about them. I wanted to die, but kept on living like a dead person for some obnoxious reason.

After several months, the news came that she had committed suicide. Her mother-in-law and father-in-law had taunted her so much about me that she had been unable to tolerate their comments. She had jumped from the third floor of their house. I banged the door of my room so hard that my parents had to let me go. I ran as fast as I could towards the village graveyard. I looked at the numerous graves around me until I finally spotted a fresh mini-mountain of mud. I went towards it and wept as I hugged the mound. Why Sumera? Why Sumera? I asked her. She couldn't have replied, not even on a *mashiq* now. I put down the wooden slate I had carried with me and wept uncontrollably. The ocean of tears didn't stop and I kept on weeping . . . All I could do was lift my hands up and ask the Almighty to return my Sumera back to me.

The silence and the beauty around me had lost its meaning . . .

Never Forget Me

RENUKA VISHWANATHAN

Love has no expiry date. I don't know who said those lines, but they sound so true today. I looked at Anandi with water dripping down her face from her wet hair. The tears from her eyes added to the water overflow.

'Do you remember . . .?' I began, but stopped in time. There was no point in asking her that.

In a different place and different time, Anandi had looked just like she was now, wet with water, her hair dripping. But then there had been no tears in her eyes. Rather, there had been anger!

'What the hell are you doing?' she had shouted at me.

She had rushed to me and caught the water hose from my hand and pushed it to the ground.

'Sorry!' I had stuttered. 'I never meant to aim the water hose at you. It seemed to have a life of its own and just slipped away in your direction!'

Her eyes were now full of contempt.

'Cheap excuse! At your age, to indulge in such juvenile tricks!' She had turned away from me, rubbing her wet face with a small slip of a handkerchief.

I had given up attempts of watering the garden and had trudged inside the building. It was a home for the elderly, where I offered my services once in a while. That memorable day, I had volunteered to water the plants in the garden.

At my age, at that time, I had just retired from a mundane career in the banking industry. I was healthy, had a good roof over my head and got a decent pension that let me live without any financial worries. Both my daughters were married and I also had a grandson. I had lost my wife to cancer three years ago, very suddenly. I had just about overcome the shock of her sudden death and with time on my hands, had begun to volunteer at this home. My marriage, which had been an arranged one, had been nothing special. My wife and I had had our ups and downs, but had been comfortable with each other. And that was how I interpreted love. Until I met Anandi.

No, it was not love at first sight. I just found her interesting and amusing. I liked bumping into her at the home and she never failed to give me a dirty look or greet me sarcastically.

'Drowned anyone interesting lately?' she would ask. 'I forgot to put on my waterproof suit, so please stay away,' she would cut me off, if I attempted to talk to her. Or she would put me down in front of others. 'Have you met King Neptune? He thinks there should be water, water everywhere.' Despite her taunts and her seeming allergy to me, I liked her and wanted to know her better.

She didn't fascinate me or occupy my thoughts totally, but

yes, I did think of her off and on. I was intrigued by her. I had managed to gather from the grapevine that she was a college lecturer. I wish I could say that I slowly but steadily won her heart! But I can't. Anandi battled with me at every step, if I even tried to talk to her. The process of getting to know her was slower than slow. I had to move a millimetre at a time. She had her defences up stiff and strong and it took me ages to wear them down. It took me almost six months to get her to agree to share a cup of coffee with me.

'I won't bite you,' I had said, as I saw that she was nervous. 'It's just a friendly cup of coffee.'

'Why do you want to be friends with me?' she had asked.

I had many answers for that. But the simplest was the best. 'I like you,' I had said.

'But you don't even know me,' she had retorted.

'Well, then give me a chance to know you,' I had said.

I was lucky she had not emptied the cup of coffee over my head.

'What a cheesy line,' she had said in disgust. 'Even my students could come up with better ones.'

'That was not a pick-up-line or whatever,' I had said. 'It's the truth. I find you interesting and want to be your friend.'

'And then you will hope that the friendship turns into something else? Look, we are not teenagers!'

'Exactly,' I had interrupted her. 'We are two mature adults, who just want to be pals.'

'I don't know about myself,' she had growled. Her defences were so high and strong, it was a wonder that she did not disappear behind them. I learnt later that there was a reason for that.

From sharing coffee, we graduated to watching a play

now and then. We saw movies once in a while. She loved reading, so we would visit the bookshop at the mall, where she would lecture me in her best professor tone on why I should read books.

'I just can't imagine how you can say that you don't have the patience to read a book!' she had exclaimed in horror. 'How can someone not READ?'

I had guiltily admitted that I was that someone.

'I love books and I can remember the characters and their lines from my favourite ones!' she went on to say. I recall her words now and want to cry as I know that the world of books is lost to her forever.

It seems a cliché, but I really don't know when I fell in love with her. There was something about her that attracted me illogically. It could be the way she dressed. It was always in crisp, cotton saris, her hair neatly tied in a bun. Sometimes she wore a salwar–kameez, in a very demure style. Nothing fancy or modern. Once in a while she tied her hair in a ponytail. Her voice mesmerised me. Even when it dripped with sarcasm while addressing me, I found the lilt of her words and her tone very sweet. I could imagine her standing on a dais lecturing to students, who would pay attention because of her voice. Her voice belied her age. It was the voice of a sweet, young girl. Not the voice of an 'almost sixty' woman. But Anandi didn't look her age. Her hair was neither too grey, not too black. I was glad that she did not colour it and make it so obvious that she dyed it!

Gradually Anandi began to relax in my company. I stepped on the accelerator and increased the frequency of our meetings and encounters, but subtly, so that she did not feel threatened. I had told her all about myself, my dull life, my past. But she hardly opened up.

'No kids, not married. I stay alone,' she had told me once in an abrupt manner, when I had questioned her.

When I had learnt that she wasn't married, I had felt a surge of relief in me. It changed things a lot and my heart dared to dream! Without a jealous husband or demanding children, my relationship with Anandi now seemed easier.

I battered at her defences and wore them away. She had now taken over my thoughts every minute and every hour. I never stopped thinking about her and wanted to always be with her. I would often end up outside her college, waiting for her to finish her lectures for the day and then we would spend the evening together.

'You are behaving like a roadside Romeo,' she had commented, as I picked her up one day from her college. But she did not resist and I was thrilled to realize that she was slowly opening out and relaxing in my company.

'I stay alone,' she had said once, when I had dropped her outside her house one night. 'So I can't invite you in at this late hour.'

Later she had told me about her life. She had lost her parents at a young age and had worked hard and struggled to educate her younger brother and sister. They had found good jobs and married and settled in life, leaving her alone. They were happy in their cocooned worlds and did not bother about the sister who had sacrificed so much for them.

'Sounds like a tale out of a film, doesn't it?' she had asked me.

'Or from one of your favourite books,' I had teased her. But I had felt the hurt in her voice. It was obvious that she had sacrificed her youth for her siblings and allowed love and marriage to pass her by.

But I was going to change that. I wanted to keep Anandi

with me for ever and ever. I wanted to wake up next to her, to hear her voice every minute. To hold her close whenever I wanted to. Sounds like some adolescent's thoughts. But love is love, whether it is at twenty-four or forty-four or sixty-four! I had been waiting and longing to kiss her. I had not wanted to scare her and had seized the right moment. Her mood was mellow after a good movie and an excellent dinner. I had stopped outside her house and before she got out the car I had leaned over and kissed her firmly on her lips. I had expected her to move away and protest, but she had responded by almost melting against me. That was the first time I was literally breathless in all the time I had known her.

'Wow!' she had said, when we both came apart. 'That was some kiss!'

'How do you know?' I had demanded. 'Have you been kissed before?'

'Maybe,' she had said laughingly and got out of the car, waving goodbye. I had stared after her, recapturing the moment.

I felt like a teenager who had been kissed for the first time. Not a senior citizen and a grandfather to boot! And I really didn't care about who had ever kissed her before. It was at that moment that I decided I had to make her a part of my life permanently.

It was not an easy task. Anandi required a lot of convincing! My arguments were endless and she had a retort for each one.

'Why can't we continue like this?' she had asked.

'Because I want you with me every moment,' I had said.

'Well, I can't let you sit in my classes,' she had teased me.

But I could see her melting, slowly but surely. And when she agreed to marriage, I really was on top of the world. I had won a major battle. But I had not expected a war to begin.

'You want to get married?' my elder daughter had exclaimed in shock.

'Dad, what is wrong with you? At your age you want to embarrass us and show the world that you can't live without a woman?'

'Stop it!' I had said. 'I want to marry Anandi for company, because I love her and want to spend the rest of my life with her.'

'She is probably after your flat,' my younger daughter had retorted. 'Nice location, prime property. With realty rates being what they are, I must say she is smart!'

'Nonsense!' I had shouted. 'You two are just blabbering and are jealous that someone can replace your mother.'

'That is just it!' the elder one had yelled.

'Nobody can replace Mom! Do you think that she would have married again and forgotten you? Never!'

'What will our relatives think? And what will my in-laws think?' wailed my younger daughter. 'Sumit will taunt me so much about what a father I have! We will not able to face our relatives.'

They both went on and on, hammering away at me and my emotions day and night, making me feel guilty of my innocent doings, casting me as a villain and a sexually deprived fiend and a womanizer. And when my sons-in-law also joined the war, I was totally defeated.

Anandi didn't have it any better. She had informed her siblings, out of a sense of duty, that she was getting married. To say that hell broke loose would be an undervaluation of the flak she faced. Like two wounded dogs, we met to lick our gashes and bruises.

'I can't take such animosity and negativity,' Anandi had said, totally defeated. 'I just want to be at peace.'

I had nodded miserably. I felt drained at all the verbal battering I had received.

So, our marriage plans were shelved. We still did meet, but now it was strained, as we were continuously under the scrutiny of our family and monitored by them. It completely took the pleasure out of it all.

'We can't meet like this,' Anandi had whispered one day, almost bent over with the strain that our relationship was causing her.

We had to break up and we did. It was convenient that my younger daughter had been posted in the USA. I went there for a few months, came back and went and stayed with my brother, who lived in a remote town, far away from Anandi. No phone calls, no emails, no Facebook or Twitter. We made the break clean, as two adults should.

Time passed. I definitely had not forgotten Anandi and I was sure that she had not forgotten me. I had resisted the temptation to try to contact her. I respected her request that we stay apart.

'Time is a great healer,' she had told me sadly.

'Words again from one of your books,' I had retorted. But I had nodded. I understood what she was going through.

One day I had found myself standing outside the old-age home. I went in on an impulse. I had recalled almost every moment I had spent with Anandi there. I had wandered over the home, seeing a few familiar faces who greeted me enthusiastically. And then I had stopped in shock. It was Anandi! In flesh and blood right in front of me!

'Anandi!' I had whispered. Then I had run to her and shouted loudly. 'I can't believe it is you!' I had exclaimed, grabbing her hands. 'What luck to meet you here so unexpectedly.'

But Anandi had withdrawn her hands from mine. There was a look of fear in her eyes.

'Who are you?' she whispered suspiciously. 'Who are you calling Anandi?'

I had looked at her totally puzzled and shocked. What was wrong? Was she play-acting? Was she still fearing the threat of her family?

'Don't you know me? Anil!' I had said, but she pushed me away and almost ran away from the room. I tried to follow her, when an attendant had stopped me.

'Sir, leave her alone. This is one of her bad days. She won't recognize you today.'

'Won't recognize me today?' I had echoed. 'What do you mean?'

'She is suffering from Alzheimer's disease. She has been here for over a year. It is progressively worsening and her family, unable to take care of her, admitted her here!'

I had collapsed on to the nearest chair on hearing this. My Anandi did not remember me! How was that possible? I had left the home in a turmoil. How did such a thing happen? How could it happen? From that day, my life had taken on a new purpose. I went to the home daily to be with Anandi. First she had refused to have anything to do with me. She insulted me, ignored me, but I gained her confidence. I talked to her, I fed her, I entertained her. I told her stories about us, but she never showed any sign that she had ever known me and had loved me.

Now, as I pick up the empty mug from the floor, I know that this time I will not be cowed down by anyone. I would stand firm on my decision, let anyone think what they liked. I wipe the water from her face with a towel. She points to the mug.

'I want to bath,' she said.

'All right, but in the bathroom, not here,' I said, leading her to the bathroom.

I have to be very careful with her and treat her like a child. She tends to forget the smallest things. But I know that she will be all right if she is with me. I will take full care of her.

'Why have you gone to her again,' my elder daughter had wailed. 'And you plan to marry her! You are really incorrigible!'

'She needs me,' I had replied.

'Oh rot!' she had exclaimed in disgust.

'She does not even know you or remember who you are!' she had exclaimed angrily.

'But I know who she is and what she means to me,' I had said gently and walked away.

I walked to Anandi, and I was going to ask her to marry me.

A Tale of Two Strangers

SWAGATA PRADHAN

Sometimes strangers are not really strangers!

Sounds insane, right? Well here goes the explanation . . .

It was mid-November last year. A very cold evening in Kolkata. An unmarried twenty-something woman, a schoolteacher by profession, struggling to board an overcrowded bus during rush hour—that's me! Diyali Pradhan. Although it was cold I was still panting and sweating as I ran almost half a mile from my school gate, not to miss the bus which I took to my house daily.

But that day, for some reason the bus was unusually crowded. Also, I could not come out of school on time due to some extra work, for which I had to run the half-mile. A distance which, on other days, I used to walk slowly, enjoying the sight of the children's chaotic scramble and their eagerness to go home while their mothers gossiped about their daily lives and their favourite serials and, of course, not to forget, indulged in a bit of bitching about women they didn't like—which we like to call 'PNPC'! Women, I tell you! So predictable. . .

As I'd anticipated, I missed the bus. Quite irritated—as I hate to wait for buses or trains or anything—I stood in the shade waiting for the next bus, when a male voice quite surprised me.

'Can you please tell me which bus I should board to reach Barrackpore?'

He was standing behind me—a handsome man, almost my age. I must say that in that state of distress, together with the irritation of having lost the bus, the presence of an attractive guy gave me some relief! He was dressed neatly in a white shirt and blue jeans—the attire I feel guys look best in—and with his hair done perfectly. He looked stunning.

'I am going the same way. You can board the bus I am waiting for.' I don't know why I gave such a weird reply rather than telling him the bus number. Maybe I didn't want to lose his company so soon. Loneliness can make you do unusual things sometimes, I tell you.

'Oh! Thank you so much!' he replied gratefully. 'Actually, I am just one month old in this city,' he added.

I hadn't asked for an explanation! But whatever it may be, I liked that he told me. I don't know why.

'Oh! So you are not from Kolkata? Well in that case, welcome to the city of joy,' I added with a sweet smile.

'Actually, I was born here but I left Kolkata when I was eight years old as my dad shifted to Hyderabad on account of his job,' he corrected hastily.

'Then let me correct myself. Welcome back!'

'Ya, thanks! By the way, I am Avi,' he extended his hand towards me.

I was stunned for a few seconds. This was my usual reaction whenever I came across the name 'Avi' as it was very close to my heart.

'And you?' he asked quite surprised by my reaction.

'Oh! Hi, I am Diya,' I replied quickly and shook his hands. I don't know why I hid my full name. Maybe because he was a stranger. 'Nice name,' I added.

'I think that should have been my line,' he winked and we smiled.

~

'Avi'—my best buddy at school. Avigyan Ray. It's a very common story. It all started with a big fight on the first day itself owing to a seat. He had occupied my usual seat on the first bench and I had, quite predictably, started fighting with him. But he had to give in due to my popularity in the class and also my position as the monitor. But it didn't end there. After that day we became regular fighters. We used to fight with each other on every small or big thing. Our fights didn't seem to end until our teachers vowed to end it and put us together in the same science project. No one could convince us to work together until the project was made compulsory for everyone. Our destiny had made us work together but still there was no end to our fights. Our views and ideas contradictory, quite obviously. It was only when the last date of submission approached that we realized it was time to work more and fight less. To everyone's surprise—and mostly to both of ours—we achieved the highest score in the project!

Everyone congratulated us. It was then that we realized that we could be friends too if we stopped fighting. Quite surprisingly and unexpectedly, we became friends. Our fights stopped. The teachers heaved sighs of relief. Within a few months we became very good friends. We used to sit together, share our tiffins and notes, go home together, play together, work together, have fun together. As if there was no one else in the class. My old friends were very jealous of him. Slowly we became the best of friends—the inseparable ones. So much so that the whole class started teasing us for our 'chemistry'—some jokingly and some out of jealousy. But we didn't care. We had no time actually to care about such silly things; our only concern was us (me and Avi) and our friendship.

It was all going well till the news of our unbreakable bond reached his parents. It is worth mentioning here that he came from a very conservative family. So his parents took our relationship—rather, our friendship—too seriously. Very shockingly he left the school—in fact, he was forced to leave—in the very next session. Four years of fighting, working, sharing, having fun—all came to end at once, and that too without any prior warning. I lost my best buddy. It was like I'd lost myself. It changed me and my life totally. Thereafter I had friends, but no best friend. I was quite scared to be so close again to anyone else as the feeling of separation always scared me.

I lost all contact with him since, twenty years ago, we didn't have mobile phones nor any social networks like Orkut and Facebook to be in touch with our friends. I even didn't know where he went and for how many days, or even whether he would come back some day or not. I had so many questions to ask, so many answers to get, but there was no one to answer me . . .

∽

My bus—or our bus, actually—arrived. An almost half-filled bus, just ten to fifteen minutes after an over-crowded bus! It's possible only in Kolkata.

I took a corner seat and he, as expected, followed me and sat next to me.

'So you are a teacher in that school?' he inquired.

'Ya, biology teacher,' was my reply.

'Oh, biology! How much I hated this subject during my school days.'

'Hmm. That's quite usual for most boys,' I said reluctantly. 'So, what do you do?' This was my first question to him.

'Well, I am a software engineer at a private firm in Hyderabad,' he replied.

'So you came here for holidays?' I asked, getting curious.

'We don't have holidays like you, ma'am. I just got transferred.'

'Okay, then you must be feeling happy, coming back to your birthplace after almost fifteen years?' I asked.

'Tell me something, do you know astrology or something like that?' he asked quite curiously.

'No. And why are you asking that?' I inquired.

'Then I must say I am quite impressed by your guessing power,' he winked again.

'I didn't get you.'

'I am back to Kolkata after exactly fifteen years,' he explained.

'Oh! I see.'

'A smart way to know someone's age! Thank you so much for teaching me this. I am definitely going to use it someday on someone else,' he joked and we laughed again.

'But it was really unintentional,' I clarified.

'Come on, it's cool,' he said.

'Where do you live?' he started again after some minutes' pause.

I told him my stop, and also informed that it was just three stops before his stop.

'Oh, that's great. Then I will have good company throughout my way,' he smiled, then continued, 'I hope I am not being a bore. Actually, I enjoy chatting. It's one of my habits,' he winked again.

'And winking after every few minutes is another,' I thought to myself. I was quite glad to discover one of the habits of a stranger whom I met hardly half an hour ago.

'Oh, no, not at all,' I said. 'Rather, I am also enjoying this conversation. Every day I go home alone. Only my phone's music list accompanies me. At least this is a different journey from the usual one.' It was true that I was enjoying his company.

'So you listen to songs daily on your way home?'

'Not only on my way home. I listen to music whenever I am free, whenever I feel lonely. I love music. It's my best friend!' I replied, wondering what question he would throw next on the topic of best friends.

'Which songs do you listen to?' his question was not on the track I expected.

'Any soft, melodious song—Hindi or English, doesn't matter. But it should be soft and foot-tapping. Not something like rock or pop,' I said.

'And your favourite singer?'

'Not one. But Sonu Nigam, Shreya Ghoshal and Enrique are my most favourite. And yours?' Now was my turn to ask.

'A.R. Rahman, the one and only,' he responded quickly.

'So you live here in Barrackpore?' I asked.

'Ya, actually I am going to stay with my mom. My dad is still in Hyderabad. I'd gone to an uncle's place in Jadavpur. I was returning when I met you,' he explained. 'And you live here with your family, right?' he then asked, becoming more inquisitive.

'Ya, me and my parents. But I have an elder sister too. She is married and stays in Salt Lake,' I told him.

'So when are you planning to get married?' was his next bolt from the blue.

'Well, I think it will happen exactly at the time when it's destined,' I became philosophical.

He smiled and I bade him goodbye as it was time for me to get off.

'See you soon!' he added which left me wondering for the next few minutes as to how we were going to meet again.

And so time passed. Then, exactly one month and three days later, I found myself standing at the Barrackpore bus stop. It was a cold Sunday evening and I was returning from a friend's place. I was almost shivering with cold. The newspapers said it was the coldest day of the season, 7°C in Kolkata, the cool westerlies making the situation worse.

'Wanna have coffee?' I was quite amazed by a familiar voice.

'Hey Avi. How are you?' I said.

'Fine. Come on, let's go there and talk.'

I followed him to a nearby Café Coffee Day.

We ordered coffee and our conversation started. I was fascinated by his looks again—he was wearing a chocolate blazer, a cream shirt and jet black denims.

'Kolkata is unexpectedly cold today. You quite vanished after that evening,' he broke the silence.

'No, not really,' I replied quickly.

'A week after we met, I went to Jadavpur for some work and was waiting at the bus stop at the same time, but didn't see you,' he said.

'Oh, you were waiting for me?' I joked with him for the first time.

'Ya, I thought I would again have an interesting conversation but I had to travel alone,' he said quite seriously.

'Hey, come on. I was just kidding. Maybe I didn't go to school that day,' I said.

'Ya. It's okay. So what are you doing here?' his 'interrogation' started.

'I went to a friend's place. I was waiting for a bus to return home.'

'School friend?'

'No, college friend'.

'Only friend or . . .?'

'Oh please, I don't have a boyfriend,' I checked him.

Our coffees arrived.

'Even I am single,' he spoke, munching on the cookies.

'What? Impossible. I mean, why so?' I was surprised.

'Hey, what makes it impossible? Even you are single,' he sounded irritated.

'No, I mean you have many reasons to have a girlfriend.'

'Really? Like?'

'You are a software engineer, handsome, smart, well behaved and, above all, such good company. What else is needed?' I gave my thoughts away.

He responded, 'Well, thanks for all the compliments. But while you know a little bit about me, you don't know what my family is like. My parents are very conservative. They will kill me if they come to know I am so friendly with girls, or that I stay alone and have a girlfriend. They are dead against love marriage. I will have to marry a girl of their choice . . .'

'Unbelievable. I mean, if the girl is fine then what's the problem? It's the twenty-first century, after all,' I interrupted.

'They will never understand. You can say it's not in our tradition to go for love marriages or affairs before marriage. In fact, none of my relatives have had one such marriage. I know it's really strange but I can't break the rules.'

'It's not any rule, just a forceful imposition of one's own thoughts,' I concluded.

Our conversation ended soon as I was getting late.

'See you soon!' was his usual farewell.

Our third encounter was quite soon. Two weeks later, in fact. At a shopping mall.

'Spring shopping?' This time I saw him first.

'Hey, what a pleasant surprise! No, no, just a casual outing. Tell me, how are you?'

'Oh, just the usual.'

'You came for shopping alone?' he asked.

'Yup, just to buy some basic things.'

That was perhaps our shortest conversation as he was in a hurry that day. He had to attend a function at some relative's place.

'Okay, bye! Have fun!' I waited for him to say, 'See you soon!' But to my surprise, he asked hesitantly, 'Hey, if you don't mind, can I have your number?' He then added quickly, 'Don't get me wrong. Just for casual chitchat.'

'Oh, sure. I don't mind!' We exchanged our numbers and bade goodbye—of course, after his enthusiastic 'See you soon!'

After that day we used to chat over the phone daily—

sometimes for a few minutes, sometimes for hours—about our regular updates, our whereabouts and everything. I don't know why I enjoyed chatting with this stranger so much, although he was no longer a stranger to me. In fact, my fear to be close to someone also vanished after meeting him.

We became very close friends, sharing each and everything with each other. We waited every day for the time when we would be free and could talk. We became restless if for some reason we could not talk. Such a small, handy thing like a mobile phone can get two people so close to each other. Both of us could not make out what was happening to us, but we never discussed it. We were scared to do so, owing to his 'family rules'.

After four months of chatting and casual meetings here and there, came the day of our last meeting, 30 April 2012. It was his birthday and we planned to spend the evening together at a restaurant which was somewhere close to the school where I used to study.

'You know, I used to study there,' I said, pointing towards the school.

'Really, even I . . .' he paused.

'Hey, what's your full name?' he asked immediately.

'Diyali Pradhan, but why?' I could not figure out why he asked.

He was silent for a few minutes.

'What happened?' I persisted.

'You know, my full name is Avigyan Ray.'

Now both of us were silent. We didn't know what to say. Our voices choked, words vanished. Our food appeared but neither of us even looked at it.

'I think I should leave,' I started saying, almost with tears in my eyes.

Usually when best friends meet after years they hug each other happily and ask so many things and say so many things. But ours was a different story. We had tears in our eyes. We also had so many questions in our minds, so many things to say, but none of us could utter a single word.

'Ya, you are right. And I think we should never meet again. I cannot afford to lose you once again,' his reply shocked me but he explained soon after. 'Let me be clear with you. You are also aware of the fact that if our chatting and meetings continue like this, we will fall in love with each other. And after knowing that you are the one I was missing for so many years, I am quite sure we will not be able to control our feelings. And, to be very frank, it's so easy to fall for you. So . . .' he paused again.

'You stole my words . . .' I could only say this much.

We bade each other farewell for the last time and left. This time there was no 'See you soon!'

After that day we never met or talked. My city Kolkata! It gave me my best friend, snatched him from me and again returned him after many years, only to snatch him away again and never give him back . . .

Now whenever I miss my bus and wait for the next one at the Jadavpur bus stop, it makes me nostalgic. Tears don't listen to me and come out without warning. I sob silently, but there is no one to care. My phone's music list has become my companion again.

Whenever I recall those moments, I just wonder, 'Why did I meet Avi that day? A stranger, or was he?'

Bittersweet Symphony

JENNIFER ASHRAF KASHMI

The first time I saw Ishita, she was wearing black. Draped elegantly in a chiffon sari, she flitted around the hall like an exotic butterfly, smiling and conversing with a multitude of wedding guests. I noticed the elegantly cut blouse she was wearing, backless and daring. The curve of her back beckoned me and I realized that I found her seriously attractive. Very disturbingly so.

A sudden move beside me made me turn. Kajal had just plonked herself next to me on the sofa.

'Enjoying yourself, love?' I nodded and raised my glass. No, I was not having fun. Being stuck in a boring wedding watching the bride and groom amidst their show of forceful splendour was *not* my idea of an ideal Friday, but Kajal had dragged me to this. 'Think of it as research, my love,' she said. 'After all, yours is in less than three months!' Kajal had no idea that my smile hid the nausea which had just bubbled up inside. My stomach felt like I was on a roller coaster, one which was picking up speed at every turn. Ah, but I digress.

Inevitably, I found myself being introduced to Ishita in a matter of minutes. 'She's just completed her masters in law from London, you guys have so much in common!' Kajal gushed before moving away to mingle and leaving us to warily explore each other. As Ishita and I sized each other up, awkwardly making small talk, I wondered how I could sneak out early without seeming rude.

'Let's ditch this party, I'm bored.' I almost fell off the sofa. Was Ishita a mind reader or a lifesaver? Frankly I didn't care. 'Let's go,' I turned to her. Kajal could fend for herself, I was absolutely fed up.

Within minutes we had stealthily made our exit and were climbing into Ishita's car. She glanced warmly at me. 'What time do you need to get home?'

'Whenever,' I replied. Ever since my *Akht* with Tushar, my parents seemed to care less and less about what time I eventually made it home. As far as they were concerned, their time of worrying and distressing was over.

'Great,' Ishita smiled. 'Let's have a nightcap before I drop you off then.'

As we shared a pot of coffee at the Westin, I soon found out that Ishita and I did indeed have plenty in common. We both abhorred artificial personalities and plastic smiles. We both loved reading horror fiction and watching comedy movies, we both shared a mutual respect and love for sushi and, last but not the least, we were both finding it difficult to 'adjust' now that we were back to Dhaka after spending years abroad studying.

By the time Ishita dropped me back home, it was way past

two in the morning. We exchanged numbers before I got out of the car and, as I lay on my bed with the covers pulled up to my chin, I found myself going to sleep with a smile on my face after a long time. The morning, upon awakening, I found a text from Ishita waiting for me on my phone: *Good morning gorgeous. How are you today? Fancy meeting up?*

Excited at prospect of seeing her so soon again, I sat and composed a message replying to her text, even before I made my way to the bathroom to brush my teeth.

And so, the texting began. . .

It's hard to determine the exact moment when I started falling for Ishita, the exact moment when my feelings crossed the platonic borderline threshold that all friends share mutually. Was it the first time she gave me the most endearing look when I had fallen asleep in her car and she had woken me up? Or the first time I felt a tinge of jealousy when she sat next to a very attractive guy? Did it happen during the hundreds of texts we sent each other every day? Or maybe the first time she invited me to her place and introduced me to her family?

I didn't know which of these was the right answer and frankly, I didn't care. All I knew was that I was falling for Ishita. Hard. We were attending all the numerous social events together now. I would wake up every morning to a text on my phone from her, and every day would seem beautiful. She would pick me up and we would head out, exploring different areas of Dhaka and sharing our thoughts on every subject, from music and literature to politics and world peace. We would talk for hours on the phone every night and I remember feeling that I had finally met the one person who understood and accepted me completely.

I can never forget the first time we shared a kiss. Ishita

had picked me up from work and we were on our way to Ichi, our recently discovered sushi hangout which had become a mandatory weekly outing for both of us. As we inched forward in the ridiculous Dhaka traffic, the radio played soft romantic songs in the background and I contentedly sipped from my water bottle, as Ishita and I shared warm smiles.

'I wish I was that bottle.'

I almost choked. *What?* Turning to her, I raised my eyebrows questioningly.

'I can't help it,' Ishita laughed. 'All I can say is that the bottle is very lucky right now. It has the pleasure of your lips, something which I am deprived off.'

Before I could even completely grasp what Ishita meant, she had leaned forward and suddenly her lips were on mine. The radio played '*Dil samhal jaa zaara, phir mohabbat karna chala hain tu* (Steady yourself, heart, you're on your way to falling in love again),' in the background. Sensations and emotions exploded within me. I had been kissed before, but not like this. Never like this. I felt like I was drowning and the only thing keeping me anchored was Ishita's hold over me.

An insistent tapping brought us back to the present. '*Apa, beli phooler mala niben?* (Would you like some jasmine garlands?)' As we both broke away, breathless, we turned to see the street hawker now staring open mouthed at us, his jasmine garlands forgotten. Undoubtedly he would have some very interesting stories for his friends tonight. The light turned green and we sped away, both grinning at each other like love-struck teenagers.

That night after Ishita dropped me home, I plugged my Ipod's earphones into my ears and danced till I was breathless. As I finally collapsed into bed, exhausted and exulted, I checked my phone and found a text from her which accelerated my heartbeat.

'Dil samhal jaa zaara, phir mohabbat karna chala hain tu . . . '

I loved dressing up for her, even though it was completely unnecessary. No matter what I wore, Ishita always made me feel like the most beautiful girl in the world. When those dark eyes looked deep into mine, I would often stop mid-sentence, unsure of what I was about to say next, my mind utterly and completely blank. It was almost like we were a couple, except that the outside world interpreted our budding relationship as a sign of friendship and female solidarity.

I know you're thinking that this can't possibly be true, how can things move so fast? Maybe it was just infatuation? With days rushing past so swiftly, the final date of my wedding ominously came closer every single day. But isn't it always how things go, how life-changing events happen when you least expect them?

A month before my wedding, Ishita picked me up from work, as was customary, and we both headed towards Gulshan. As the car sped through the familiar Dhaka landmarks, I recognized that we were heading towards Baridhara, a spot where we had spent many evenings together, chatting and kissing, getting the requisite privacy that no other place in Dhaka provided. These diplomatic residential areas had their benefits; as long as you looked the part of sophistication and elegance, no one stopped you or even dared to check up on you inside the intimidating darkly tinted windows.

Ishita silently and efficiently parked in our favourite spot, turned off the ignition and turned to me. She seemed to be searching for the right words and I waited breathlessly, not really sure I would like what I was about to hear. After what seemed like an eternity, Ishita finally took a deep breath and started to speak. 'I can't do this any more,' she said. My heart missed a beat. 'Do what?' I asked her with a cheerful smile, deliberately attempting to keep the atmosphere light.

Ishita exhaled sharply. 'I can't see you any more,' she said. 'You're getting married in less than a month. For God's sake, you're already legally married! In a month you'll be heading to someone else's house, you'll be spending your days with him. You'll be sleeping with him every night! You will belong to him in every sense imaginable—legally, religiously and socially! How do you think that makes me feel?'

I was starting to have trouble breathing. Ishita's words seemed to float right over me; my mind was refusing to see reason, refusing to let her go. *You can't leave me, I won't let you.*

Taking a deep breath, I weighed my next few words. 'I will still belong to you wholly in my mind, you know that,' I whispered. 'Things will not really change. I will still be yours and you will still have me.' *I love you*, I screamed silently in my mind.

My carefully chosen words seemed to fall on deaf ears; she was getting increasingly agitated by the minute. 'No, Raina, things *will* change. Will you be able to come out and meet me on half an hour's notice every time I call you? Will you be able to stay out with me till two in the morning? Will you be able to answer your phone after midnight when I want to talk for a couple of hours before heading to bed? No, you won't. So please don't tell me that things are not really going to change, as I know better!'

I was speechless. We had never talked about this before. I knew I was falling deeply in love and I knew that Ishita loved me too, but I could never grasp the extent of her feelings. Whenever she told me she loved me it was always in a very light manner, and I always had the feeling that I loved Ishita a thousand times more than she loved me. *I love you*, my heart whispered again.

'You never told me you felt so strongly,' I stammered. Ishita gave me a look of pure exasperation and I immediately realized that I was being silly. 'Right,' I muttered to myself. She did not have to tell me; ours was a most unconventional relationship, words were not necessary between us. We sat silently, each of us lost in our own worlds. Finally Ishita started the ignition and we turned towards Gulshan.

I turned to look at her silent profile as she drove wordlessly. My beautiful Ishita—so full of life, so full of love.

'Come to London with me, Raina,' she suddenly said.

I blinked in confusion. I knew she was heading to London for a short trip to take care of some family business, but she was leaving a couple of days before my wedding and would be staying abroad for a couple of months.

Ishita looked at me again, sideways. 'I'm serious, Raina,' she said. 'Come with me, let's just run away together.'

Run away, run away. . . my heartbeat accelerated. But didn't that just happen in the movies? No one I knew had ever run away before. Could I really do that?

Why not?

I looked at Ishita, trying to assess whether she was serious. She met my gaze squarely, steely determination in her eyes.

I will follow you to the ends of the Earth, my soul whispered.

Yet, just as I was about to tell her the same, my mother's innocent face flashed before my eyes. The words I so desperately wanted to speak out suddenly lodged themselves in my throat. My parents' love, their trust, their faith . . . the consequences of my fleeing the country were unimaginable; all the preparations were going ahead at full steam, all the invitations were in the post, relatives abroad were making their way back to Dhaka after decades. Was I brave enough to take the step?

I never got the chance to find out.

In the next instant Ishita gave me one of her cheerful smiles and floored the accelerator. We did not speak of running away again.

That night I went back home and waited for Ishita to call. When she did, we talked about everything, everything except what had transpired between us that evening. By some unspoken agreement, neither of us mentioned it.

I went to sleep feeling lonely, frustrated and unfulfilled.

It was Wednesday evening and I was waiting for Ishita at Hotbrew Café. Ishita would be leaving the next day and we both wanted to simply spend our last evening together, as none of us were sure about what the future held for us.

An hour, two coffees and a plateful of peanut-butter cookies later, I was tired and crabby and just about to leave, when Ishita finally walked in. As I waved her to the table, I couldn't help wondering what had kept her so long. However, as usual, I didn't push. Ishita had a tendency to get very defensive if I started asking questions.

I also couldn't help noticing that her eyes were bloodshot. She had been crying and drinking, I could smell it on her breath. Leaning across the table, I reached for her hand. Usually warm and soft, it felt cold and clammy. Something was definitely wrong.

'What's the matter?' I asked gently.

Ishita didn't answer. Minutes passed. We sat in silence.

After fifteen minutes had roughly elapsed, Ishita finally spoke up. 'I love you,' she whispered.

'I love you too. So very much.'

'Please don't get married.'

Her words hit me like a blow. My wedding was in less than three days and she was asking me to back off *now*? I sat speechless, in shock. 'What?' I managed to croak.

'Please don't get married.'

For months we had been dating, growing closer and closer, falling more and more in love with every passing day, and she chose to drop this bombshell on me now? When my wedding was in less than three days?

'You know I can't escape it,' I whispered. 'It's too late.'

Ishita shook her head vehemently. 'It's never too late. You can. Just tell your parents you don't want to get married. Please, I need you. Just be with me. You know you can do it.'

Could I? My heart soared with the thought. Just Ishita and I, being completely free and enamoured with each other; we could be so happy. And then my heart sank. This couldn't happen. Relatives from all over the world had already flown in, the hall was paid for in full, the event management crew and the caterers had been working together for months, the wedding invitations had been distributed personally all over the country just a couple of weeks ago!

Roughly five thousand guests had been invited to the wedding; I dreaded to imagine the phone calls cancelling the event. Why, oh why, did Ishita wait till the last minute to ask me to walk away from my wedding? Or was this just another cruel joke?

In the last few months that I had come to know her well, I had begun to realize that she had a penchant for stirring up excitement. Ishita did have a thing for drama. Maybe this was just another one? A misguided attempt to 'test' my love?

I shook my head. 'It's too late,' I repeated. 'Give me a year?' I whispered.

'A year? What happens in a year? Did I miss something?'

I shook my head. 'If you really do love me, give me a year. Have faith in me. Things would have calmed down by then, and I would be able to end this travesty of a marriage.'

'You want me to wait around for you for a year? An entire year?'

'One year—that's all I'm asking.' I nodded. 'Have faith in me.'

'You won't be able to,' Ishita challenged me.

I smiled inwardly. Ishita had always witnessed the soft side of me. She had no idea how ruthlessly determined I could be when I set my mind to something. 'One year,' I repeated. 'I believe in us.'

After what felt like eternity, Ishita nodded. 'One year,' she replied. 'I love you. I believe in us too.' She grasped my hand firmly.

That night, when Ishita dropped me home, we exchanged goodbyes the way we always did. 'Kiss me,' she challenged me in the car in front of my gate, whilst the guard held the door open, a bored expression on his face. I stuck my tongue out at her. If I knew then what I know now, I would have kissed her, guard and society be damned.

'Call me tomorrow, before you leave?'

'You know I will,' she promised.

The last time I saw Ishita, she was wearing black. Draped elegantly in a chiffon sari, she flitted around the hall like an exotic butterfly, smiling and conversing with a multitude of party guests. Only this time I was not admiring her elegantly cut blouse or the smooth curve of her back.

I was too busy dying a thousand deaths every time she flashed her beautiful smile.

At the end of the day it was Ishita who didn't have either

the guts or the courage to go through with the relationship, to go through with 'us'. Funny, she always said that I was the one who lacked the necessary conviction.

I remembered weeks of waiting for her to get back from her trip abroad. I remember the distant attitude that she had adopted, her aggressive comebacks which were triggered by the simplest questions I asked her. I remembered the nights I had spent crying over the loss of our beautiful relationship.

Score: one for society, nil for us. Game over.

As I lay in bed that night, with Tushar snoring gently beside me and my tears to keep me company, I mourned the loss of the Raina who used to be full of life. I mourned the loss of the dreams and hopes we had cherished. I mourned the loss of beautiful nights under the stars, on a nameless road in Baridhara where we exchanged kisses while the crickets sang.

And, my eyes focused on the streetlamp light ray that shone through my open window, I said goodbye forever to the love of my life; I said goodbye to Ishita.

Heartstrings

Dr ROSHAN RADHAKRISHNAN

I saw the ring today after all these years. I hadn't seen it in ages. My heart skipped a beat as a silent crescendo of emotions washed over it, leaving me short of breath even as the world around me continued to function uninterrupted. I could hear a familiar tune playing in my head once more—a song I'd not heard in years. Slowly, as I stared at the gold ring, the present crumbled and the past peeked through.

~

'In whose name shall I bill it?' the jeweller asked, his eyes never leaving the computer screen.

'Mine . . . I mean, Roshan.' Try as I might, I could not take my eyes off the ring. It held no sparkling diamonds, rubies or intertwined swans. To anyone else, it was probably your run-of-the-mill gold ring. But for me, it represented a year of my hostel allowance saved—on account of skipped meals and taking xerox copies rather than buying the original texts. More importantly, it represented feelings I'd held in my heart for too long. Involuntarily, a smile passed my lips again as I saw the two letters carved into the gold: 'M.R.'

M. Megha Balakrishnan. What can I tell you about her? We'd known each other for years. It had all started innocuously enough with us being stuck in the same medical course. My first impression of her was that she was just another snooty NRI brat. She, in turn, had found me standoffish. In time, we both understood how wrong we were. Being assigned as each other's lab partners would prove to be the ice-breaker—we realized how alike we actually were. Our initial aloofness had been nothing more than a common inability to make new friends easily. The truth was, we were both naughty as mice with a wicked sense of humour. Perhaps that, more than anything else, strengthened our friendship.

As the years passed by and life threw various hurdles our ways, we learnt to watch out for each other. I could count on her to be my 3 a.m. wake-up call to study during our exams just as she could count on me to stand up for her if anyone badmouthed her. Our assignments were invariably carbon copies of each other's papers. Bunking classes, making mnemonics only the two of us could understand to remember drugs and classifications, tic-tac-toe marathons on the table while the lecturer droned on about myopias and cataracts—this was our life. In a world where two teenagers had been abruptly thrust from a fawning school life into an unforgiving medical-college life of books, blood and diseases, we were each other's comfort zones—a place where we could be the people we once were without being judged. We were the best of friends.

When did I fall in love? I don't know. It's hard to define

the exact moment, really. Sometimes, you just realize that the person you've been walking beside all these years suddenly looks different—her natural charm is enhanced by the radiance of her personality. You find yourself missing her jokes, her laughter and her voice—even if you've just spent the day with her. You envision what life could be like: the two of you together—the posh villa, the pet dog and cat who would grow up mimicking the love they see in their owners, the holiday trips where you actually live the dream that travel brochures paint for everyone . . . and the stolen kisses that would still promise a lifetime of love and trust. You see yourselves growing old together. And it feels just right.

I guess, that's how it was with me too. One fine day, I woke up and realized that all these days the dream girl I was looking for was right beside me all along . . . I had just never thought of her like that before.

The recent exams had been our last. And while we'd gone our separate ways for the holidays, we would be returning to the college for our one-year internship together soon. We had kept in touch via the phone sporadically over the month, but it just wasn't the same.

As luck would have it, we both ended up clearing our exams. In fact, she topped the batch in two subjects. And I was amongst the top five. Whoever said those who bunk classes wouldn't prosper had obviously never met us. As part of the celebrations, we decided to have an afternoon out for ourselves the Sunday after we joined back. Just me and her . . . and a heart dying to reveal itself.

'Roshan. Yoohoo, Earth calling Roshan!'

I looked up. She looked beautiful. I know how silly it sounds, but sitting there, tired after a long day, furiously attacking the ice cubes in her cold coffee with gusto as she searched for the ideal spot below the air conditioner, she just looked beautiful. That was the only thought that came to me.

She arched her eyebrows, reminding me that I had not yet responded.

'Ya, Meg. I'm here!' The ring in my pocket weighed a ton . . . as did my heart. Everything had gone great up until now. The movie had been sufficiently romantic without being melodramatic. Lunch had been skipped to devote more time to the usual post-movie shopping ritual. After two hours of trekking across the length and breadth of the mall, seeking my opinion on everything she tried on before vetoing it, we now sat at what we had once labelled our own personal ancestral home—the familiar coffee shop. I watched her as she leaned forward, her fork dipping into my Chocolate Fantasy cake, even as her eyes stayed on me.

'Megha?' I ventured.

'Hmm.'

'I need to tell you something serious.'

She stared at me for a moment. 'Actually, there's something I need to tell you too.'

For the first time, I noticed a nervousness in her voice. Suddenly, there was an awkwardness in her tone that I'd not seen in years—not since the time we had first been paired together.

'Sure, you go first.'

She stopped chewing as she pondered her words carefully. 'This last month after the exams, being at home, away from . . . well, it made me realize something. I guess . . . Damn, I don't even know what to say!'

'It's me, Meg. You can say anything you want.'

'That's just it, Rosh. Sometimes it's so difficult to say these things to the people who matter the most. Rosh . . . do you believe that you can spend your whole lifetime being with a guy and then suddenly, one morning, everything is different? You find yourself looking at that guy differently, noticing things about him you'd not seen before. Suddenly . . . you want to be with him more and more. You miss him when he leaves; you wait to hear from him again. You know?'

I nodded, my heart beating wildly within.

'This past month being away . . . something changed for me, Rosh. The feeling was probably there for a while, but I guess I just didn't want to think about it while we were still students. I don't know how you'll take it or how it'll affect us, but I need to tell you. In fact, I've been wanting to tell you ever since we came back. I didn't want to do this over the phone. I guess I just wanted to tell you face-to-face.'

As I watched her, I realized how true the saying was: the eyes really did reveal what the heart wants to say. I could see it in her eyes—the trepidation of a girl in love—and I knew in that moment that this was meant to be. This was what it had all been about. Destiny had brought us together from different parts of the country, landing us in the same college, pitting us against heartbreaks and group studies, across cultural programmes and dissection tables, medical cases and go-karting races to this one moment—when we realized how incomplete we were without each other.

I forced myself to let it play its course. I held her hand on the table. They were tiny, I thought to myself. They were also trembling. In all these years, being right beside each other, the truth was, we had never even held hands.

'What is it? You and I, we've been through so much. Trust in me to understand what you have to say.'

She looked into my eyes for a hint. She must have found

what she was looking for, because moments later, she smiled, a smile I'll always remember till the day I have to leave this world for another. I can see it even now when I close my eyes—a moment frozen in time in the memory book of my heart.

'Roshan, I'm in love with Rahul. We're going to get married next year.'

I didn't flinch.

I listened to her as she told me of the long conversations she had with our batchmate, Rahul, during the holidays—the online chats, his proposal, the meeting of the families. The engagement date. And God help me, I didn't betray myself to her, not for a second. I laughed at the right moments, consoled her as she spoke of the fears she had telling her parents and cooed like old times as she giggled her way to the end of the story. Even the clichéd watering eyes at that moment seemed so appropriate—a friend overjoyed for his best friend's happiness.

As she gushed and giggled, I watched the nervousness vanish and the familiar, confident woman I loved reappear. And when it was all over, she waited for me. 'Your turn. You had something to say?'

I looked at her. This was Megha. I couldn't lie to her. She'd see through me immediately. We didn't do the 'oh-never-mind-forget-it' routine. That wasn't us. But what could I say to her?

Two small hands enveloped my own. I looked up at her. That smile, never meant to be mine. Unless . . .

'Come on, Rosh. Trust in me to understand what you have to say.'

I saw in her eyes the love that shone and all that we'd shared together. I saw my love and hers too and what we both stood to gain . . . and lose. And suddenly, everything seemed so simple. I knew what I had to do.

I withdrew my hands from hers and reached into my pockets. I took out the little blue box and placed it in front of her on the table. I opened the cover, revealing the gold ring with the artistic 'M and R' forming two sides of a gorgeous heart.

She looked at it, her mouth agape. Time stopped, if only for the two of us, in that familiar corner chair in this familiar coffee shop that had hosted us for years. She finally looked up at me in puzzlement. I looked down at her hands and once more placed mine over them.

This was my moment.

'I knew about you and Rahul, Megha. Do you really think you can keep things like this from me? Come on, yaar. I had this made to give it to you as a present on your engagement, but well . . . I guess this is as good a time as any.'

Her grin widened and I could see her eyes grow moist. She turned her palms over, held my hands and squeezed them tightly.

'Oh, Roshan . . . this is amazing. I love you.'

I'd like to think my voice didn't crack as I finally revealed my heart that day. 'I . . . I love you too, Megha.'

She wiped away her tears. 'Gosh. Look at us. People are staring at us. And this ring? They'll think you proposed to me. These guys in the cafe must be expecting us to hug and kiss now!'

'Perverted rascals . . . Pur-vur-ted ras-cala. Chee, chee,' I said, accentuating the South in my dialect. She giggled at the impression of a professor we both despised immensely.

'I know. Pur-vur-ted ras-cala.' She giggled. 'Come. Let's pay the bill and get out of here. Rahul's birthday's coming

up before the engagement and I need your help in finding
him a gift. Break's over. It's shopping time again.'

Picking up our shopping bags, we left the coffee shop
that day; two hearts in love—one heart freed over a cup of
coffee, another destined to be hidden for ever.

~

*Six years have passed since that day. Seeing the pictures of Rahul
and Megha on Facebook as I sit here waiting for my next patient
to be shifted into the operation theatre, I can only smile. Life would
eventually find other ways to separate us—soon after her marriage,
she would move to a different country with her husband and lose
herself in her new environment and lifestyle. I would find a way
to lose myself too, not entirely unintentionally, in the endless ocean
of my postgraduate years and the new challenges that the life of a
surgeon brought. The promises of being friends forever would remain
what they always were—college promises scribbled in the sand. Over
time, we've become just one out of hundreds of friends in each other's
Facebook list. We are not strangers, I know, but we can never be
what we once were. What we could have been.*

*And yet, I still find solace in her smile. In her happiness that
radiates through these pictures, I find it easier to sleep at night.
Because that was what I'd always wanted for her—to be happy.*

*As for the familiar ring tied around the neck of their little girl,
Deepika . . . well, it's fulfilling its promise even today. A promise
of unconditional love.*

The Most Handsome

KAVIYA KAMARAJ

Divya inquired from the receptionist about the X-ray report that she was supposed to get that day and also mentioned her appointment with Dr K.C. Balan MD, who also happened to be a family friend. The receptionist requested her to wait after sending one of the assistants to the medical superintendent's room to get the attested report.

A small introduction about Divya could probably make you feel more comfortable. Divya was in her sophomore year, studying psychology at the University of Madras. She was rather tall for a girl, had a slim figure and a slender waistline that most girls would envy. With alluring eyes, a Roman nose and fleshy cheeks, she was very attractive. She didn't need any ornaments; she wore those inimitable expressions!

She was searching for a suitable chair—rather, an appropriate position to sit—when she saw this lovely couple. In particular, she noticed the handsome husband seated in front of her.

Divya's parents had been looking for the right guy for her; and ever since the search for her prince had started, she'd started dreaming of her ideal man. This guy who was sitting there matched almost all the parameters she'd set. He was tall, fair and well built with a minimal frame. And with a clean-shaven face, sharp nose and penetrating eyes, he was one of the most handsome guys she'd ever seen. She immediately felt jealous of the girl seated next to him, his wife. The girl looked like a model, the kind you can only see in advertisements and some expensive magazines. If you had taken an international flight, maybe, you could have seen some one like that. They were the kind of couple people call 'made for each other'.

Since there were a couple of chairs right behind them, Divya thought settling in there wouldn't be that bad an idea. She went unnoticed—not deliberately, though—and sat in the chair right behind the charming couple. However, the pair didn't notice her arrival and continued to chat loudly enough to be audible to the person seated behind.

'Why should you not reconsider this?' pleaded the girl with her husband.

'There's nothing to reconsider here, Maya. You know that my salary has been cut by almost 50 per cent and I don't feel safe at all. This is an emergency measure that is very much required!' He sounded very desperate.

'But, Kabir, even with the salary you earn now, we can raise our child. It's enough. It's just our mindset. Don't you think?'

'What's enough!' He didn't allow her to complete the sentence. 'Look. It isn't enough. I want my son to grow in the best possible environment. I want him to eat the best food. I want him to attend the best school. I want him to live in one of the costliest apartments and I want him to wear clothes that not many are blessed to even think of. This is how I want my son to grow up. I don't want him to grow up seeing his father suffering from the financial crisis. So it's better you have an abortion now. I am sure things will get better in a year or two; we can have a child then.'

Divya felt that though his manner was gentle, as if one hand was cradling the new baby, the actual content was harsh, like using the other hand to choke the same baby to death.

Maya continued crying. It was a rather 'cultured crying', to which people like Maya are conditioned inherently. It's impossible for anyone to notice unless one sits at a close proximity like where Divya was seated.

'I feel really insecure. This is our first child. Who knows? This abortion could take my life. I am afraid!' She said. Her voice trembled, echoing the emotional turmoil she was going through.

'This is just a minor operation. There's nothing to worry about, sweetheart. I have spoken to the doctor.' His efforts at consolation, for no reason in particular, reminded Divya of the plastic flowers used for decorating a room—all looks and no fragrance.

'You dirty liar!' hissed Maya. 'Don't lie! I spoke to the doctor myself. She said there's a huge risk involved in this, now that I am psychologically not ready for this and all. Generally, doctors don't talk like this to expectant mothers. This is our first child. How can you be so monstrous?' Words didn't come out of her as comfortably as she wanted it to. She was on the verge of losing all the culture to which she had been institutionalized since her childhood.

'Look,' began Kabir. 'On this issue, we've had long discussions before and the conclusion is what has made us sit here. If you are still adamant, you can probably go ahead and have this child. But prepare yourself to live without me. Period.' Saying this, he turned his face away from her, sealing the argument. It was then that he noticed a stranger sitting behind him. His expression changed completely in a way that Divya was unable to comprehend. The same face that looked so handsome until few minutes back now looked so ugly that she felt bad for having seen that face in her lifetime.

Suddenly there boomed a voice that almost shook the entire block: 'You mindless idiot! How many times do you want me to repeat this?'

It was spoken in strongly accented colloquial Tamil which people like Divya don't get to listen to pretty often. It came from a guy who was sitting right at the front, while Divya was sitting behind the couple who were some good ten to fifteen seats away from him. Almost all the seats were vacant as it wasn't a weekend or a peak time in the hospital—or probably people were too healthy.

'How many times do you want me to say this!' he continued yelling. Everybody near the reception and also this young couple looked at this shouting man who seemed completely oblivious of his surroundings. The person at the receiving end was his wife. She was a lean woman with a swollen face. She was wearing a wrinkled sari. A yellow thread was around her neck and her face was too swollen to describe the attributes.

Her husband, the one who was shouting, was tall, massively built, with red eyes and a large moustache that occupied almost all of his face. He had a daunting stature. He was wearing traditional village attire, white shirt and a white dhoti—not all that white though. He was holding some old leather bag with probably a bottle in it.

He possessed exactly the features that Divya hated in any guy. 'All men are barbarians,' thought Divya to herself. 'Some of them conceal their brutality very graciously, like the one in front of me, while the others like this villager are openly barbaric.' She thought that the word 'barbarian' described that man precisely.

She wanted to know the story behind this verbal lynching. 'Eavesdropping isn't ethical,' she told herself. But curiosity got the better of her and she shifted herself slowly and discreetly till she was sitting right behind this village couple. The gap between two rows was large enough to go unnoticed and small enough to make the conversation audible in the rear. This helped Divya's cause.

'Drink this. You haven't eaten anything since today morning!' he said, offering his wife the bottle he was holding. Divya assumed it probably had sweet lime juice.

The woman continued crying. Divya wasn't sure if she wasn't in the mood to accept the bottle or if she was too weak to! The woman had been crying and looked really tired. Divya wouldn't have been surprised if she had fallen dead ten minutes from then.

'Why are you crying? Nothing has happened,' the villager tried to console her. His pleading was so incongruous to his looks.

'I've given birth to a dead baby boy and doctors have told me I can't conceive again. Your parents are going to make you divorce me and you will get married to another woman,' she said, weeping uncontrollably. 'I am probably a sinner, the biggest sinner ever in our village!' she shouted and continued, 'I shall not be spared. Punish me, my God. Take me. It's better that I die rather than giving difficulty to my husband and his family.'

Her tears were genuine. Not a single iota of any of it sounded dramatic. Divya could empathize with her. She had been to a village to meet her grandparents and she knew what it was to lose a first child there—when a woman was declared sterile, she naturally became untouchable. So all the emotions that this female was displaying—they could be insane and even seem specious when analysed logically—made all the sense in the world to Divya who realized it was more than just logic. Now this woman would probably be thrown out of the family by her husband and she would have to lead the rest of her life as a destitute. How sad!

But her husband held her hands, giving her warmth in the process, and said, 'Look! I am not going to marry anybody. I swear. Now, trust your husband! Stop crying. I can't be disloyal to you.' He then patted her hair and called somebody, probably his wife's sister, and asked both of them to wait at the bus stand as he had some formalities to complete.

'Hold her tight, lest she should fall,' he loudly instructed his wife's sister and then disappeared from Divya' s sight.

Divya waited for some time. After a few minutes, the receptionist called her, handed her the X-ray reports and asked her to meet her family doctor, who was waiting for her on the first floor.

As Divya entered the doctor's room, she saw one huge figure leaving the room and she craned her neck and saw it was the same village guy whom she'd seen below.

'Hello, Uncle! How are you doing?' Divya asked Dr K.C. Balan, who was their family doctor and, incidentally, the chief medical superintendent of the Nila Hospitals.

'Hello, Divya! I am doing great. How do you do? How's your father? Hasn't he come out of hypochondriasis yet?' he asked jovially.

'He is fine, Uncle. As usual complaining about those silly pains here and there. You know.'

'I saw the X-ray report and he is completely all right. Just ask him to do his regular exercise and stuff. That would suffice.'

'Uncle, it could sound intrusive. But, can you tell me something about this guy who just left your office? I am interested in knowing about him.'

'That's a very sad story, Divya. I am not supposed to share my patients' stories with anybody. However, this one is extraordinary; I want you to hear it. I hope you don't share it with anybody else. This guy's name is Ilamcheliyan and he is from this remote village from the south. His family is a prestigious family in his village and they are fondly called the 'Velakkarapadayiner'—that roughly translates as 'guardians of the village'. His family has been considered as the defenders of the village for generations and the first male child in each generation takes the mantle of defending the village from his father. Now, after Ilamcheliyan, his son is supposed to become the Knight of the Village, with the mantle passing from Ilamcheliyan to his son.

'Ilamcheliyan's wife had a small accident and hence there was an unexpected complication in the delivery and the baby was stillborn. Because of this accident she's lost her ability to conceive again. She's become infertile. Now, given this scenario, you can easily expect the next few scenes. The powerful family of Ilamcheliyan and the whole village will force him to ditch his wife and get remarried to some other girl. It doesn't matter how much Ilamcheliyan resists or how much he doesn't want this to happen; he will be forced to do it. Imagine, when thousands of people are pushing you in a certain direction forcefully, is it possible to run in the opposite direction? You can try; but what will happen? You will have to eventually give in. I mean, it will not be practically possible for Ilamcheliyan to say no to them forever. They are really influential and Ilamcheliyan will be overwhelmed at some point of time for sure. But, this is where you've got to give it to this guy. A salute. An incredible gesture!'

Dr Balan paused and took off his glasses.

'What is he going to do?' asked a puzzled Divya.

'Vasectomy,' he said and stopped abruptly.

'What! Good God, is he crazy!'

'He's asked me to keep this a secret. He's fixed the appointment with our surgeon for today evening itself. If any of his people comes to know of this, all hell will break loose and they will go to any extent to stop this. I know his family. I've been following them for quite some time. They have a different set of values altogether. Ilamcheliyan's father himself had three wives and innumerable concubines, and he used up almost all the assets in the process. Their culture and their way of living could look odd and probably even nasty to some of us. But that's how life is defined there for them, and that's how they have been living all along. And to see an absolutely truly civilized man like this from that kind of place—it's awe-inspiring!'

Divya was so taken aback that she didn't have anything further to say on that topic. She was speechless, to say the least. They had their normal chat for some time and Divya later left the hospital.

While she was waiting at the bus stop to catch an auto, she could hear a familiar voice behind her. Turning back, she saw it was the man with the big moustache, Ilamcheliyan. His stature intimidated her, as usual.

'We have to go to Saidapet. Can you tell me the bus number?' he asked Divya politely. Then pointing at a bus, he inquired if that will take him there.

'Yes, it will! Kindly hurry up!' Divya said urgently. She saw him board the bus with his wife and her sister. Ilamcheliyan was holding his wife's hand carefully and guiding her inside.

She looked at Ilamcheliyan's face for probably the last time ever. She couldn't remember seeing somebody more handsome than that!

A Pair of Shoes

MANASWITA GHOSH

Rishi lay on a rock on the banks of the river Beas, listening
to the thunderous gush of water speeding past him—a roar
that contrasted sharply with the deafening silence inside him.
His eyes moved about the night sky in an unfocused way,
bringing up tears now and then. His lips would never stop
smiling. As if he was happy. Really happy. In the most sad,
unmentionable way. Happy over something that never existed.
Or perhaps did, a long time back—somewhere so far away
and so far back in time that it was barely a memory; and yet
it brought out a smile and secret burning tears every time
his mind raced back to it. For him it was a source of some
consolation, of support, of strength . . . It was strange how
the gravest of reminiscences had the power to heal things,
to rejuvenate life, shaping every lost and broken bit in a way
that makes everything appear perfect again . . .

But it was over. Nothing could be shaped now. He knew she was gone . . . After he met her today . . .

~

Eight years ago:

'Do you know how much those shoes exactly cost? And you thought you could buy them!' Adaa nudged him in the arm. 'And besides, who wears shoes like that? All hi-fi people buy them! Not us!' She promptly looked away, backing off the glass showcase.

He considered for a while. 'You never dreamt of wearing them? Ever?' he asked, not taking his eyes off the pair.

She hesitated, 'Err . . . what's the point? When you know you can't have something, why go after it?'

'But how do you know you can have it or not if you don't go after it at all?'

'You talk a lot, you know that? Enough of this, let's go, we're late for school . . .'

'You can't lie to your best friend! I saw you ogling them last evening on my way back from the grocer's . . .'

'Liar!'

'What were you doing then? Admiring the glass?'

'Shut up! Just walk silently. Can't you?' She elbowed him, and together they ran down the winding path.

~

He remembered a shadowy evening and a familiar face . . . The dark sketch of a girl . . . Somewhere inside, he felt a sting, a nudge that hit hard and sharp.

Adaa sat on a rock, her cold feet dipped in the ice-cold river water. She had her shawl on, the only one she had. An *angithi* burned beside her, the red-hot coal sizzling softly. Her long hair was tied in a loose knot and fell all the way to her waist. She turned to look when she heard his steps. She had smiled in a sad, beautiful way. The kind of smile that ignited a million questions and yet you feared to ask a thing out loud. He took off his dirty shoes and dipped his feet in the river too, cringing a little as the water touched his skin. Adaa watched him, smiling shyly. She then looked away.

'So, are you going to tell me what's with you?' he asked.

He looked at her. She didn't. She was staring somewhere far off, a place his eyes couldn't fathom. The river reflected the yellow lantern lights from the houses above, the mountains, forests, stone houses, rocks, stars and the sky—everything drowned in its depths. A broken sun had drowned too, not much time back. She heaved a sigh, weighing her words.

'I am getting married.'

'What!'

She looked at him directly now. 'They are marrying me off, Rishi.'

He sat there, bewildered. She looked away again. He just looked at her, listening to every single sound that reached his ears except that one beat that came from the girl who sat beside him, her heart screaming silently somewhere inside.

'But you are just seventeen—and so am I . . . If I can't marry now, so early, you too can't! You are still in school! Your parents can't just marry you off!'

'I wish it worked that way . . .' she had said. He thought he heard her voice quiver a little.

They sat there quietly, feeling lost, both suppressing the storm that rose up inside. He had watched her eyes well up, her face glowing in the moonlight. She sat there, looking everywhere else but at him. He had watched her wipe a tear from the corner of her eye.

It grew dark; slowly they walked their way home—she silent, he lost as ever.

~

It was the darkest, yet the sweetest, of his memories. And the saddest of them all—one he had recalled repeatedly over the years. He couldn't get rid of it. He couldn't live with it either. He smiled, wept and burned at the same time, every single time it crossed his mind . . .

It was dusk, and fluffy gold-hued clouds filled a rather brilliant blue sky in the background; perfectly picturesque. The sun set behind the mountains. Tiny dots of light started to appear as the sky turned to navy blue and then to the regular pitch shade. He thought of the darkness and emptiness this universe is filled of. A deeper, more infinite universe was swelling inside him, a vacuum only he was capable of living with—perhaps.

He wore his best suit, a white cashmere kurta with brown patterns all over, topped with a rather mismatched khaki overcoat. The kurta smelled of mothballs even after a few washes. He had poured half a bottle of jasmine water over himself to ward off the stink. His eyes were red and puffy, from staying up the night before. He had never actually thought of this day, not enough for it to be real. His mind couldn't register the fact that he was going to witness his best friend marry and leave him. *Just a best friend, was she?*

Confused. Sad. Happy? Even more confused. He entered her house. It was bursting with people—uncles, aunts, cousins, friends, neighbours. Everyone happy, everyone dressed in their best. Laughing their hearts out. Children ran around, the house was festively lit up. It appeared her parents had spent every last penny of theirs on her wedding. Smiling at anyone who smiled at him, he slowly made his way to her room.

She sat before the mirror, looking every inch the bride. He was mesmerized by her reflection itself. Her red and golden attire gave her a mystic touch he had never known her to have, the jewels dazzled her even more. Her heavy hair was tied up in a knot at the back of her head, a few strands of white flowers pinned underneath them. Her blood-red lipstick contrasted with her fair skin, as she nervously bit her lip. She turned to look at him. Her hands were all done up in mehendi, ending a little above her wrists. Her glass bangles jingled as she moved one hand to tuck that one lock of hair which always fell on her face, no matter how well her hair was done.

'I am glad you came. I thought you won't show up.'

She looked curiously at him. She seemed kind of happy. But somewhere, deep down, she told him she wasn't happy at all. She was sad. Unbearably sad.

'I miss you, Adaa. It's like I am never going to see you again . . .'

She lunged at him; he felt his lips against hers, fierce from something he couldn't relate to. It was something he had never felt before; a strange, new, unexplored horizon that joined more than just the lips. That spread its tentacles far and wide and brought every tiny little insignificant soul it felt worthy to fit in its small vastness. There was more than just a kiss. There was a heart, confused and hurt from the effort of wondering how far it could go in love just for love's sake. There was a soul, intimidated till it had lost its individuality, and yet on its way to finding another which would help retrieve its own true part. There was a silent dream, a flickering hope, that burned with a rather steady intensity and looked for just the pair of eyes which would hold him back . . . Just this one last time. And make him believe he could love too. And never be out of it. It would be a 'forever and ever' thing. Just the way it happened in fairy tales. Where fiction went real and truth became irrelevant. That madly in love feeling. And he had found his princess. Perhaps. He told her. In a thought, a silent one.

It was the way he pulled her in an embrace, the way he ran his fingers through her hair, looked into her eyes or kissed her. Something about it told him it wasn't going to be a goodbye kiss. There would be more of them. That they would part and meet again somewhere far and forgotten with just a momentary passionate thought to cling to till they did . . .

And she loved him. For everything he was. For everything he was not. For being the guy who had made her daydream and brood over the way he smiled on semi-dark evenings as she sat on the river bank—the very thought would make her smile to herself. And it had been so for many an evening—she had lost track. Sometimes at night, or during the day, thoughts of him kept mushrooming in her head and she would shoo them away with a twinkle in her eyes, yet wait for another to pop up—it was that kind of a mad love. But now, it wasn't madness that defined this love any more. It was pure sadness that clung to every single memory of him. She could never think of him with a smile on her lips again . . . It would be just tears. Silent ones she couldn't even stop. Yes, it sure was some sad, mad love.

She was gone, leaving behind a part of her with him no one owned except him—and taking a part of him with her that left him with barely anything.

~

We live in a society that has always laid down rules for almost everything—affection, love, hatred. Every single reply to what, how, when, where and how much—it's not for us to answer. It's predefined. There's something untold about every known thing and it's untold because it's very well understood. Something that fairly defines whom to love, when to love and how much to love. And when to be out of love too. For your own good—if you want to fit in this place, if you want to live a fulfilling life, die a respected man.

But somehow, it didn't mould the seventeen-year-old boy in a way he could learn to fit in. He particularly didn't want to. He wanted to live, not survive. He wanted her safe in his thoughts, so he left to be in the army with just a suitcase and her memories.

His heart—he had lost it a long time back.

Eight years went by. Adaa could no longer smile. Not even when the snow caps turned a brilliant gold and rainbows danced after the rains. She couldn't remember who she was. Who she use to be. She didn't know she was married. Nor that she had a six-year-old son who had died along with her husband. It was in an accident—the same accident that has made her forget everything. Amnesia, the doctors called it. Things that ought to be in the present couldn't even find their way into her memories. They were lost, breaking all those fairytale promises they had ever blinded her with. She lived in a helping home in Kullu now, lost in her own empty world. She didn't remember anyone. Rishi—her best friend, *her first love*—she knew not . . .

Eight years in the army had disciplined him well. It had managed to train his mind, but not his heart. It had successfully driven the child out of him and pushed in a responsible man, capable of serving the nation. It had beaten every single pain out of him, but the heartache was something it hadn't yet managed to touch. He had thought of her each night as he lay in his tent. What would she be like? Did she love him still? Somehow his heart could never register the fact that she had a husband and perhaps a child too . . . For him, she was always the seventeen-year-old girl in her bridal attire—the girl who had his heart.

~

Rishi stood in the garden, waiting for Adaa, holding a bouquet of white daffodils and a white box. Something about the helping home nauseated him, even though he knew it was a home for people who had nowhere else to go. Adaa would be here any moment now. He was here despite his family's efforts to keep him away. He was determined to meet her. His Adaa. He knew she would remember him no matter what. It didn't matter that she was suffering from amnesia. She would know.

He had begun to feel the moistness of the flowers when she finally came. Clad in a clean white sari, was she really the girl he had known all his life? He knew not . . .

He stood there, looking at her. Just the way he always did when she wasn't looking at him. Her long hair was loosely tied into a knot at the back of her head, just the way it had been on her wedding day. But that single lock of hair was gone—the strand which somehow always fell on her face. Rishi was amazed. Here stood the girl right before him, his best friend whom he had known forever—and yet she was now a stranger he felt he had never known. Something about the way she looked at him told him she had no clue who he was. He felt a cold chill go down his spine. Somehow, he mustered up the courage to frame the word, 'Adaa.'

She stood there, gazing at him with a serenity he had never known her to possess. She was amazed. Finally, after what seemed like a lifetime, she smiled. His heart heaved a sigh. She remembered him after all!

'Do I know you?' he heard her say. The words rang in his ears. He went numb, robbed of every single thought he had. He felt something break inside him and heard someone else speaking through him.

'I . . . I am afraid not. I am a friend of the family. We used to be friends when we were kids. It's a long time now—I am sure you do not remember.'

She smiled in the most compassionate way.

'I am extremely sorry. I am unable to recall. But meeting you today, I am sure we must have known each other. You seem to be a good man . . .' She paused.

'Roshan,' he heard himself say.

'Roshan,' she smiled. There was an awkward pause.

'I return to my town soon. I thought I would visit you while I was here. I am sorry if I troubled you.'

'Not at all. It's good to have visitors. This is the very first time that someone has come to visit me. I feel I belong somewhere—but where exactly I don't know . . . I am sure someone will come soon to take me home—to where I must have belonged before I came here . . . I am sorry, why are you crying, Roshan?'

He felt his cheeks wet. 'I am sorry, something must have got into my eyes. I should leave now. I have a train in an hour. Oh, here, I got these for you . . .'

He handed her the daffodils and the box. She smiled in a way that broke his heart once again.

'It was nice to see you again, Adaa.'
'My pleasure, Roshan. Take care.'

⌒

Was I never yours to save?
I wonder as I lie in my grave,
Why did your eyes brim up with love,
Were they for me? The tears that you shed?
Or were they because I was gone now, so dead?
Why did your lips touch mine?
Was it because there was a love that you once felt?
Or was it because you thought we finally parted,
a final touch that made all boundaries melt?
Why did you turn to me with that longing gaze?
Or was it because you knew this was the last time we met?
I thought I knew love, or did I know something that you just framed?
Was it my fault to draw you among the stars,
* and dream with them as they came and went?*
Is that love finally gone, the one you framed?
I do not know, but it still remains, hiding somewhere underneath.
Were there no hidden promises after all?
Not a single fake tale to read to my soul?
Not a single touch that silences my screams,
No forged dreams to make me sleep?
I know it's over now, you're gone and so have I,
Now that I have a forever to think of you, in my grave as I lie . . .

⌒

Somewhere in the dark, Adaa was up in her bed. Turning on
the light in the room, she took the white box in her lap and
opened it. Inside lay a gorgeous pair of white shoes . . .

'Rishi,' was all she could say . . .

The Smiling Stranger

LALIT KUNDALIA

It was yet another day today, the same as the past three years had been. I got out of my house at 9 a.m., maintaining the consistency of my departure. After going to the temple, which was on my way to the railway station, I ended up on the railway platform with all my clothes wet. It was the sweating season and the source of all energy was on an all-time high.

I went up to the chai shop. The owner saw me and in micro-seconds he handed me over my regular burning cup. As usual the trains were running on IST or Indian Standard Time, i.e., fifteen minutes behind the scheduled time. It was a quarter-hour's journey and ended up quite comfortably. There's one thing special in the local trains of Kolkata—the people in there, standing around you, will never let you get bored. The gossip, the chit-chat, the debates and the cold fights never fail to entertain. Though, most of the gossip is preoccupied with 'Dada' and 'Didi'—i.e., cricket and politics respectively.

The journey in the train was at par with a sauna bath, the only difference being that it wasn't voluntarily done and I wasn't enjoying it, of course. Stepping down from the train I headed towards the nearby bus stop, looking towards the long queue of slow-moving buses. I was searching for a bus that was empty enough to at least allow me to stand comfortably. Expecting an empty seat, that too at this hour of day, was at par with expecting a politician to be non-corrupt. After around ten minutes, I managed to board a semi-empty bus and even found a corner to stand comfortably in. For a journey from the suburbs to the main city, one has to cross the mighty Hooghly river. The bus started crossing the Howrah Bridge, a wonder in itself for the city of joy.

The breeze blowing on the bridge was the only relief for the heat these days, though in effect it actually acted as a drop of water on a hot frying pan. I was standing near the window, just behind the driver, facing the crowd at large in the bus. The cool breeze, nonethless, became a source of some comfort to me as the bus gained speed.

I looked around, as I generally do to observe people, read their faces and capture their vivid expressions. Looking around, I ended up with nothing interesting to invest time in and focus on, except one thing in particular. There, in the middle of the bus, was a girl occupying the window seat facing the great Hooghly.

The breeze was constantly playing with her hair, causing strands to move on and away from her face. It felt like these strands of hair were playing a piano on her cheeks. She had a vibrant face, a fair complexion. Her eyes were closed and she was enjoying the breeze. It looked as if she was in a new world, a world she has always wanted to be in. I was getting irritated with her hair, which was constantly flying around her face, not allowing me to observe her. I felt like investing the rest of my day gazing at her. I was drawn to the aura around her, the aura that she had created, that of love and peace. But this gazing did not last too long; it ended as soon as she opened her eyes and looked straight towards me. Our eyes met for a second and I instantly averted my eyes away from hers as I wasn't interested in being tagged as a stalker.

Oh God, what a moment that was! I was out of my mind. I had never ever seen such eyes in my entire life. They were bright as pearls, nicely curved and had deep reserves of innocence in them. They were doe-like eyes. This hobby of observing people, I say, can really be risky at times—you can be branded as a loafer from a gentleman in a matter of minutes.

By then the bus had crossed the bridge and was back on the city's populated streets, crawling through traffic once again. New passengers were clambering on to the bus, making it more difficult to stand in comfort. I tried to keep my eyes away from hers. But there was a part of me—an inner voice—that was constantly opposing what my mind had decided.

The new passengers soon occupied the space between me and her and I could barely see her now. The voice within me had won at last; I made up my mind to try my luck once again. With a few adjustments to my height and inclination, I tried to catch a glimpse of her. She was looking at her cellphone, a smile playing on her face. I could barely detect any signs of artificial make-up on her face and still she looked eternally beautiful. Any trace of make-up would have been washed away with sweat by now. This in turn reflected her purity and simplicity.

Suddenly, today had become a special day, different from last three years. I was happy! I was enjoying the bus journey irrespective of the overcrowded bus, the unbearable temperature and the crawling traffic. I'll have to admit that she made a real difference to my daily monotonous life.

Oh, not again! I was caught red-handed, looking at her again. Now I was assured that I had lost my gentlemanly image completely. I was accusing that voice within me for pushing me to this; I felt guilty. But all that guilt vanished soon as I found no signs of irritation or frustration—as one normally expects—on her face; instead I saw a well-concealed smile this time.

I felt relieved, but still I was not sure about my standpoint. As the old saying goes, 'A single hand is never enough to clap.' The only way I could be sure was to check if she too was watching me. I hid myself behind the passengers in the bus in such a manner that she couldn't see me anymore. I also managed to find a way to keep an eye on her without making her aware of it. I was happy to get that childish streak back in me.

Going by my plan, for the next few minutes I behaved as if I was least interested in looking at her. I took out my cellphone and started playing with it to show that I was busy with some serious stuff. I wasn't sure whether I was right or not—it may be that I had misinterpreted the whole thing about her possibly showing interest in me—but I still wanted to continue with this just to make sure.

From a distance, I kept an eye on her constantly and noticed all her actions. For the first few moments, there were changes as she was busy with her cellphone. After that, once she looked towards the place where I had been standing moments ago and instantly went back to her cellphone again. Then again, after about twenty seconds or so, she looked back at that place with her cellphone pressed to her ear. Probably that was a fake call, an excuse to look in my direction, because she put her cell down as soon as she didn't find me standing there.

I was getting more and more excited as her behaviour was making me more and more sure about myself. Not finding me there, she now started looking around with a different excuse each time, making it appear as if she had only been looking at those places incidentally and not intentionally. I noticed that the frequency of her looking at that vacant spot where I had been standing had increased, and the curve of her smile had straightened somewhat.

Her eyes were constantly moving around in search of something in particular and then she fixed her gaze on something. But what was it? I looked down to see that it was my briefcase. I had been holding it in my hand throughout, and it was visible to her now. Clearly I'd left a loophole in my plan. She must have earlier seen my briefcase and that helped her to spot me now.

In a second she noticed me looking at her from the hideout. This time her eyes moved away as soon as they met mine, but her face immediately broke into a cute smile. That was the 'key moment'. All doubts in my mind were cleared by now. I knew she was interested in me.

I was happy; I no longer felt guilty. I was no more a stalker, but was merely a party to a 'two-way arbitrage'. This staring game had now changed into a sort of hide-and-seek. Everything was going fine, until the conductor came and asked me to pay for my journey. It was not that I had any problems in paying him, but the interruption of this uninvited guest reminded me of several things at a time:

- The bus was moving at a moderate speed (which I had hardly kept in mind)

- I had a destination (which was hardly two minutes from here), at which I needed to leave the bus
- She was a stranger . . . and I was not sure if I would be lucky enough to see her again.

All these days I had been cursing the traffic system for ill-maintenance which consequently resulted in wastage of precious time, but today, for the first time in my life, I had no grudges in my heart against the system. Neither was I bothered about the scorching heat and nor was the overcrowded bus irritating me today. I wished the world somehow stop right there, so that I need not part with her.

After paying the money, I prepared to get off. A number of thoughts had sprouted in my mind by now, mainly categorized into two streams—one that said, look at her, capture as much as possible in your mind so that you can be happy recalling this time; and the other that said, stop looking at her or else you'll be feeling sad remembering her, as you might not meet her again.

I was confused and time was slipping away fast. Stepping down the stairs I was still debating the two thoughts in my mind. Each was a valid viewpoint in its own way. I had to take a decision real fast.

Ultimately, I tried to look at it from her point of view—though it was difficult—and came to the decision that, if she made me smile all that time, if she made me feel good all that time, then she for sure deserved to smile and feel good too. The driver pulled the breaks and the bus came to a stop. Getting down there, I looked back at her; she too was looking at me. I gave her a smile and waved my hand to bid her goodbye. She returned the smile—that was all I'd wished for at that moment.

Eleven days had passed since I last saw her. During these days, I had thought of everything that would enable me to meet her again. I was going along with the blueprints that I had created the very first day after bidding her goodbye. I was trying to recreate that day—I departed at the same time, took the same train, went by the same route and even went up to the same bus that I had travelled that day.

In spite of my sheer dedication, nothing positive turned up. I even tried my luck on social networking sites but that too turned out to be useless as the only specifications I had of her was the mental image of her that I had carefully stored away—non-retrievable, non-printable, no ctrl+c or ctrl+v options available. Sitting on my bed, having my tea, I turned around the newspaper. All it had was the same boring news full of negativity, crime, corruption and scams all over. Then I came across an open letter posted by a student to the then honourable chief minister of the state.

In the said letter the student had opposed the latter for making a statement in which the former was tagged as a 'Maoist'.

At once, an idea occurred to me! I stood up, opened my laptop and started typing away at my best speed. About an hour later, I ended up with a short piece titled 'TO THE SMILING STRANGER'.

Yes, I was actually up to it, and it was my only hope now. I wrote everything that I had experienced that day and ended the extract with the statement: 'I wanna smile again'. Saving the document I added an email ID at the end for responses. Then I Googled for newspapers which allowed readers to share their experiences, but ended up empty-handed.

Then, I moved to Plan B. I took my cellphone and dialled a colleague who was then associated with a reputed city newspaper, that too at a high post. After about fifteen minutes of requests, inquiries, etc., I finally managed to prove to him that I had not gone insane and even got his answer in the affirmative. After sending the text via email, I was more than happy. I kept my fingers crossed.

Next morning I woke up early, went downstairs bought myself two copies of the newspaper. Reading my column, I felt some positive energy flowing from within. I went to the office, completed my job real fast and took an early leave. Getting back home, I logged into my personal email ID. '70 new mails', it displayed. My heart was beating fast as I started looking into each of them. I was searching for one special email in particular.

It took me about twenty-five minutes to get through all of them. There were about twenty-five spams, twenty-five casual mails from friends and the rest were responses to my article. I was happy reading the positive responses for my extract but on the other side it was depressing as the main purpose behind the column remained unfulfilled.

My mind was, in no time, occupied with depressing thoughts. Maybe she did not read it, or in case she did, maybe she was not interested enough to reply. Ignoring these thoughts, I made up my mind to wait for another couple of days before settling on any conclusion. I posted that very extract on all the social networks I was attached to, trying my best not to leave any stone unturned.

The next three days passed like centuries. I opened my email almost two hundred times. Even my activity level on social networking sites reached cent per cent, which in the past had never even crossed the twenty per cent mark.

I was broken—broken into pieces . . . for a stranger.

This is a step forward from my side. I'm trying my best to reach her. Yes, all this anxiety I feel is still a part of me, and will be so until this message reaches her. I feel that, if in your lifetime you have ever experienced something like this or if you had been through any experience close to it, you would be aware of this anxiety very well.

This whole extract has been written by me to thank that stranger for making me smile, for making me happy, for making a difference in my daily monotonous life, for soothing me during my lonely hours, and for helping me rediscover that hidden child in me.

Oh, how can I forget to mention:

'I wanna smile again.'

The Last Note

AMRIT SINHA

The station was bustling with people. Passengers and their relatives moved around busily on every platform, some lying down on sheets of newspapers, waiting for the arrival of their trains, while a few others stood patiently near the edge of the platform, peering and craning their necks, hoping to catch a glimpse of the arriving lights of the engine. The porters were running about in full swing, shouting and bargaining with the passengers.

Luckily I found an empty chair on platform no. 2 as I waited for the Howrah–Delhi Rajdhani Express. I was travelling to Delhi to my son's place. 'Mom, both you and Dad have to come,' my son Rahul had said. It was the occasion of my grandson's first birthday. However, Kunal, my husband, couldn't accompany me as he had to go for an urgent business meeting in California.

My train arrived right on time, and I boarded the assigned coach, S-5. I moved towards berth no. 9, which was booked in my name. I didn't have any heavy luggage, just a small bag and a purse. You don't need much stuff when you are travelling alone to visit your son.

I managed to get the lower berth and thus had full right to sit beside the window. Through the glass window, I witnessed the hullabaloo of the busy station in a muted ambience, reminding me of those age-old movies without sound.

The train roared to life at the designated time, and the fruit sellers and bookstores and porters and platforms all raced away in the opposite direction. The compartment was relatively empty. A newlywed Bengali couple was sitting opposite me. Probably on their honeymoon, I thought.

'Excuse me, ma'am.'

I looked up and saw a pot-bellied man, probably in his early forties, addressing me, 'But this seat, berth no. 9, belongs to me.'

Why are people so weird? They should properly check their tickets before boarding the train. 'I guess you are mistaken. Coach S-5, Berth 9 has been allotted in my name,' I replied confidently.

'Perhaps you won't vacate my seat like this. Let me call the TTE.' He walked to the other side of the compartment. Soon after, he returned with the TTE.

'May I have a look at your ticket, ma'am?' the black-coat-wearing TTE requested.

'Sure,' I handed over my ticket with aplomb.

The TTE looked through his glasses, like a scientist examining a biological specimen, and after careful examination, finally spoke, 'Ma'am, you have to leave this berth. It indeed belongs to this gentleman standing over here.'

I was shocked. How could that be? 'The ticket clearly mentions my name and the berth number,' I fought back.

'I agree, ma'am,' the TTE was as cordial as ever, 'but probably you have made a mistake. The ticket is for Sealdah–Delhi Rajdhani Express, not Howrah–Delhi Rajdhani Express.'

Sealdah and Howrah were the two big railway stations of Kolkata. It then struck me what a stupid thing I had done. I had accidentally booked the ticket for the wrong train. Why hadn't I cared to verify the ticket after booking it online? So stupid of me, and I deserved the embarrassment. Was there a way out? I looked at the TTE with pleading eyes.

'What should I do now?' I asked nervously.

'In normal cases,' the TTE replied, 'travelling without the correct ticket is regarded as a punishable offence. However, I trust you did this by accident, and without booking you for the offence, I request you to kindly get down at the next station.'

I got up from the seat and the fat man soon came and occupied the place near the window. 'Can't I get another berth?' I asked, my eyes now moist with the thought of being stranded on an unknown station all by myself. There was no way I could get a reservation for another train before the next morning.

I needed a saviour now, to get me out of this mess.

'Probably she can travel with me,' I suddenly heard a strong, booming and familiar voice behind me. It felt as if I had heard this baritone before, but wasn't able to recollect where.

'We are acquaintances. I guess she made a mistake, but probably you can let her travel. I will pay the fine,' the voice spoke again.

I turned around and my eyes popped out in disbelief.

This was definitely something I was not prepared for, nor had ever expected. But for a moment, my mind was filled with relief, a unique sense of joy and satisfaction of finding company in this forlorn circumstance.

He went ahead with the TTE and signed a few documents. Soon, he was back.

'Hi,' he smiled, his eyes beaming with joy.

'I never thought we would meet like this,' I replied, my heart fluttering in excitement.

He didn't stop smiling. 'Come over to my seat. It's towards the left.' We moved as he guided me to berth no. 33, which again was a lower berth.

'You can take the window seat here too, it's all yours now,' he offered.

We sat. There was an old man chatting with his young grandson on the seat opposite us, and another corporate type busy-looking guy fiddling with his laptop on the upper berth.

Where to start? There was so much we didn't know about each other. I was seeing him after over thirty years. He looked fit as always, the greyish hair and those wrinkles beneath his eyes now adding a tinge of maturity to that innocent face. He was wearing a brown jacket over a white shirt, which complemented his faded jeans perfectly.

Framing the first question was difficult. I kept quiet, and started playing with the straps of my purse.

'You are still so shy,' he chuckled.

'Is that so, Mr Akash?' I laughed and looked up at him. 'Well then, tell me, how are you?'

'What a vague question that is. You very well know how I am—decent, good, hard-working, trustworthy, smart, dashing, intelligent . . .' he answered.

'Stop, stop. At this rate you will use up all the adjectives that are there in the English dictionary,' I joked.

'Not all the adjectives, mademoiselle—only the good ones,' he smirked.

'You are still the same,' I said.

'Same with you, Sapna,' he took off his jacket and hung it on a hook, 'How long has it been? Thirty-two years?'

'I guess so,' I calculated.

'Strange how time flies, and yet you still look twenty-two,' he smiled.

It felt odd receiving such a compliment from him. I nervously turned my gaze away and looked out of the window.

'You won't be able to see anything. It's dark outside,' he grinned.

I turned towards him, 'Oh God. You are still so talkative.'

'On the contrary, people tell me I have grown quiet. Maybe that's because I couldn't find anyone with whom I can talk,' he shrugged.

His words suddenly left me with a question, 'Don't you talk with your wife, or your kids?'

'I have a life without a wife, and thus there is no chance of fathering kids. Of course, kids could have come by alternate ways, but wouldn't that have risked my reputation?' he laughed.

That sounded strange. 'Why didn't you marry?' I inquired.

My question had probably left him in a state of discomfort, and he reached for his bottle of water. I waited for him to answer.

'Sir, here is your dinner,' a railway staff came up with a plate of food, interrupting our conversation.

'Thanks. Can we order an extra meal too?' he asked, probably for me.

'No, sir, that's not allowed by the rules. However, I will talk to my manager and let you know,' he said, and took his leave.

Akash laid the plate carefully on the seat, and asked, 'You haven't become a vegetarian yet, I hope?'

'No.'

'Good. Have it then.'

The contents in the plate looked fresh and delicious: rice, roti, daal, chicken and curd, a complete dinner. However, there was no way I could accept it. Akash had already offered me his seat; I couldn't take away his dinner too.

'I am not hungry now,' I tried to counter his favour.

'Cool. Neither am I, but let's share. We have to eat anyhow,' he suggested.

We quietly picked up bits and pieces, our fingers brushing occasionally against each other. It felt strange sharing a meal with him after several decades. I couldn't even refuse. There was something magical in his smile—there always had been—which never let me decline any of his proposals.

And perhaps that's how I had said 'Yes' on that rainy evening when he suddenly bent down on his knees and proposed:

'Rain being the witness,
As it pours down upon us,
I confess my love to thee,
Will you accept my love, and me?'

'The only thing lacking today is a Coke,' his voice disrupted my chain of thoughts.

We always had a glass of some soft drink or another with our meals whenever we went out on dates. Yes, that's true—a single glass of Coke, with a straw, as we took turns sipping. Coke was just an excuse, though. Actually, it was a way to display our sense of belonging, the desire to love each other, the dream of becoming one, that made us enjoy drinking from the same straw.

'Why didn't you marry, Akash?' I repeated my question.

We finished our dinner. Wiping his fingers with a tissue paper, he explained, 'I had had my share of love already, Sapna. I couldn't love again. In fact, I wasn't interested in loving someone else, and maybe that's why I never had the urge to get married. I started writing and kept on writing, and in the process interacted with the love that was buried deep within me. I miss being in love, but I wish to be in that same love always. That's why I never thought of finding someone else.'

I couldn't reply. The break-up had been harsh on both of us at that time, but perhaps it was he who felt its impact more. Was I guilty in some way? Could we have sorted out our problems and restarted our love life in a fresh and organized manner? But then, love can never be organized; it's the madness encircling it that really makes it what it is. It's only when you try to play with your mind that love starts becoming a burden—because love resides in your heart; it's not to be tampered with the silly thoughts that run in your brain. Perhaps we were too young then and our unnecessary egos really came in the way of our love.

A note he had written to me then flashed once again before my eyes:

'Me the fire, you the rain,
How does it matter whether we lose or gain?
So stupid of me to imagine us together,
Your downpour turned me to ash forever.'

'What are you thinking?' Akash asked. 'Come on, life shouldn't be lived with regrets. Every experience teaches us a lot. To be honest, I have become a changed and better man now, and that's only because of what I faced. The same happened with you too. Don't dwell in the sad past. Tell me about your family.'

I told him about my son and my husband, and how they had prospered in their respective fields. I myself had stopped working around five years ago.

'That's a wise decision,' he smiled. 'There are so many other things in life than working in the corporate sector. You never get enough time for your family or for fulfilling your own wishes. Also, the crazy competition really drains your mind, and you keep toiling without any rest. Ah, that reminds me—it's time for you to sleep. You can lie down on this berth.'

'What about you? Where will you sleep?' I was filled with a sudden feeling of concern for him.

'My friend is travelling in the other compartment, I will share with him. You don't worry. Have a good night,' he replied.

I remembered how we used to stay awake late, talking in hushed whispers on the phone. Those days were lost long ago, and so were those nights.

I slept in a whirlpool of myriad dreams—some comforting, while a few others disturbing. There was this snake that suddenly crept out of nowhere, ready to bite, when an eagle pounced upon it and flew skywards. I was soaring high up in the sky, above the clouds, with the snake held tightly between my claws, and was surprised to realize that I was the eagle. I crashed against the sun and landed on the moon.

My dream broke as the moon hid itself behind the other majestic planets.

Daylight was peering through the window. I checked my wrist, the watch showed 8 a.m. I sat up. The old man was reading a newspaper, while his grandson was busy turning the pages of a Hindi comic. 'How long will it take to reach Delhi?' I asked the old man.

'Around thirty minutes, I guess,' he replied back.

I looked around me. There was no sign of Akash. I walked up and down the compartment, and he was nowhere to be seen. So foolish of me, I should have asked for his mobile number.

I came back to my seat and opened my purse. As I lifted it on to my lap, I saw a folded piece of paper that was hidden underneath the purse. I unwrapped it and read the words:

Oft have I heard the preachers say,
'Time and tide wait for none.'
This is false, quite untrue,
'Cause time and tide do wait for some.

Memories flash, moments of joy,
A glint of a smile, a fateful cry;
Your heart very well knows the truth,
Love is one hell of a sinful fruit.

And yet this fruit I silently tasted,
Fought with the devils, then I rested.
An eventful journey life has been,
Dreams so pretty I've always seen.

A jolly fate I do possess,
Meeting you again was beyond my guess;
Thanks for the company through this mile,
Just never give up on that sweet smile.

Time to say goodbye, a warm farewell,
Enjoy your life, truly, without any fail;
Someday, somewhere, we will cross again,
Perhaps on a sunny day, or a night when it will rain.

The teacher still preaches,
'Time and tide wait for none.'
Yet I couldn't agree to it anymore,
'Cause time and tide has indeed waited for one.

I wiped the tears from the corner of my eyes and placed the note carefully in my purse. The Delhi station was fast approaching. I took my bag and walked towards the compartment door. I saw my son waving at me from a distance.

'How was the journey, Mom?' my son asked as I got off the train.

'Good,' I said, and then added, 'probably the best train journey ever.'

The Uncertainties of Life

ARPITA GHOSH

I was all dressed up for the party and stood in front of the mirror admiring myself. Putting on the white XXL shirt, a clean-shaven eligible bachelor like me looked no less than a Cinderella's Prince Charming. It was the last day of the college reunion. I was very excited to meet my old friends: Vikramjeet, Pratik, Atharva, Emily and Maitrayee. Everyone was to come to attend the party, as all had confirmed on the phone.

It was seven o'clock. My coffee had almost got cold recollecting the memories from the past with my photo album. Almost fourteen years had passed. How quickly the time progressed! But it seems it all happened just yesterday.

When I had reached at the party I met some old classmates of mine. I introduced myself as a teacher of literature in my own school. Pratik had become a banking agent; Vikramjeet continued his family business of fertilizer, Emily was a librarian, whereas Maitrayee remained a housewife and a mother of two. The information that shocked me most was that Atharva was employed in a private firm, because during college he used to tell us that he would be taking the civil service examinations after completing his graduation. He had always been wanted to be a bureaucrat. However, his scornful smile created some doubts in my mind. Despite being curious, I refrained from asking him, imagining perhaps my curiosity might embarrass him. But it was obvious that something had gone wrong with him.

'Hey Samrat! Wazzup?'

The voice of the woman thrilled as well as elated me. It was Emily Stewart, my best friend at college.

'Excellent.' I said, 'And what about you?'

'Leading a normal life, as usual,' she added, 'I have been a librarian for the past two years.'

Emily and I had been best friends since we were children, as we used to live in the same neighbourhood. After my father's promotion, we shifted to a new flat, leaving the rented house. But I remained in touch with her as we were studying in the same collegiate school. In college we were joined by our new friends. Although we had separated from one another almost eight years ago after graduation, we'd remained in touch through the phone calls and emails.

During the schooldays, sometimes I used to wonder that how a jolly, impulsive and outgoing girl like Emily could be friends with a boy like me who was very emotional, quiet, and shy of course. During college, when Atharva, Pratik, Vikramjeet and the others made fun of me, or addressed me sarcastically as 'Sam' or 'Sammy' instead of my original name, i.e., Samrat and I looked a bit emotional, Emily stood in my defence. That is how a true friend works.

When we completed our graduation and to be separated, all of us were sad because we would seldom meet but we promised to keep in regular touch with one another. And so we did. Before this reunion, I had had an opportunity to meet them on the occasion of Maitrayee's wedding ceremony. But I couldn't attend the occasion because of my examinations.

However, after leaving college something made me feel that perhaps I had a soft corner for my childhood friend. In fact, I thought of proposing to her more than once. But I never dared to proceed with my feelings. I was gripped with panic everytime I thought about it. What if she were to reject me? What would I do then? I didn't want to lose her as my best friend. At that time, I thought it was better to suppress my feelings than to bring them out in the open. We also belonged to different religions. There was fear in my mind that our families might not agree to blessing our union. This reason was sufficient to prevent me going forward.

Years passed. On the occasion of the college reunion, Emily was dressed in a black kurti and pink skirt. She was as jovial as she used to be in school or college days. She continued babbling about herself and her family. Others were also looking very attractive.

'My dear Emiline,' said Vikramjeet, 'I think you should talk about your parents' recent most desirable task—of which I'm already aware—because you promised me that you will reveal your secrets to all of us today.'

'Of course. I was about to tell everyone about it,' said Emily.

'But you didn't.'

'Okay, I'm telling them now . . .' she said smiling.

'After my speech?' he asked.

'Vikram, don't be a moron.'

'I refuse to understand,' Vikram said, showing mock annoyance.

'Then I'm gonna murder you, man!'

'Then you'd be in jail.'

We laughed at their banter. Vikramjeet was still being a prankster as years back. Then Pratik intervened, 'Stop quarrelling guys! Will you please come to the point?'

After a few moments pause, Emily spoke out, 'Finally my parents have stopped searching for an eligible bachelor for their daughter.'

'You must have threatened them,' said Maitrayee.

'No, dear,' she said, 'actually. . .' she paused and then taking Atharva's arm she said, 'We've decided to get married.'

'What?' Maitrayee and Pratik asked, surprised.

'Yes, dears,' said Vikramjeet. 'I've know this for the past two years. They were secretly messaging, mailing and dating. Atharva had shared this with me earlier as he proposed to her. Atharva, tell them about it,' he said looking at Atharva.

'It's true,' said Atharva. 'Emily and I are going to get married next month and all of you definitely have to come. And don't worry; I'll personally invite you all,' said Atharva excitedly.

'This is really exciting!' said Pratik. Maitrayee also expressed her delight and congratulated the couple.

'Congratulations to both of you,' I said. She was holding Atharva's arm.

On returning home that night, I felt went to my room with a sense of loss at. I thought of Robert Browning's lover from 'The Last Ride Together' and realized that I should allow my beloved to choose her own path of happiness. If she wished to be happy with someone else, I should not put petty obstacles in her path by telling her about my love for her. If I do love someone, it's not necessary that she has to be in love with me. Sometimes little injustices happen in life. But we have to go through such sufferings and pains with courage. I decided to overcome my frustration and attend my best friend's wedding.

A month later, on their wedding day, I went to attend the function. As my family and that of Emily's used to live in the neighbouring area, my parents were also invited by her father. To my surprise, I could see no one from Atharva's family as long as I stayed there. I assumed they would come later. But what could have held them back?

Our group of friends had also come together to attend their wedding and wished the newly married couple a happy and prosperous married life. Another day, Atharva arranged a get-together as a treat for his friends instead of a formal reception.

Almost one and a half years had passed since our college reunion. One day, while coming back from the post office, I met Vikramjeet. During this time I had not visited either of my friends. Even phone calls, emails, messaging were infrequent among us. He recognized and called out to me from his car. I waved and went to meet him. I told him I was happy to see him after such a long time. I asked him about his life, his family and about the others in our group. Then I could not help but ask him about Atharva and Emily. A shadow of pain and sadness passed his face. Instead of answering my questions he asked, 'Sam, don't you know anything?'

'About what?' I asked.

'About Emily and Atharva?'

'Actually I heard about Emily's pregnancy from Pratik a few months after their marriage. Once I had called them up to, but no one answered the phone. So I didn't call again, thinking that something must have happened. They didn't answer Maitrayee's calls too. So I just . . . Anyway, what happened?'

Vikramjeet spoke with a lot of pain in his voice, 'Well, last year Emily had a boy. He looks a lot like his father but. . . ' his voice turned gloomy, 'Atharva and Emily are no more.' He paused, 'They died in a car crash a fortnight back.'

'Oh dear God!' My head reeled with the news. I put my hand on the car's bonnet for support. All I could see was the happy face of the couple in front of my eyes.

'Are you okay? May be I shouldn't have . . .'

'No, no, it's okay. I needed to know this,' I said. Then it suddenly struck me, 'What about the baby?'

'The boy survived miraculously,' he said. 'Both of Emily's parents had died last year. Her father had a massive cardiac arrest. Her mother couldn't take his death and completely broke down. Then she passed away within six months of her husband's death. As for Atharva's parents, they denied any responsibility of the child because they said Atharva had married against their wishes to a non-Hindu girl!'

'Is that even a reason? What sort of cruel people are they? They've said no to their only grandchild! The kid is after all their dead son's only representation.'

'Mm . . . So horrible!' Vikramjeet said shaking his head. Then he spoke again, 'Do you know they did not even take his body from the morgue! It's all because of religion. And that was why he chose to work at a private firm. Atharva's family had refused to provide any sort of financial help for his study of Public Administration only because of his being in love with Emily. He had been abandoned by his family forever. After leaving the college, I had always remained in close contact with Atharva. And that's how I knew about his family disputes and stuff.'

This came as a shocking news to me. I could not imagine they had gone through so much in order to stay together. But my heart was going out to the child. 'What about Emily's cousins, uncles or aunts? Are they not taking care of the child?'

'They were informed. But I don't think they would care for the infant as the neighbour told me. As a result, the child had to be sent to the nearest orphanage. Emily and Atharva named the boy Devraj before they died.'

Once I had seen the little boy in photographs which had been sent to me by Pratik in his emails. It was pretty obvious that he'd got them from Vikramjeet, as Pratik too hadn't been in touch with the couple. So there was no direct contact of the couple besides Vikramjeet.

'I was just thinking about paying a visit to the boy after taking the address of the orphanage from the local police station,' said Vikramjeet. 'I want to go but I couldn't . . . because I'm just scared, you know. I have a family to look after . . . So I couldn't make up my mind for that.' I nodded my head in understanding.

After talking some more, Vikramjeet went away. I remained there, thinking of the shattering blow life had given the infant who'd lost both his parents just in the beginning of its life! Why had that happened? Why does the life become so ruthless and merciless to most people?

~

Suddenly, a loud gust of wind coming from the open window hurled me back to reality. I finished the last sip of my coffee. It was entirely cold and almost turned tasteless. I closed the album that contained the last meeting of our entire group at the college reunion ceremony. How quickly thirteen summers have passed! My father died a couple of years ago. I did not think of marriage throughout these years.

I heard footsteps running down, and an elated voice cried out, 'Dad, it is raining outside! Let's get drenched in it. C'mon!'

'Dev, if it rains outside you should shut the doors and the windows instead of running out!'

'Which I already did, for your information,' he said sarcastically. 'Now let's have some fun in the rain; c'mon, Dad.'

'No.'

'Dad, please Dad. Even Grandma's not letting me go outside.'

'Dev, if Grandma asks you not to then you shouldn't go outside.'

'Why?'

'Because you'll catch a cold! Besides your mid-term examinations are coming. What will happen if you fall sick?'

'You know what!' he said excitedly, 'In school our teacher has told us that he used to have a lot of fun in rain while he was in the school. If he could do it, then why can't I?'

'Because I told you so. I don't want to know what your teacher did in his schooldays. I've never stopped you from watching TV or playing games. But not this. I'm worried about your health.'

'Honestly, Dad. You're being really mean!'

'I don't care.'

'But Dad. . . can't you let me go? Just once. . . '

'No.' I got angry. 'Haven't I told to you to be inside when it rains?'

His face turned gloomy as I scolded him. So I had to soften my voice, 'Dev, I want you to listen to me. Do you get that?'

'Yes, Dad,' he said calmly.

'Then no more arguments. No more questions. Go upstairs. You are a good boy, aren't you? I know you are.'

'Yes, I am.'

'Then go upstairs. Good boys always obey their fathers.'

'Fine. I'll go,' said Dev and he went off. The excitement on his face had disappeared. I didn't mean to hurt his feelings, nor to spoil his fun. But sometimes strictness is necessary for raising a kid properly.

Now I realized that life isn't so unfair for those people who have gone through the dark phases of life. I got the most precious and dearest reminder of my best friend (or my supposed beloved) Emily by adopting her only child. Now I am his father. I am happy with the partial fulfillment of my desire. When I go out for work, my mother takes care of the kid. Although the boy takes after his father but in his deepest nature he is as jolly, spirited and impulsive as his mother once was.

~

Moral: Fulfillment of a desire on earth is bliss. But what doesn't happen according to one's wishes is even better. Because then it is the wishes of the Almighty Himself. So whenever one gets upset with something, it should be kept in mind that He has already planned something else for that person.

Another Time, Another Place

SOWMYA AJI

The much-wrinkled, too-often-read letter was in his pocket as he got off the train. They had read about such letters in old war-time novels that were a dime a dozen at the school library. Both of them would go there during every free period and pretend to be engrossed in books while sneaking glances at each other. Still, some of what they read had also gone into their heads and, conveniently, provided 'discussion' topics!

Such letters used to be called 'Dear John' letters during the Second World War, when the soldiers—away on the war front for years—were informed by their sweethearts back home that they were moving on in life and not waiting for them. He had made up funny situations for triggering such letters, like 'I am sure every letter he sent from the war front probably just had the word "Duh" in it' or 'Maybe he sent her gunpowder instead of face powder as a gift'; and she had giggled all through. She had also added her bits of absurdity, like 'Maybe the sweetheart thought the neighbourhood tomcat was better groomed than her John'. Neither had ever dreamed that she would have to write such a letter to him.

He touched the letter in his pocket, as he did always. 'I am sorry. But I can't wait for you any longer. I don't have a choice in the matter. I have waited and waited, but have run out of excuses. I am getting married tomorrow. I wish you all the best in life. It's goodbye. Yours, once . . .'

He did not blame her. He had not been there when she needed him, had not been in a position to even write and let her know that. She had waited as long as she could. Their being together was just not to be; it was not written in the fates.

And yet, after three years, there was a gap in his being, a loneliness that gnawed away at him. She was never far from him; that letter was always in his pocket. He had blocked her vision whenever it had floated into his consciousness—so what if he cried out for her in his sleep? He went about the business of living and was perfectly fine, thank you.

But today, out of the blue, he had to go back to 'their' place, on work. He had managed to avoid going there ever since he got her letter. And he had been very successful at that. Now, he had to go, for just a day. But what a day!

Going back to the place where it all had been—where they had known and loved each other—had not helped at all. He had been swamped with memories which just sharpened the pain. Still, though he went and though he missed her with every breath, he had not sought her out. That letter had been very definite.

It didn't matter that he yearned to see her. It certainly wouldn't have helped to seek her out now. He had convinced himself and come straight back, as soon as his work got done. And he was certain this gloom had come on only because he had gone back to their place. Of course he was perfectly happy and content. He would be fine. He went out of the railway station, looking for a taxi, carrying his bags in one hand.

~

He had strong hands, very capable. She remembered them so well. She had been standing behind the window of her rickety apartment opposite the railway station, just emptily gazing out, when she saw him in the distance. Unexpected, and yet daily expected, ever since she and her husband had moved to the city. She had not informed him that they now lived in the same city as he did. After all, she had said a very definite goodbye.

But now here he was. So near and so far. No, not a good idea to catch his attention. It would interfere with her life and her husband would definitely not like it. She screwed up her eyes, her nose flattened against the dingy pane of the window glass, gazing at him with hunger. She could see him, standing just opposite her window, waiting for a taxi, carrying those heavy bags in one hand.

In his strong, capable hand. She smiled. That had been such fun. She had fallen into this hollow between the rocks, as they had made their way across the hillside to the beach. Left to herself, she would have looked upon rocks just like she now saw their doorpost or her typewriter. But he was with her then. He had given a special enchantment to those commonplace, regular rocks.

With him, for the first time in her life, she had gone exploring there. She had discovered mysterious caverns, interesting crevices and wondrous rock formations. Every time they went to 'their' place, they had found a different route to the beach. On that day, on one of these pioneer routes, she had been gazing at him, starry-eyed, and was not watching where she was going. Of course, she had overbalanced and fallen into this hollow.

She had scrambled back up to her feet, laughing at her own clumsiness. He had smiled at her and, stretched out his hand, reached into the hollow. Ignoring her attempts to scramble up, he had—in one breath, without any trouble—pulled her out one-armed, up and out, straight to his side.

He had teased her wickedly, of course. She smiled again now, as the glaze cleared from her eyes. Oh no, of course she wasn't crying. And he was still standing there on the kerb, with no taxi in sight. Could she . . . do you think she could just go across and say . . . hello? No. It would be a betrayal . . .

Nonsense! Just to say hello? What harm would it do? Yes, but she had written that letter to him . . . and had got married . . . and . . . Well, that was because of circumstances! But what would her husband say? He wouldn't like it! I mean, past loves should stay past!

But . . . he looked so tired and grim. And his shoulders were still broad . . . Aha! A bit of grey in that lovely hair? It suited him though . . . Just to say hello? He was still standing there! . . . Please, God! Forgive me! Just this once . . .

She made her way rapidly to the door. As she reached it, it opened into the face of the milkman. Oh heck! She had to pay him the monthly dues. She ran into the kitchen, rummaged into the box where they kept their meagre cash, blindly dug out the last few notes and ran back. The milkman placed that day's milk bottle just inside the door, took the money, touched his cap and went.

Distractedly, she ran to the window again. He was still there, standing on the kerb, looking up and down impatiently. Oh God, don't let him go away!

Praying under her breath, she went to the door. Ghastly stairs. Very treacherous. One had to balance carefully to get down. It was a lousy two-room tenement, of course, in the worst building in town, but it was all they could afford.

She crossed her fingers. She couldn't see the kerb from the stairs and could only hope that no taxi had turned up and he was still there. She was as careful as could be, but on that last but third step, she slipped, as usual, and landed in a heap near the exit from the building. The man just coming in exclaimed, 'My dear! Are you alright?' and solicitously helped her up. It was her husband.

She quickly looked past him, at the man across the street. He was still there, but no, he hadn't seen her or her inglorious slide down the staircase. Smiling an empty thanks at her husband, who was still fussing around her, she ran out through the door.

Just then, a taxi blocked her vision and slowed down in front of him. He was getting in. She raised her hand, her lips forming his name. He didn't see her. The taxi moved away. Her hand dropped down and she stood looking at the taxi as it sped down the road.

Her perplexed husband bustled out behind her. 'What's the matter, dear? Don't run into the street like this. And have you locked our door? Look, go out later, please. I need some coffee.'

She looked down and let her husband lead her back in.

Maybe the stairs could substitute for those rocks. Maybe her husband could substitute for him. After all, the taxi had gone away without a backward glance. She looked up at her husband with a hesitant smile, and slowly climbed the stairs again, holding his hand. Thank God, the milk had come for his coffee.

~

As the taxi turned round the corner, the man in the back seat glimpsed a woman, being led into a building by a man. Oh! Could it be . . .? Quickly, his hand moved to the driver, then stopped. It couldn't be her. She was not even in this city. Hell, he should never have gone back to their place. Now he was hallucinating, seeing her everywhere. This was just the limit.

His hand reached into his pocket. He pulled the old, almost-tattered piece of paper out again and read her last letter to him, every word of which was engraved on his heart. After all, he had read it at least once, every day, for the past three years. Should he crush it and throw it away? Tear it up? His hand hesitated. Then, with a sigh, and a resigned smile, he folded the letter and put it back into his pocket.

He looked out of the window, at the wide tree-lined streets in the upmarket area of the city. They seemed to be nearly home. He leaned forward to give directions to the driver. The taxi stopped, he carelessly dragged his bags out, paid the man. He stood on the kerb, looking at his home. An apartment in a three-storey building, neat and well-built, with a swanky kitchen, huge hall, swish bathrooms, three big and empty bedrooms. And no one to fill them. Oh, why had he not gone to her when he knew she needed him? How could he blame anyone but himself for what had happened?

The old lady who lived downstairs saw him arrive. She came out eagerly. 'My son, I am glad you are back. I have made sure that your apartment was cleaned today, and the electrician had come to fix that switch for you. I went and stayed with him all through till it worked and he left. Do you want a cup of coffee? Will you come in?'

He shook his head, smiled and carried his bags up the smooth, marble stairs. The old lady stood at the bottom of the staircase and looked at his back, climbing up and up. Such a nice, thoughtful boy, so well-mannered and gentle. She only wished that he didn't always look so sad.

~

Things finally began to look up, when the crisp, thick-papered letter came in the post late evening. She had got the job. It was another typing job, true, but at least she would be called a secretary. It was a new job at the same office where her husband worked, though for a boss she was yet to meet. She would get more pay, more respect. And maybe, if she hoarded everything and cut some of their groceries' expenses, they could move out of this dump. Her eyes shone.

She quickly cleaned up the house the next day, got ready and climbed carefully down the stairs. She gripped the broken rail at the last but third step, her husband helped her and she gingerly crossed it. Ah, at last, she had managed to get off those stairs without slipping! They went out and began walking the seven-kilometre distance to her new office. After all, they had to save bus fare and now it was for two.

The office was an imposing building, in the middle of the city's main, extremely busy thoroughfare. Her husband kept reassuring her all along the seven-kilometre walk that the new boss, though young, was a very nice person and she would not have any problems at all. Naturally, the more he fumbled and reassured and asserted, the more nervous she got. The new boss's former secretary had done all the formalities and hired her. He hadn't even bothered to meet her. What if the boss didn't like her?

She clutched her husband's hand, as they climbed the steps and made their way into the office. He ushered her in like she was a total dimwit who didn't understand anything. He dumped his bag on one of the desks along the way and took her straight to a cabin door. 'I have to leave you here,' he said, licking his lips. 'He is inside. Please go in and please don't mess anything up for either of us.'

She started trembling. This job was so important to both of them. It was their ticket to survival. She didn't look at her husband. She dropped his hand and drew a deep breath. She thought of the boy she had sneaked glances with in the library, who had held her hand through the rocks. She thought of the boy who had smiled at her and lifted her, effortlessly, out of a deep hollow, single-handed. The moment glittered in front of her again. She straightened her shoulders, smiled, pushed open the door and went in, leaving her still-fluttering husband behind.

The new boss looked up. And touched his hand to his pocket.

Clumsy Cupid

REUBEN KUMAR LALWANI

Have you noticed the way men make complete idiots of themselves around women? It is not intended, of course. In fact, the intention is quite the opposite but, sadly, it just happens.

Which one of us has not approached a beautiful woman (in our own distinctive estimations), only to trip at the last moment, spilling half the Bloody Mary—originally intended as an ice-breaker or conversation-starter—on her pristine white sari, the balance to be ingested internally (if she stops screaming and accepts it thereafter).

Which of us have not seen a beautiful woman pass in front of our car at a traffic light, and blown the horn. Blowing the horn? Come on, have a heart! For a lot of us, this is a reflex reaction. Something way beyond our control. Our hands at that time have a mind and spirit of their own. What exactly are we trying to do here? Telling her to get out of the way? No, we can safely rule that one out.

Then what? Are we trying to get her attention? Probably, but then, what after she disdainfully looks at the driver and gives him a 'drop dead' look. What is the next step, buddy? Good question, but of course we have not thought that far ahead. Remember the hand moving of its own volition? It's just something we do.

Which of us have not given soulful looks across a crowded restaurant or pub at a gorgeous woman, only to quickly look away when she is joined by her boyfriend/husband, who incidentally looks as if he has nothing better to do except work out at the gym and have protein shakes?

This brings us to Ranjit.

The above instances are real-life examples, directly lifted from Ranjit's young but hectic life. He lives in Kolkata, a city with quite a few million people living—or rather existing—in it. He has a job selling vacuum cleaners of a famous brand who believe in direct sales, depending on people like Ranjit to take them door to door demonstrating them and hopefully selling a few of them in the bargain and thereby earning a livelihood (if one could call it that, he used to often think). He had done his school final and also thereafter graduated in economics. He was sometimes gullible and could be fooled, but he believed steadfastly in honesty. He was a hard worker and though fairly street smart, he accepted as true the motto—Honesty is the first chapter in the book of wisdom. He lived by this maxim.

Ranjit was twenty-nine years old. He was a sardar and all of 5'4" tall, weighing a steady fifty-eight kgs, which in the land of the sardars made him downright puny. But he was a spirited lad, charged and filled with the zest for life. He did not just get out of bed every morning—he actually sprang out of it. Once he leaped out, he would go straight to his parents' bedroom and do their 'charan sparsh'. (To the uninitiated it means touching feet.) He rigidly believed the blessings received after charan sparsh of his parents were like invisible armour. They motivated him and gave him strength. The blessings this gesture of respect included, he staunchly believed, was protection and gave him vigour and self-confidence. He had not missed this routine even once in the last twenty years except on his only unaccompanied trip to his organization headquarters in Mumbai, at the time of his product and marketing training.

At the party during his above-mentioned training he had seen Geeta, his counterpart from Mumbai, and had really liked her. And there was a lot to like. She was a healthy twenty-six-year-old sardarni who was reserved and aloof almost to the point of being unfriendly. She was tall (an inch taller than Ranjit at 5'5"), and at a slim 54 kgs, looked taller much to Ranjit's chagrin, but it did not bother him enough to keep him away. However, as he watched her from across the room, what attracted him the most to Geeta was the dimple which formed only on her left cheek whenever she smiled. Maybe they formed on both cheeks, however from his vantage point he could only see the left one, standing as he was on her left, which for the purpose of riveting his attention on her, was well and truly enough. He was mesmerized by her singular dimple as she smiled often, conversing with Mrs Shukla, the general manager of the company. He thought she looked so unattainable, perfectly attired in her yellow and green salwar suit. In fact, he thought, she looked so far out of his league, she might well have been from another planet!

But, if anything, Ranjit was a fighter. And in Geeta, he saw something well worth fighting for. To break the ice, he thought he would get her a drink.

He remembered the old catchphrase of Coca Cola, "things go better with Coke" and hoped it would, while getting her one and negotiating the distance between them. While attempting to get close to her to give her the Coke, he overlooked that the end of the carpet had curled up, and this caused him to go flying into her lap as she was seated (by this time) on a steel fold-out chair—and spilled half the 200 ml on to her lap. He sheepishly tried to offer her the balance 100 ml, except that she on receiving the cold beverage on her lap, Geeta jumped up and this caused Ranjit to spill the remaining 100 ml on himself.

It did not help that thoughtfully, Ranjit had put four cubes of ice in the glass and both Ranjit and Geeta stood staring at each other, gasping as the freezing cold drink soaked their respective attires. Ranjit, holding a now-totally-empty glass in one hand, wracked his brain for something to say to salvage the situation. One might have thought that the situation was beyond redemption, sunk completely like the Titanic. It was the most socially awkward moment he had faced in his life, and there had been quite a few. But being the fighter that he was, picking up his masculinity and raising himself to his full 5'4", Ranjit came up with, 'Umm. Hi, I am Ranjit, I know you are Geeta, and this was the Coke I was getting for you (*inadvertently offering her the empty glass*). I am sorry, I actually intended you to drink it and not bathe in it. Can I get you another? And I do hope you won't call the cops and press charges?' Ranjit cursed himself at his weak attempt at wittiness. *You might as well just come out and tell her what a joker you are*, he thought to himself.

Then without thinking, he whipped out his handkerchief to offer her a means to dry off, forgetting completely just a few minutes earlier, being the thoughtful son that he was, he had placed two small serving spoons of sugar-crusted saunf in it to take for his mother, who was very fond of the substance. The brightly coloured stuff went flying all over Geeta, with some of it sticking to her clothes and adding topping to the dark stain and decorating it further. Geeta looked at Ranjit incredulously. She saw the look of panic on his face and burst out laughing. Her earlier aloof look dissolving instantly, she said to Ranjit, 'This time, Ranjit, please get me the Coke in a sipper with a straw.'

Ranjit looked at her and soon both of them were guffawing wildly. Those in their immediate vicinity, who were keen spectators, joined in, clapping loudly. Then on, in spite of being in different cities, they became good friends. In thinking about this instance, Ranjit gratefully thought later, adversity had indeed changed to triumph.

The second and third occasions, which had not-so-happy endings, happened in Kolkata, much before the aforementioned incident, and oddly on the same day.

The first one was when he was merrily travelling on his scooter, humming the latest Shah Rukh movie song, *Chamak Challo*, and even doing an occasional body movement which he called dancing but, those who had seen him dance called a spasm. While waiting for the lights to change to green at the Park Street traffic lights, he saw a vision in the shape of a woman, of small built and wearing a salwar suit (his favorite choice of dress for the opposite sex). Involuntarily his hand went to the horn on his scooter and it went 'peep'. He was horrified. Two things happened simultaneously. He immediately regretted his action, cursing himself in the most colourful Punjabi phrases possible, which is saying something, and secondly, the girl gave him such a murderous look that he shrunk and tried to hide behind the front panel of his scooter (which even for his small 5'4" frame was no mean task).

Later the same day Ranjit went to a small Udupi restaurant. His mother had failed to pack him his usual home-cooked lunch and instead asked him to grab something wholesome. If there was one culinary preference of his, it was South Indian food. Very unlike sardarjis you might think, as they are voracious meat-eaters. But Ranjit's liking for this kind of vegetarian fare went well with his diminutive frame and, also suited him well since he suffered from irritable bowel syndrome.

As he ate, he happened to notice a woman seated diagonally across his table. And then lo and behold, he shivered, she was looking at him. Was she? He could not believe it. He looked at his side tables—empty. Behind him was a plate glass window, overlooking the park. There was no one else but him in the vicinity and line of her vision. What happened next almost caused him to fall off his chair—she was actually smiling bashfully at him. The first thought that came into his mind was that the years of charan sparsh had paid off. He was being blessed now. And then the bubble burst. A huge burly dark young man about the woman's age joined her, proprietarily putting a hand on her shoulder. She looked up lovingly at him, as he sat next to her on her side of the bench stuck to her. Women could be cruel, Ranjit thought. She was playing him all along. He should have known. A puny specimen like him and a gorgeous babe like her. Ranjit, if anything, was a true fighter and believed that the speed at which a man bounced back from an impediment demonstrated the true worth of a man. Paying his bill and without a backward glance at the woman, gathering up his well-worn helmet, a sticker on the back which read—'Super

Ma' (the N at the end of the sticker had been disfigured and was essentially unreadable), he strode majestically out of the small Udupi restaurant.

Sitting in his small cubicle at office at about 4.40 p.m. one afternoon in late November, Ranjit was depressed. With no sales in the last two days, he was feeling terribly down. They said it was darkest before dawn. Ranjit was in the 'darkest part' vicinity of that adage. And then dawn loomed. Beautiful dawn loomed in the form of an email sent to his email ID: SS(SuperSardar)@gmail.com.

He read it once and then read it again and would have continued reading it had it not been time to shut office and go home, where he would no doubt reopen his mail and read it a few hundred times more. It was not that it was an intricate mail, in fact quite the contrary it was a two-line mail which read:

Dear Ranjit,
I have been posted to Kolkata. I am going to be working with you. I will be arriving tomorrow and would be grateful if you could suggest some place to stay for a couple of weeks till I get something permanent. More later.
Best Regards,
Geeta.

The world was suddenly full of the sound of music. Even though it was 7 p.m. he could see butterflies fluttering all around him. Or maybe they were just fluttering in his heart. Geeta was coming to Kolkata and they were going to be spending most of their working days together! There was a God in heaven and he was smiling down on him, Ranjit thought. The angels were on his side. On his way back home, riding his scooter, he sang his favourite song *Chamak Challo* with renewed vigour at the top of his voice, causing a startled dog near his gate, calmly resting just a few seconds ago, to jump up and run away yelping.

'Hi Ranjit! How have you been?' asked Geeta. Ranjit had been expecting her all morning and here she was, a dream in cream (the colour of her salwar suit) standing at his desk.

'Hi Geeta!' said Ranjit. A simple enough greeting and the logical rejoinder to her 'Hi,' one might think. But no! Ranjit had been practising the saying of these two words in a million different ways since even before he had brushed his teeth that morning. But when he actually said it he forgot everything and could just about get the two words out, her beauty tongue-tying him instantly.

She looks even more beautiful than I remember, Ranjit thought to himself. He instantly stood up with a jerk, hitting the back of his knees to the rim of his chair and sending it flying behind him. 'Clumsy, clumsy, clumsy,' he told himself, 'I am just confirming how gawky and bungly I am,' he said, continuing the conversation with himself. Geeta turned around to say hello to another colleague, turning back in time to see him picking up his chair. It was a bit of a funny scene, Ranjit struggling to pick up the big executive chair, almost lying prone on the floor.

Geeta could not help remarking tongue in cheek, 'What's the matter Ranjit, wrestling match with your chair?'

'No, Geeta, just trying to murder it for putting me in this embarrassing position,' Ranjit sombrely replied.

And once again both burst out laughing, recalling the Coke incident that had brought them together.

Over the next two months Ranjit and Geeta had been working together and spending a fair amount of time together.

When two young souls are thrown together in the cauldron of life like this, both unattached and both outgoing, things are bound to happen. Geeta was unattached and was looking for opposite-sex companionship. She was a sensible girl, who had long decided that the two qualities she would be looking for in a mate would be honesty and a big dollop of humour to make a partnership faithful and fun. In Ranjit she realized early on that she could find both. She could see he was scrupulously honest and this endeared him to her. His sense of humour was also becoming increasingly apparent. In fact it was linked to his honesty. His responses were so genuine and from the heart that, in this world of appearances and display, she found them endearingly funny. It was true he was small built, and was not putting stock in the world's accepted standards of good looks, but she found him adorably attractive. She wanted a solid man and she now after two months of pretty regular association, believed she had found her soul mate.

In between their work, Ranjit had found her a room to stay, in Rashmi Auntie's flat which was in the same building as his house, on the floor above his. The close proximity fostered regular visits to his house. She had become very close to his father and mother, with his mother telling Geeta one evening, 'Arre beta, no need to go out and get dinner or to cook your own, you eat her with us from now on. *Apna ghar samjho.*' She felt more comfortable here, than she had felt in her own place in Mumbai, as her parents were so busy most of the time, either working or socializing, she barely saw them on a daily basis.

Ranjit too was having the time of his life. His dream girl was becoming his girlfriend. This was so unreal. At one time he had thought she was totally out of his league and now he was not only spending time with her socially but when they went to see the movie—*The Dirty Picture*, the storyline of which he did not remember at all—all he could think of was holding her hands and what happened in the few minutes before intermission.

He had kissed her.

Her constantly squeezing his hand had emboldened his resolve and he took off his glasses for the hundredth time to clean them (they kept fogging up possibly due to the fact that his body temperature was in the early hundreds and his BP had shot up dangerously). Putting his glasses back on, he decided to take the plunge. Puckering up his lips he leaned across and almost reached her flawless cheek when she excitedly turned to him to say something and he landed the kiss square on her mouth. It was more than he could handle. Her cheek he was prepared for, her mouth he was not. He almost fainted and would have, except suddenly the loud dialogue on the screen jolted him into wakefulness. '*Kutte main tera khoon pee jaoonga!*' Nasseruddin Shah bellowed at the villain and Ranjit did not know what effect it had on the receiving screen persona but it kept him in the present moment. Geeta tenderly kissed him back, that too on his lips and he knew then—*baat ban gayee!*

Geeta and Ranjit resigned from their jobs and had opened an agency to undertake turnkey assignments to clean houses and offices on a contractual basis. A natural progression one might say, from selling vacuum cleaners. Both loved each other and were thankful for the abundant blessings the heavens had showered on them.

Exactly a year after Geeta came to Kolkata, they were married at the Bhawanipur Gurdwara.

It was a smallish affair with only twenty invitees. It was

how both Ranjit and Geeta wanted it. Geeta's parents found time from their very busy hectic Mumbai schedules to be there for their only daughter. Ranjits parents had invited only close relatives.

The reception held at the Punjabee Bradree hall was another matter altogether. There were 200 invitees and it was in true blue Punjabi style—full of pomp, glamour, food, music, balle-balle dancing and the common denominator liquor. Geeta and Ranjit both danced till the wee hours of the morning as did most of the guests. It was a night to remember. Sometime during the evening, Ranjit picked up a tray of drinks to offer his aunts. However before he could even take it to them, Geeta gently put a hand on his shoulder and said, 'Ranjit, it's safer for your aunts if the waiters take them the drinks, especially after the couple of beers that you've had.'

Appreciating that there was truth in what his wife had said, Ranjit willingly handed over the tray to the waiter who had suddenly materialized. Geeta smiled adoringly and gave her husband a warm loving kiss.

All was well in their world.

Here's How It Goes

ARKA DATTA

Ravinder Singh lifted an eyebrow as he noticed the story started with his name. With a little more interest he checked the name of the story and the author again. The name was 'Chance', and it was written by Rudra Sengupta. There was even a short note before the story, which was to set the motion of the tale that followed:

My name is Rudra Sengupta, and this story is the truth that I cannot live hiding any more. This story is not about a contest, or getting printed in a book, or to even reach thousands of people. It should reach only one person at least, the one who matters the most, the one I am writing this for, and, most importantly, the one I love. This is the story of my life—not the life that others see, but the one I live within.

Ravinder started to read 'Chance', by Rudra Sengupta, knowing it will be nothing but a pile of messed up feelings . . .

226

PART ONE

'Ravinder Singh gave an interesting treatment to the book. Not that you will agree to everything, but give it a read,' Ree said with a smile as she put *Can Love Happen Twice?* on the table.

Rudra picked it up and said, 'I won't? But I thought I will agree to it. At least the title says so. Love can happen hundred times if you are ready.'

'It's not that. Just read it, will you?'

'Sure, I will,' said Rudra, as he pushed his coffee to Ree and went to get another one from the counter.

It was another typical Sunday and, just like any other one, Rudra and Riyanka were sitting on their favourite table of the café near Rudra's apartment. They had never missed a Sunday for last four years, not when they were in college, dating other people, busy with interview preparations or busy on weekdays with the new jobs. Everything has changed since they first came here, but not the ritual of their meeting—talking about life, getting older and everything else that happens to them.

'So, tell me about the new one,' Rudra said as he came back, 'He is real, right? I sure hope he isn't another one of your soap opera stars.'

'It's not that all the time, you know that. Ujaan is a colleague, HR department.'

'Oh! So this one has a name, and belongs to a department too. Good girl, you are improving.'

'I am. Am not I? And the crush is stronger too.'

Rudra looked at Ree's eyes. They were wide with excitement, even her cheeks were getting all red, but she had that crooked smile of hers, which, Rudra knew by then, was a sign of anticipation. She was expecting it to be something real. She had been single for almost an entire year, and for her it was more than she could take. Rudra took a sip from his coffee mug, choosing his words carefully, and said, 'You know what you are doing, right?'

'When did I ever? Come on! Tell me what I want.' Ree threw herself back on the chair.

'What's that now? It's your crush and I am done telling you what you need. It never works anyway.'

'It works just fine, you dumbo, but any boy I like turns out to be just the same, every time. I don't expect you to be spot on all the time, but you often know better than me what I need.'

'What you need now is a fling. You are not ready for a relationship. You are just lonely and living alone makes it harder.'

'I suppose it's true. I am not ready, but the boys I know are not good enough for flings. They are a little too simple for that.'

'Then you need a man,' Rudra said standing up, 'and I have to leave now. The apartment is a mess. I need to unpack.'

They came out of the café and it was raining heavily. Ree took her umbrella out and asked, 'Can I offer you a lift, mister?'

Rudra took the umbrella from her hand and they walked in silence towards his apartment building, which was about a five-minutes' walk away. Ree returned from the doorstep, denying Rudra's proposal of coming in, 'I don't want you to trap me with all the unpacking crap,' she reasoned, with a wink.

Rudra's apartment was only few kilometres from his home, where he lived with his parents and young sister till a few days ago. He moved in here because it was closer to his office, which gave him a lot of time to spend with his own self, which was, as Rudra always put it, 'fundamental for writers'.

It was a small apartment with two tiny rooms. What made him take it up was the large, open terrace attached to it. He stood at the door of the terrace, watching the rain slowing down. He used to get wet every time it rained even till few years ago, but now he felt satisfied just watching. Rudra was a tall, well-built man, with dreamy eyes. He was among the witty ones who could cast a spell over people instantly. His charming smile attracted everyone, especially the girls, but what made him a real charmer was his understanding of women's minds. He was as close as a man can ever be to knowing what women wanted, and he loved that about himself.

The more he undid the layers of women's minds, the more he fell in love with them. He loved everything about them, right from the complexities to the confusions of their minds, and he never failed to let them know that. Rudra knew girls were attracted to him and he enjoyed that. He never left a chance to make them fall for him, but he kept himself from committing. He found himself falling in love with most girls and so a relationship with only one girl seemed a waste of a beautiful life to him. There were a few women who moved him more than the others, but despite trying honestly, he was unable to continue with the ones he dated. Sooner or later, he figured out all of them, and that ended the chance of any long-term relationship.

All he needed, always, was a woman who would make him work, who would not be charmed by him and who would never be easy enough for Rudra to understand. The only girl who had ever made him feel this incapable was

Ree. The very first day he tried to make a move on Ree in college, she looked back on him with a playful smile, and said, 'I am happily stable with a boy, but I sure wish I wasn't, so I could just reject you for no reason.'

He was shaken by her forwardness, but he managed to say, 'I wish that too, so I could finally meet a challenge worth running for.'

For some strange reason, Ree kept him close. They were fast friends, and it didn't take Rudra much time to realize that she was off limits. She was smart, strong and funny, and she carried a certain weight that he'd never felt in any woman before. He was fascinated by her beauty. Her deep brown eyes, soft and everlasting smile, voice, glowing skin and her playful yet controlling way of treating him made Rudra go weak in his knees, but he knew too well where his limits were. Ree loved to make him envious of the man she dated, or the men who showed interest in her. They shared a strange bond. They were friends with potential. They stood on the transition line of friendship and devotion. They both enjoyed their strange friendship, but never crossed the line even for a weak moment.

Rudra kept himself busy with the attentions he got from the other girls. Even when Ree broke up with her long-time boyfriend, Rudra didn't try to woo her. He helped her to get over the man and move on quickly. He even fixed her dates with his friends, and it was not long before she was in another relationship. He was comfortably happy with the way everything was; and apart from the playful flirting and occasional affectionate poems, he never tried to disturb the order.

Just in the middle of Mass Comm and Journalism, final year, Ree decided to be on her own for some time. Rudra was supportive again, but it all changed on the final day of college. The farewell party of their college was the wake-up call for him. Standing in middle of the hall room, watching her dancing with other students, moving her body with the music, Rudra realized that life, the way he knew it, would never be the same again. He knew he couldn't trick himself any more. He had been in love with Ree for years, but he was afraid—afraid of the girl he could never really figure out, the girl who was better than him in every possible way. On the way back home that evening, Ree gave him a hug and said, 'It will be weird not seeing you every day.' And all he could do in response was to sigh deeply.

Sitting there, watching the last few drops of rain—like the silent tears at the end of a tragic love story—Rudra realized how helpless he was. The empty terrace was crashing into him from all around, and all he could think about was how his life, journalism and dreams of being a writer would all be meaningless without Ree being a part of all that. She was the kind of woman who had inspired great creations since the very beginning of mankind. It was women like her who always forced great paintings, songs and poems out of men. All these feelings were kept inside him for a long time, trying to find a way out. And when Ree talked about her screwed-up relationships to him, all he did was to tell her that the right man was just on his way.

His thoughts were broken by the sound of his phone. He read the message from Ree: *Check ur facebook. I hv sent u ujaan's pic.*

Rudra wanted to reply with a lot of things, but when he typed, all that he wrote was: *Sure.*

A message came again: *He will like me, rite?*

Rudra: *Of course he will.*

Ree: *Hw can u be so sure?*

Rudra: *When was I wrong ever?*

Ree: *I knw! Bt hw?*

Rudra: *I know because you are the most beautiful person, inside out. You are smart and messed up in the most beautiful way possible. You are challenging, and you are like a glacier that stays a feet over the ocean and goes a mile within it, existing but invisible.*

Making Rudra wait for few heart-stopping minutes, Ree finally replied: *Oh! I almost fell in love again ;)*

'Almost it is!' Rudra thought in his mind, and just replied with a wink. He started his laptop and signed in to Facebook. There was a message from Ree, with a picture of a boy, whom Rudra found extremely flat. His cute smile seemed immature to Rudra, and his bright eyes looked blank. Rudra was jealous and he hated that more than he hated Ujaan, but, like always, he replied, 'Not bad . . . not bad at all.' He turned the laptop off, and started unpacking. He had an apartment to decorate, to live by himself only.

That night, Rudra was chatting with Ree on Facebook, hearing about how great Ujaan was, when an update from Penguin India caught his eyes. They were arranging a love-story writing contest, and Rudra, right at that moment, knew what he needed to do. He could not speak his mind, but he could always write it out. He knew that if it failed then he could always escape with the 'it-was-just-a-story' excuse, but if it worked then he would have everything he needed. For some strange reason, the idea of his story not getting published at all never hit his mind.

He took his laptop and sat on the terrace later that night. Before doing this, he wanted to be sure that it was what he actually wanted. He knew life with Ree would be challenging, and there would be a constant struggle to keep up the peace, but that excited him the most. Words were everything Rudra needed. He felt most comfortable with them, as long as he got to write them but not speak. He knew what he needed was a way to make Ree understand what he felt, and there was nothing better than telling their own story, with his true feelings. Even a little bit of love could give birth to unreasonable hope and courage. For him, there was desperation with love, and that made logic obsolete. He knew all too well that only irrational truth could get through to Ree, the girl who had always believed in reasoning. He emptied his heart out with each of his words and wrote the story, which he believed to be his only chance to reach the one he loved.

PART TWO

Ravinder Singh scrolled down to check if the story, if he could call it that, had actually ended. He immediately fell sorry for Rudra. He thought Rudra Sengupta neither knew the art of storytelling nor did he understand women, which he thought he was good at. If he had, then he would know that all Ree wanted was for him to act like a man, and speak up. Ravinder Singh knew what he had to do . . .

By the time of the final announcements from Penguin India, Ujaan was already history and Ree was constantly pushing Rudra to find her a real man. All he was doing was waiting for the day to come when his story was published—so that she would realize that the man who loved her had always been there in front of her!

On the day the contest's results were to be declared, he logged into his email, and the obvious results were in front of him. His story had not been selected and, for the first time, he realized that he'd never even considered this possibility, which was the only one all along. He felt numb and stupid. He wished he had never written the story, and he thought he had a snowball's chance in hell to do anything about it any more. Just when he was about to get up, a second email entered his inbox. It was from Ravinder Singh, who had asked Rudra to check Ravinder's official Facebook page. Rudra didn't have any idea what he was doing. His hands took over as he logged in to the page. To his absolute surprise, his story was posted on the page. For a moment he though it was all a dream, but he sure wished it was not. Ree was a member of the page, and that kept Rudra's hopes alive, which grew faint with every passing moment, as Ree didn't try to reach him.

He was standing on the terrace that evening, watching the busy street below him, full of people walking together. He felt even lonelier, and the street lights were becoming blurry slowly. Rudra closed his eyes, clutching the railing. He almost felt like throwing his phone away as far as he could, when it suddenly rang. It was Ree. He had heard about the feeling of fluttereing butterflies in the stomach, but what he felt were not butterflies. They were angry eagles. He gathered all his strength to pick the phone up, and said, 'Hey!'

Ree replied with a clear and strong voice, 'Why me? Choose your answer wisely, mister!'

For a moment Rudra's heart stopped. He took a long, deep breath and said, 'I have no clue, Ree.'

'You know,' she said with her playful voice, 'for a man who wants to make money by writing, you are awful with words.'

Rudra felt too weak to stand. He sat down, with his back on the railing, and said with a trembling voice, 'Because I don't understand you, and I want to spend my life trying to do that. Is there a better way to spend your life with someone than to discover that person little by little every day? I know every day with you will be a new adventure and that is all I need with you. I can't promise you eternal happiness but I can assure you that our life will be a carnival. Just give me a chance, for once . . .'

'Okay! You are not that bad. Now tell me the magic words, and I will think about it,' she said with a laugh.

All Rudra could say was, 'I . . . umm . . . Can I message you that, maybe?'

Faking a disappointed voice, Ree replied, 'Oh dear lord! I have a hell of a lot of work to do with you, Rudra!' And there was nothing but silence from his side.

PART THREE

Three years had passed since that phone call and Rudra was sitting beside Ree's bed, watching their newborn baby sleep.

Ree took his hand in hers and said, 'Sorry I kicked you! I was in pain and you were the one to blame.'

Rudra looked at her, and said with mock anger, 'Ya right! It's my baby only, right?'

Ree pressed Rudra's hand and he said, 'She has your eyes, deep and brown.'

'Ahh! Thank God for that,' said Ree, as she laughed out loud.

He took a notepad out of his bag, wrote 'I Love You' and gave it to Ree. She read it with a smile and looked at him as she said 'Oh dear lord! I still have a hell of a lot of work to do with you, Rudra!'

Love, Beyond Conditions

ASMA FERDOES

Sujal had never felt so lost before. He just couldn't believe what he saw—everywhere there was smoke, confusion, debris and the smell of raw flesh mixed with gun powder. His eyes burnt with tears and the surrounding heat. He had to keep wiping them away to be able to see. He didn't know which way to go, which way to see. Where was his Aastha?

She had been here just few minutes ago covering the inauguration ceremony of the new park for her news channel and he had seen her live on TV; and it was just a few minutes ago that he had seen an explosion a few yards behind her. Now the whole place looked the same. The air was thick with smoke and everywhere there were clusters of remnant fire, scattered chunks of clothes and flesh, pools of blood and men in uniform working intensely amidst the chaos and the cries to restore some sort of control.

He didn't realize how he had reached that spot; nor did he know where to look for his wife—his life—now. All he knew was that his Aastha needed him and he must rescue her at any cost. He wiped his tears once again, took a deep breath. He ran to where his legs led him, digging where there seemed even a slightest hope of finding her, all the while calling, 'Aastha! . . . Aastha!'

In the process, he saved a few people buried under the debris of fallen walls and broken wooden planks while unearthing a few others who couldn't survive. People rushed to take over and help, but where *was* his Aastha?! Sujal felt drained now. He knew his wife was alive. She couldn't die! Not now, when he needed her the most! Not when their life was just beginning to blossom! She could not desert *her* Sujal! *'Where are you, Aastha?!'* Just then he noticed Sunil Bhatia, Aastha's cameraman, sitting outside a rescue camp, heavily bandaged and crying, with his hands over his head.

Sujal rushed to him as hope flooded his heart again. *Maybe, he knew! Maybe he could help!* 'Sunil! Oh, Sunil! I'm so glad to have found you! Thank goodness you are safe . . . where's Aastha? You were with her, right! Where is she?'

Sunil seemed overcome with increased pain at Sujal's sight and refused to even look his way.

'Look at me, Sunil . . . please, look at me . . .' Sujal pleaded his reactions stabbing at his heart. 'Don't hesitate even if she's hurt. I'll take care of her . . . but tell me where is she, please. Listen! Don't cry . . . please don't cry! Tell me, where's my Aastha? Please tell me, bro . . . please.'

But Sunil cried even more and could only manage to look at Sujal with sorry eyes. This merely increased Sujal's desperation and he looked around, inside and outside the camps, yelling out her name. But she was nowhere. He returned to Sunil and said sternly, 'Look! Stop crying. We are here. Everything's going to be alright. Tell me, where is Aastha? At least show me where you saw her last, man!'

At this Sunil looked around like a broken navigator and at last pointed in a direction. 'There . . . '

'There! By that rubble?!' Sujal asked with hope.

'In . . . that . . . rubble . . . I think.'

As Sujal broke into a run, Sunil called out to him and said, 'I'm sorry, bro . . . but there's no hope.'

Sujal had to fight the tears that rushed to come and, deciding he had not heard Sunil's warning, ran to the place the cameraman had indicated. He sought her in the rubble and all around it, with only her name on his lips, pushing aside every bit of wreckage he came across—broken slabs of wood, shattered glass panes, mosaic wall pieces. But still there was no sign of Aastha. 'Aastha! Are you in there?' he kept calling out to her. 'Don't worry, your Sujal is here. He will save you. Hold on, dear . . . hold on.' As he pushed aside the last piece of rubble, all that he met was warm feeble ground. His hope left him, his limbs gave way and he collapsed to the ground, shouting for one last time, 'AASTHA!'

Sujal had never cried like this before in his life. He looked at the silent chaos around him. His family and friends, like so many others, were still searching through the wreckage. There were others too—the volunteers and officers still searching for survivors, the media still covering the incident, the survivors and family members still crying for their loved ones. There was a lot of activity all around him. Then why did only his world suddenly seem to have come to a standstill? Why had it suddenly fallen silent? He could even feel his heart slowly cease to beat, one beat at a time, as his tears flowed in such a rage as if determined to kill him.

Just then something glittered in the sun and caught his attention. It was a little diamond ring on a hand buried under debris a little away. He immediately recognized it to be the same ring he had gifted Aastha on her last birthday. His heart lifted at its sight and he quickly crawled up to it. After a few more laborious minutes of moving aside the debris, he found his life again. There was his Aastha—limp, badly injured and soaked in blood! He didn't know whether to laugh or cry. He pulled her up and held her tightly to his chest. He heard a meek 'Su–jal!' escape from her lips before she passed out.

She was rushed to a nearby hospital and the doctors immediately took her into the operation theatre. Many hours passed, and they were still inside with her. Their family and friends sat over the benches in the corridor, waiting and wishing for the operation to end successfully, but Sujal couldn't afford to move away from the OT's door. He stood outside it and looked on as if he could see all that was happening inside—the nods and gestures of the doctors, the exchange of surgical equipments, the questions and confirmations in their eyes, nurses using cotton balls after cotton balls to control her bleeding, the monitoring of her heartbeat and other vital signs through machines, the cuts, insertions and stitches made on her body. He twitched at the last thought, feeling the prick and pain of scalpels and needles. It must hurt her too, won't it? Only that she wouldn't feel it. She had long been unconscious and he wondered if they had even needed the anaesthesia for her; and all the while, he wished for a miracle. He wished his heartbeat would reach her even as he stood here in despair while she lay there in distress; and like a fairytale effect her spell would break, her eyes would flutter open much to the amazement of the doctors and nurses, and she would murmur, 'Water' or 'Sujal'.

He waited long moments for the doors to fling open and the doctors to emerge, beaming to declare, 'It's a miracle! Aastha's completely fine. You may take her home now.' But no such thing happened. The red light continued to glow overhead, the door remained closed and every moment continued to be an ordeal. The air suddenly grew thick around him and he couldn't stand there any more. He rushed to the window across the corridor and stood there looking at the commotion below and the setting sun further beyond, fighting his tears that hadn't dried yet. His mind moved over everything that had happened—how so many people's lives had changed in a split second, maybe for ever too, because of one senseless and mindless act of violence inflicted on them by some heartless brutes; and how nothing made sense anymore, except the little life, now threatened, flickering or extinguished within their loved ones.

He didn't turn back even once to look towards the door. He neither had the courage nor the need for it, but he immediately knew when the red light was switched off at last, and he was there by the door before anybody else could reach and before even the doctors could emerge. Dr Mayank Sharma emerged, looking his usual composed self. Mayank was Aastha's close friend and Sujal knew friends never spelt doom. He forced a faint smile and conveyed to them in his casual doctor-like tone, 'The operation was successful. We have removed almost all the foreign particles from her body and treated her wounds. Second phase of the operation is under way, but we need to discuss few urgent matters. Can any two among you come into our senior doctor, Dr Sethi's, chamber?'

He went away without further talk, and Sujal wondered as to what it takes for someone to be this composed even after seeing his friend caught between life and death! Maybe years of dedicated practice as a top surgeon! But what were these urgent discussions he talked about? A sudden fear gripped his heart and he couldn't manage a thought, as his father led him along.

The few minutes they had to wait outside Dr Sethi's chamber were some of the longest in Sujal's life—enduring every moment, fearing every moment. At last, Dr Mayank ushered them in, every part him being the epitome of composure; only his eyes seemed to betray him. There was restlessness behind their calm. Sujal sat looking at them suspiciously, ready to talk on Aastha's behalf while knowing that he should let his father handle most of the discussion.

'We are lucky to have found her before too late,' assured Dr Sethi. 'Our team is still attending to her and we hope she responds well.'

'I hope Aastha isn't critical, sir!'

'She's gone into coma and we need to keep her under observation.'

Coma! Sujal looked stricken.

The doctor continued, 'We, however, can't wait for her to revive and there's an important procedure we need to do to save her.'

Another blow hit Sujal hard on his heart.

'What procedure, sir?' Even his father's voice couldn't hide the fear behind them.

'We all have seen her right hand. She's lost a major portion of her forearm from wrist to elbow . . .'

'Replace it,' Sujal suddenly spoke up realizing what Mayank was referring to, the feeling of something tearing that he had felt when he had pulled her out of the rubble, returning to him. He clenched his fist to suppress it.

'I'm sorry Mr Raiwal, but that's not—'

'There are so many ways,' Sujal interrupted again, 'grafting, re-building, whatever.'

'That's not an option here. It will only increase further complications. Her hand's lost its life.'

'Revive it then.'

'Try and understand, Sujal. She's in a very fragile state and we need to do this operation,' Mayank broke in.

'There'll be some way out . . . please find it,' Sujal pleaded.

'Her blood isn't clotting, Sujal. Our team is at present trying to help her achieve that.'

Sujal only shook his head in denial.

'We need to save her and amputation is the only way.'

'I deny the permission,' Sujal said in a cold voice and left without letting them say another word.

Sujal stopped by a little fountain in the hospital's yard, his helplessness killing him. He knew he'd be approached again and he wasn't escaping. He only wished Aastha had somehow escaped this attack. Mayank came and stood beside him.

'I can't let this happen, Mayank,' cried Sujal, sensing the friend in him.

'I can understand,' Mayank replied gently, 'Come with me.'

Mayank led him to the ICU. where Aastha lay. As Sujal entered, clad in a surgical robe, he found her lying still, a dome-shaped cover over her body. She was heavily bandaged and looked so delicately brittle. There was swelling in most parts of her body and her wounds still seemed ready to burst. She was being supplied with glucose and blood intravenously and an oxygen mask helped her breathe. He yearned to touch her, yet the fear of harming her turned him numb. Mayank moved the white sheet a little aside to reveal her hand. The sight of it brought Sujal's hand to his mouth and he looked away

'You need to be brave, Sujal,' began Mayank, his desperation finally evident. 'You can see the degree to which her bones have suffered burns. Her nerves . . . blood supply . . . everything's been cut. The pain must have been horrible for her. It's a miracle she's alive.'

'It's . . . so blue!' Sujal blurted out in fear.

Mayank nodded. 'It's turning toxic. Doctors don't consider comatose as a good thing, but I'm glad she's not witnessing this part of her life . . . We can't wait for more than a hundred minutes now.'

'Then do it,' Sujal said, sounding really lost and walking out of the room, a part of him dying with those words. He didn't cry anymore, tears didn't have the power to console him or comfort his heart anymore. A nurse approached with a statement to sign, which he did without another thought, even as his family looked on. 'We are helpless, Dad,' was all he could say.

As two wardens wheeled Aastha again towards the OT, Sujal whispered, 'I'm sorry, Aastha . . .' The last drops of his tears finally fell.

The next few months passed away in a haze with lots of visitors coming in and offering him words of encouragement, and Sujal not being away from the hospital for more than a couple of hours every day. Aastha's condition improved at a very slow rate and Sujal stopped paying attention to what the doctors had to say after the first week of her operation. Before the operation they said it was necessary in order to save her life and, after it, they said they needed to wait for her to revive in order to rule her out of danger. He, instead, chose to sit by her whenever they allowed, listening to her breathe and the beeps of the monitors as if his own life depended on them, and pick signs from her condition. Every day that passed gave him only one report—his Aastha held on to life and she was in pain, immense pain. Though her wounds and burns had begun to heal, she showed no signs of revival. The tumult inside him threatened his entirety but on the outside he was the paradigm of calmness. Only those who knew them well could see the storm he battled within him. After all, their love had withstood the test of time, distance and trust.

The pain filled her as she slowly regained consciousness one evening, and Aastha moaned even before she could open her eyes. By the time doctors rushed in, she was crying profusely. Outside, though Sujal had found his heartbeat again, he realized he didn't have the courage to face her. What was he going to tell her! A few hours later, after her situation was brought under control and Mayank turned to leave, Aastha called him back, saying, 'How long have I troubled you?'

'Not long enough to tire me, sleeping beauty.'

'My whole body aches . . . but I don't feel anything in my right hand.'

'Don't worry; you won't feel any pain anywhere else too by morning.' It was too early to shatter her with the truth. Her family was then allowed to visit her. Sujal crept in last and the others kept their meeting short—to allow her to rest and give the couple some time together.

When they were finally alone, Sujal slowly sat beside her and embraced her.

'Don't ever leave me again, all right!'

'When it happened . . . I feared I'd never see you again.'

'Hush! Don't say that . . . Thank you for coming back.'

Aastha tried to smile despite her pain, relief flooding her. *But she is not able to lift her right hand!*

They softly talked into the night even as apprehensions gnawed at his heart, as he noticed fear and panic slowly settle in her eyes.

'Sujal, can you do me a favour?' she requested before too long.

'Say,' he managed, fearing the worst.

'Remove my cover . . . I don't have the courage to.'

He froze for an instant, too shocked to react. 'Aastha . . . listen . . . ' he stumbled.

'Please!' she pleaded, gripping his hand and nearly in tears.

He silently acquiesced and, moving closer, he gradually lifted it just enough to confirm her fears. The next moment she had buried her face in his arms, stifling her cries and denying what she had just seen.

He cocooned her in his love, letting her cry her heart out.

'How am I going to manage without it, Sujal?' she lamented between her sobs, as the first wave of shock slowly passed away.

'We'll work it out somehow,' He assured her. Prosthetics was an option. But he didn't tell her that. It depended on how much mobility her arm regained. Nothing was certain yet.

'But it'll never be the same again.'

'Then we'll start afresh,' he added, smiling faintly for the first time in months.

She nestled in his arms, shutting her eyes to the trauma, finding strength in his warmth and life in his love again.

Notes on Contributors

Amrit Sinha is working with Genpact as a software engineer and is also pursuing his MBA from Indira Gandhi National Open University. He loves reading. His favorite authors are Dan Brown, Sidney Sheldon and Chetan Bhagat. In his free time, he writes poems and short stories.

Anjali Khurana is a content manager who writes for celebrities and plans their digital presence. She creates their virtual diaries in the form of voice and web blogs and also writes press releases at the time of events. She has a bachelor's degree in hotel management and lives in Mumbai.

Arka Datta is a trained multimedia animator. After working as a freelance graphic designer for an advertising agency, he dropped everything to follow his dream of becoming a writer. He started an online blog magazine and took up content writing. Currently he is a freelance graphic designer, content writer and creative writer.

Arpita Ghosh lives in Uttarpara, a small town near Kolkata. Having finished her graduation in English literature, she is now pursuing a master's degree. For Arpita, the achievement of true love lies in its non-fulfilment.

Asma Ferdoes holds a B.Com degree. She is twenty-four years old and hails from Kolar Gold Fields (KGF), a small mining town in Karnataka. She enjoys reading and teaching. She has published short stories, articles and poetry in several magazines.

K. Balakumaran is an existentialist, a movie-lover and an occasional but passionate reader. In his free time, he likes to pen what he observes, sometimes inspired by the weirdness of intriguing real-life characters. Balakumaran is currently working as a consultant with Infosys, Chennai. You can get in touch with him at balakumarann@gmail.com.

Haseeb Peer was born in Sopore, Kashmir, in 1991. He has been contributing articles to the local dailies of the state. He is currently pursuing a bachelor's degree in engineering and intends to pursue journalism and full-time writing in the future.

Jennifer Ashraf Kashmi has been the publisher and editor of *Sticks & Stones* anthology series. She is currently a university lecturer, a corporate lawyer and writer for the *Daily Sun*. She is also the health columnist for *Groove Magazine* and features writer for the *Morning Tea* magazine. You can contact her at jenniash@yahoo.com.

Jyoti Singh Visvanath is the managing editor at SHRM India and the regional advisor (India) for the Society of

Children's Book Writers and Illustrators. She has authored five books for children, has been published in several Indian national dailies and magazines, and has developed Internet content for children. Her short stories have been featured in *The Asia Literary Review.*

Kaviya Kamaraj is an extrovert, a bharatnatyam dancer, an ex-NCC cadet, a passionate cook, a shopping fanatic and someone who loves television serials. In her leisure time, she likes to write what she experiences in her day to day life. She is currently working as a software engineer with Infosys.

Lalit Kundalia (Jain) is a chartered accountant from St. Xaviers College, Kolkata. He is crazy about reading novels and loves debates. He loves to pen down day-to-day incidents that he observes around him. He can be reached at lalitkundalia@ yahoo.co.in or www.facebook.com/kundalial for feedback and interactions.

Manaswita Ghosh is a writer, poet and avid blogger. A final-year student at the Institute of Technical Education and Research, Bhubaneswar, she is extremely passionate about writing.

Manjula Pal is a multidisciplinary person, having worked as a postgraduate lecturer of philosophy and as a scientist in research projects at AIIMS. She has written articles and columns in Delhi Press publications, has published a storybook for children in Hindi and is currently working as a freelance journalist.

Mohan Raghavan is an engineer based in Bangalore. After spending many years in the IT industry, he is currently pursuing an inter-disciplinary doctorate, bridging engineering and life sciences at the Indian Institute of Science, Bangalore.

Omkar Khandekar is a journalist from Mumbai. He made his debut as a fiction writer in 2011 with a short story in the anthology *Not Like Most Young Girls*. When he is not busy reading and looking after dogs, Omkar likes to watch movies, visit the theatre and occasionally write.

Renu Bhutoria Sethi is an avid reader and a budding creative writer and poet. She lives in Mumbai and enjoys writing love stories. She has a creative blog http://day-to-daystories.blogspot.in/. She can be contacted at sethirenu27@gmail.com.

Renuka Vishwanathan is a freelance writer and editor, and has published several short stories and articles in *Femina*, *Woman's Era*, *Savvy*, *Times of India* and *Deccan Herald*. She has won the All-India Competition for Writers of Children's Books by the Children's Book Trust, New Delhi, four times; and has also won the first prize in the short-story-writing contest *Somewhere Sometime*, conducted by Tumbhi.com in 2012.

Reuben Kumar Lalwani works with the West Bengal office of the United Nations Children's Fund, based in Kolkata. He's passionate about writing and photography, and has compiled two volumes of photographs of children for the UNICEF. Sukanya, his wife and sounding board, is his one uncompromising critic. 'Clumsy Cupid' is dedicated to her.

Dr Roshan Radhakrishnan is a blogger, foodie and an anaesthesiologist (not necessarily in that order) who believes in the healing power of love and laughter but practises medicine just to be on the safe side. He blogs at www.godyears.net.

Sowmya Aji is a journalist by profession and has worked as a reporter for newspapers, TV and on the Internet. A single mom, she currently works for *India Today* in Bangalore and covers politics, crime and culture as her main beats.

Sujir Pavithra Nayak is an amateur writer who discovered her passion for writing by sheer accident. Having graduated from ICFAI, Hyderabad, with a master's degree in finance, marketing, operations and entrepreneurship, she is currently working for an IT company as a business analyst. She aspires to become a famous novelist someday.

Swagata Pradhan is a pursuing an MSc in Zoology from the West Bengal State University, Kolkata. She enjoys reading and listening to music. 'A Tale of Two Strangers' is her first attempt at publication.

Vandana Sharma has finished her BSc and is now pursuing an MBA from Sikkim Manipal University - Distance Education. She loves to read, write, paint, design clothes and watch movies. She lives with her parents in Ajmer.

Vinayak Nadkarni is an engineering graduate from Hubli, Karnataka. He is employed with one of the IT giants of India but his primary love lies in theatre and writing. He has also completed his Level-1 acting course from Ratan Thakore Grant Acting School. His hobbies include blogging and writing scripts. He is an ardent follower of Indian cricket and loves playing it on the field as well.

Yamini Vijendran hails from Pune. She is an engineer by education and an IT techie by profession. After leaving her software job, Yamini started exploring the world of freelance writing. Her stories and poems have been published in literary journals such as *New Asian Writing, Six Sentences* as well as the poetry anthology *A World Rediscovered.*